Barry Pilton is the author of *The Valley*.
He has written scripts for radio and TV,
including *Weekending* and *Spitting
Image*, and numerous plays; in addition to
having worked with a large number of
stars of British light entertainment including Griff Rhys Jones, Brenda Blethyn,
Richard Briers and Nicholas Lyndhurst.
Barry is currently working on the TV
adaptation of *The Valley*. He lives in
Bristol.

THE TOWN WITH NO TWIN

Abernant is an idyllic rural town . . . except for the simmering hatreds, crooked politics and sexual debauchery. The mayoress, to elevate her social status, commissions a statue for the town. But the local sculptor is a drunk, who loves to shock. Duly shocked is the butcher, who has a vendetta with the deli owner, who in turn hates the mayoress. The statue's prospects seem dodgy. Meanwhile, the commodore has hired out his mansion to a film company, which has been less than honest about their plans. Watching all this is *The Mid-Walian*, a newspaper with a desperate need to increase its sales . . .

Books by Barry Pilton
Published by The House of Ulverscroft:

THE VALLEY

BARRY PILTON

THE TOWN WITH NO TWIN

Complete and Unabridged

ULVERSCROFT
Leicester

First published in Great Britain in 2007 by
Bloomsbury Publishing Plc
London

First Large Print Edition
published 2008
by arrangement with
Bloomsbury Publishing Plc
London

British Library CIP Data

Pilton, Barry, *1946* –
    The town with no twin.—Large print ed.—
Ulverscroft large print series: general fiction
    1. City and town life—Wales—Fiction
    2. Humorous stories 3. Large type books
    I. Title
    823.9′14 [F]

    ISBN 978–1–84782–215–4

Published by
F. A. Thorpe (Publishing)
Anstey, Leicestershire
Set by Words & Graphics Ltd.
Anstey, Leicestershire
Printed and bound in Great Britain by
T. J. International Ltd., Padstow, Cornwall

This book is printed on acid-free paper

FOR JAN

Spring

1

It is possible that if Mrs Hartford-Stanley had not needed to take three practice back-swings she would not have been struck by lightning. Her first love was bell-ringing but, since centuries of unsuitable subsoil had caused the church to collapse into the river, Rosemary had concentrated lately on lowering her golf handicap to single figures. Golf was not an easy game to perfect in Abernant, as the small market town had only one golf course, sublet from a farmer and shared with his sheep. This caused an added hazard on competition days, for then the greens were ring-fenced by a double strand of barbed wire, to prevent dung pellets interfering with the roll of the ball. Already, on the outward nine of the 1987 Nightingale Cup, Mrs Hartford-Stanley had drawn blood to her inner thigh by attempting a slightly vain vault for a lady of her years. By the twelfth hole, a par 3, this scratch had undermined confidence in her stance, and she had paused to rehearse the tricky use of a seven iron across the phlegm-like waters of the duck pond. This was her first tournament, a ladies-only event, and she was lamenting her bad luck at being fifteen over par and in need of a Band-Aid when her raised club was hit by 300,000,000 volts.

★ ★ ★

The abandonment of the Nightingale Cup was a troublesome headache for Clydog, who was now short of a lead sports story for *The Mid-Walian*. At first, Miss Nightingale, the autocratic seventy-two-year-old who owned the weekly paper, had been reluctant to forgo the annual photo of herself presenting the family's silver cup to a grinning lady with stout calves; for many years a player at county level, she felt that her readers' prime need was to experience life through the prism of golf, and no edition of her *Mid-Walian* was without an account of shanks and bunker shots. However, the combination of a tropical storm and a corpse (charred) had reduced the jolliness of the day's proceedings, and many of the match pairs had favoured an early return to the clubhouse.

Clydog leaned back in his chair, a move that edged his profile from rotund to obese, and with a weary hand he let out another button on his old tweed waistcoat. Not for the first time in forty years of chronicling the events of mid-Wales, he was short of copy. Tribulations like this left him secretly glad he had been turned down three times for the job of editor, although he still maintained that he had hidden depths of dynamism. Yet he was not a great believer in the fearless pursuit of truth, if only because it put a strain on his heart and made him sweaty. Clydog's type of news came about not by investigation but by osmosis, by the gentle gathering of gossip as he pottered the streets.

The Mid-Walian was not very keen on hard news. 'Golfer Incinerated!' was the sort of story the paper tried to avoid, as it was felt to be upsetting for the readership. Indeed, no news at all was put on the front page, for fear unseemly facts might ruffle the calm of country life. All eight columns of page one had, since the days of Victoria, been an advert-only zone, the Nightingale family long holding the view that tractor parts and the competitive rates of hedge-layers offered the best lure for the locals. Which is why the late Mrs Hartford-Stanley made just a paragraph at the foot of page seven.

Clydog gazed out of the first-floor window in the vague hope that something newsworthy might happen in the square below. His was a wide brief, and should he see an outsize vegetable, or a prize bullock, or an unusual hobby, he had the authority to set his copperplate hand to work. And besides, he liked to gaze. The newspaper occupied a one-time Georgian town house which, though its internal elegance had been lost to plasterboard, still retained a view almost worthy of bardic verse on a clear day.

In the foreground was the small square, the hub of town, where traffic jammed on market day and flat-capped farmers gathered to mutter their monosyllables. Here stood the War Memorial, strangely off-centre, in a formal setting of gravel and grass. Beyond, the sky spread wide as the high street dropped down to the narrow stone bridge over the Nant, the river that gave the town its name. Further beyond, a long green scoop of hillside and a great white skein of hawthorn blossom marked the valley where the River Nant gushed its way down from the heather on the high moors.

But today Clydog found no journalistic inspiration, in the hills or the square. The only sign of life came from a cattle truck that mooed as it ground its way up the sharp incline from the river.

Clydog looked again at the blank sheet, struck out the words 'Sports Page', and thought some more. He would get no credit for his thoughts. There were no bylines, not

6

even for Clydog, since articles materialised as the work of nameless specialists. To the casual reader, *The Mid-Walian* was puzzlingly overstaffed. Last year, unusual climatic conditions had created clouds of Painted Ladies, a fact that was learnedly commented on by The Butterfly Correspondent. In his time, Clydog had been the correspondent for almost everything, including Suez.

Clydog turned his mind to the arts. There had been no arts in mid-Wales that week, apart from a WI talk on Rudolph Valentino. But he vaguely remembered a press release from the Welsh Arts Council. He retrieved it from his bin.

There was, it seemed, concern in Cardiff at the lack of new sculpture in the regions. In response to this crisis, sums of money were to be made available, to prompt rural communities to think in terms of plinths. '*With preference given to concepts or individuals that best expressed the nature of their locality, by converting the world of dreams into solid form.*'

Clydog had no idea what this meant. But his deadline was pressing and he at last had enough for a filler.

2

The Air Commodore had been in the river for over two hours. Despite a lifetime of tying flies, of tweaking fur and hair and feather into tasty shape, it was a day when nothing remotely aquatic had been tempted by his lures. Gaunt and arthritic, the old man stood motionless in the water like a stick insect, and still there were no takers. The trout were elsewhere.

So were his thoughts. Commodore Powell had not been happy since breakfast. In fact, he had been depressed since 1942, but medication helped disguise this as the usual upper-class difficulties with coherent speech. Normally, the Commodore left the problems of reality to be sorted by others, by his sister, by his gamekeeper, by his bank manager, by passing motorists, but that morning the world of the Powells had found troubles that could not be wished away. So, pausing only to tap on his great-grandfather's barometer, he had slipped out of the manor house and decamped across the meadow.

The Commodore did not follow the sheep track that he had trodden for sixty years, that

Rupert had pissed on for twelve, but instead he and his gun dog had aimed downstream, bypassing the remnants of St Brynnach's. Since their family's church had subsided into the Nant, as if victim to over-zealous baptism, the river had rethought its ways, reworked its backwaters. The familiar eddies had gone, the fish-rich weed beds were crushed, and he no longer even paused by his favourite pool as it was full of pews. The Commodore had yet to locate where his trout now laid up, and as he plodded past his herd of Welsh Blacks he longed for an oxbow with ripples of promise. Only a tug on the line would blot out the warning words of his sister, only rising fish would help him forget the threat to his heirlooms.

It was the porridge that had been the harbinger of trouble. Like the dog that did not bark, it had boiled in silence. No lipsmacking bubbles broke its surface, no terrain of volcanic mud formed in its saucepan. Ten minutes of boiling, and a baby's bum could have safely been immersed. Indeed, the pan could have boiled in vain for a further ten minutes, but the Commodore always began his day with the obituaries, and as *The Times* contained few dead that morning the lack of warmth in his breakfast came quickly to his attention.

The fault lay somewhere within the ancient Aga. The model was fired by solid fuel, cause of the smoke-grey veneer that covered the walls and ceiling, and mornings often found it at a low glow. The Commodore had got up to see what was wrong. He soon discovered the problem to be not a lack of coke, but an absence of updraught: no air was being drawn into the flue. To remedy this, and better heat the hot-plate, the Commodore slid back the small rectangular vent on top of the Aga.

And a scorched, sooty, very angry jackdaw had hurtled out as if fired from a cannon. Cawing vociferously.

Half-blind and hotter than porridge, the bird bounced off the walls like a squash ball in a killer rally. Black imprints of all its body feathers began to appear in every part of the kitchen. It crashed into each of the window-panes and fell repeatedly to the floor. The Commodore waved *The Times* about in a pointless panic and the bird's beak tore a hole in the lifetime achievements of an Anglican bishop.

Hearing the ruckus, his sister had come in.

The Commodore cast again. There were no willow trees downstream, and he gained no help from the trickery of shade. But he was also up against the isobars, and he cast not in hope but from habit. The large print on his great-grandfather's dial had left no doubt he was in the low that follows a storm, that barometric moment when depressed fish sink to the bottom.

'Looks like rations for us, Rupert,' he muttered miserably.

His sister was efficient, even the Queen knew that, though the OBE citation made no mention of bird control. Whenever he wanted to know anything about the twentieth century, she was always the one he asked. This was also because his wife was never sober and could only be asked about gin. Of which she had thirty years' expertise. He often wished it was his wife who lived in the stable block and his sister who lived in the house.

The swirling water pressed hard against his waders as he stood looking ruefully back at the ancestral Powell pile.

The jackdaw had been no match for Dilys. By the use of calm and an opened window the barbecued bird was quickly gone. But the cause of its coming was the greater alarm.

To check the chimney, Dilys and her brother had gone into the cobbled yard, where horses for the hunt had once clattered up and down. Few would have picked them out as siblings. Dilys, with a chilly authority to her manner and a faded formality to her clothing, appeared to have stepped from a Pathé News broadcast; a trim woman with the spinster gene, she sat on public bodies — their duty the doing of good works — and wrote memos that had to be obeyed. Julian was nervy and awkward and withdrawn, and he wore, as every day, his much-patched cordwear, all in the autumnal colour-coding of country sports. He appeared to have escaped from an internment camp for failed gentry.

They had expected to find the cowl thrown to the ground, its wires bent silly by the jackdaw's mischief.

But what they found on the ground, and under their feet, was chimney plaster and broken brick; and what met their upward gaze was a roof whose slates had slipped.

'Yesterday's wind,' said the Commodore, who knew a thing or two about wind.

'Next year's income,' said the sister, who knew a thing or two about builders.

With the river still running quite high, the Commodore opted to cast long and shallow, beneath the undercut bank where the sand martins nested. This time his mind was on his dead father, whose disapproving features swam before him whenever another bit of the estate fell into disrepair. As it did, year by year, now almost day by day. His father's portrait loomed and lurked throughout the crumbling Queen Anne house, the second grandest home in the valley, and — as the psychiatrist once allocated by the War Office had explained — paters with high expectations could be dashed bad for morale when it came to the old guilt thing.

But what he felt to be his father's greatest reproach hung above the dinner gong. At the foot of the grand stairs, in sepia, was the framed photo of his father's proudest moment. It weighed in at 4lb 7oz., and had been caught just above the old mill (now ruined). Not only was it the heaviest brown trout ever taken from the Nant, but it was six ounces more than the Commodore had weighed as a baby. His birth, however, was a family event only found in mildewed albums, and the Commodore had never quite shaken off the thought that, in his father's eyes, he had come second to a fish. Even now, in his late sixties, he was driven on by the need to exorcise this personal demon and catch a five-pounder before he died. He flicked again at the line, ruffling the water with a rare impatience.

Dilys stood in her brother's squalid kitchen — a room she never visited for purposes of food — and wondered about tarpaulin. The answer to dry rot had been their grandmother's cutlery. The solution to woodworm had been two Persian rugs and a cannon from the terrace. The remedy for half a roof and a chimney would probably be the china, the piano and a chesterfield. This did not appeal. Faced with the loss of more heirlooms, she would sooner have sooty jackdaws and indoor rain.

Three hundred years of wear and tear had taken their toll. Where once the smell of polish infused every room, now the air was musty, with the added bouquet of bat droppings. The house was decaying around its owners, the retainers long gone. Even the suit of armour had lost a kneecap. And it did not help to have an alcoholic in the house, whose every foray from bed threatened the life of some vase or antique side-table.

Dilys hovered, for once uncertain what to do. She gazed around at the smudged jackdaw imprints that randomly covered the room. Perhaps more pheasants, she wondered, and more rich and vulgar townies down to massacre them . . . ? She bent to pick *The Times* up from the floor, to read some world news as distraction. But the paper was too bird-damaged and dirty for a person of distinction and she left it where it lay.

14

And then she noticed the latest issue of *The Mid-Walian* upon the table. It was not a paper she often read, for she disapproved of its punctuation. But, on some whim, she picked up its eighteen Clydog-packed pages.

The Commodore's line had gone taut and hard to reel. The tension on the line told him he was holding an object of substance, and he edged cautiously toward it across the stony river bottom. Two hours of earnestly gripping his rod had left him with no reward, and so he played this mystery catch with a grim determination. The water under the far bank was a muddy brown and kept its secrets hidden, but little by little he could feel his unknown prey succumb.

Dilys did not reach the inside pages. The Nightingale theory of rural readers was proved correct. Initially she had paused to read the offer of high-grade bull semen for Welsh Blacks, but then, just below, her eye was caught by an odd-sized box with bold type. The advert had presumably been lumped under Livestock because it belonged to no category known to the typesetters, but its contents were intriguing . . . and seemed to hold out a prospect of financial salvation from a most unlikely quarter.

Dilys rummaged in a drawer for the kitchen scissors.

It sprang from the dark waters without warning, as if abruptly released from the vice of vegetation, and caught the Commodore off balance. The great weight of the catch hurled it in an arc over his head, and the old man struggled to keep his footing. The thing was pink and blue and yellow, and he recognised the words 'Jesus Loves You' along its side. It was number twenty-seven in his sister's series of embroidered kneelers.

3

1. Vomit
2. Hire of the fairy
3. Decline in bin-bag quality
4. Loss of trade caused by Oxfam
5. Pizzas and the wrong kind of visitor
6. Resignation of President

Hubert the delicatessen owner affected a yawn, to indicate his weariness with the predictable agendas of the Chamber of Commerce, and to disguise his bitterness at being asked to resign. Hard-backed chairs scraped across bare boards as the sixteen apostles of business moved closer to the aggregation of bar tables. A teenage minute-taker on a work experience scheme sat blushing nervously in the corner. Apologies for absence were announced from Knick-Knackery and Celtic Militaria.

This was a bimonthly meeting and, as always, took place in the bleak upstairs room of the Brown Bear, the type of room where receptions are held for marriages that are destined to fail.

'You could even count the chick-peas down

the shop-front, it was that disgusting,' began Mr Devonald, the boutique owner. 'What lady is going to want to buy a blouse if she has to wade through curry?'

'Every weekend it's the same,' lamented Mr Johnson of Johnson's Modern Sportswear. 'I've had projectile vomiting from as far as the Belisha beacon,' he said, adding, 'I think it's some sort of competition.'

'You're lucky,' said the baker. 'I've had excreta.'

This was how most meetings began.

Although sixty-two, Hubert still fancied himself as a rebel and sometimes took up sympathetic postures on puke in the high street, but this evening he lacked the will for such provocation. Or for any intervention at all, as of late he seemed to have lost his lust for power politics.

The delicatessen owner had worked hard on his image, laconic, sardonic, iconoclastic, and had developed a body language that was spare and a bit seigneurial, as was fitting for a tall, bald man with a Gaullist nose. He had built up a reputation for unfamiliar groceries — the only recorded sighting of avocado in the county — and the black-inked calligraphy on his labels spoke to shoppers of a man of character. He even had a pipe that he puffed like a patrician.

So when *The Mid-Walian* had published a misleading photograph of Hubert lying in the gutter chained to a parking meter and apparently looking up the dress of the mayoress, he was more than a little upset.

'We need an anti-drink campaign for these young tearaways,' said elderly Mr Fortescue, the homeopathic chemist.

'And shorter opening hours!' added Mr Bufton the ironmonger, who lived in a flat above his town premises.

'Yes, why don't we *all* go bankrupt?' sneered Mr Clement, the publican of the Brown Bear.

'Maybe I should sell bleeding paper doilies instead?' suggested Mr Armstrong, owner of an off-licence chain, and already several cans the worse for wear.

'My customers don't urinate through *your* letter-box,' replied Mr Beavan, a second-hand bookseller specialising in Welsh mythology, poetry, and royal photo albums.

There then followed the usual argy-bargy between the town's vested interests. The anti-vomit lobby made their usual proposals to bring in youth ID, increase the drinking age, cut the opening hours, and raise a local militia. The pro-alcohol lobby made their usual counter-proposals (there were seventeen pubs in town, who all denied any connection between drink and drunks) and reiterated their usual belief in the freedom of the landlord, the rights of the individual and large profits. There was the usual failure to resolve anything.

The meeting moved on to discuss the fairy.

The Mid-Walian had, of course, published Hubert's letter, explaining how he had, dropped his padlock key down the drain and was trying to retrieve it, but the damage to his reputation had been done. His principled stand against the introduction of parking meters to Abernant went unnoticed when the public gathering accidentally became a riot — and then later his photo had somehow got converted into a very popular poster by the enterprising new photocopy shop.

'Apparently you could see through her ballet dress,' said the treasurer, Mr Lloyd, whose garage had the town's first carwash. 'Town hall says she arrived with moth holes.'

'Well, she left me in perfect condition,' snapped Mr Devonald, who became a little camp when roused. 'As always.'

'But the council won't pay for a fairy if she's shop-soiled. They say she has to be in perfect condition to go on a tree.'

The state of the Christmas fairy had been a sore point for some months. The Chamber of Commerce prided itself on the quality of their annual fairy, centrepiece of festivities in the Abernant high street, and were insistent that blame for the lacy air vents lay with municipal negligence. But there were no witnesses to the manhandling of the fairy and the hire fee remained in dispute.

'I'm surprised you don't accuse her of getting pissed and falling over,' sniggered Mr Clement, who considered that ownership of the room gave him the right to be offensive.

'Could I say a word about bin bags?' asked Mr Beynon, the town's leading haberdasher, who was always eager to avoid controversy.

Hubert blamed Clydog for his disgrace, and had barred him from his shop for nearly a month. The posters of the President of the Chamber of Commerce upon his back in the mud had been seen in various public places, including toilets, and had done much to undermine his power base. In his mercantile desire for free parking, Hubert had become a meter martyr. And now the tectonic plates of the Chamber of Commerce were shifting, and new forces would rule.

Yet it could all so easily have been avoided. Had the trainee photographer possessed more skill (or had Miss Nightingale's nepotism not awarded that post to her young nephew Auberon), the lad's photo of the tape-cutting ceremony would not have depicted the mayoress as being short of an ear and the end bit of her forehead. Had Mrs Myfanwy Edwards been captured with all her body parts, the town's biggest news item since the Rebecca Riots need not have been illustrated instead by the flailing figure at her feet.

Clydog had, of course, apologised for the scoop. He and Hubert went back many years, and Clydog was the biggest purchaser of at least three of his confectionery items, sometimes buying Mississippi Mud Pies in bulk. He was unwilling to fall out over some trifling issue of press freedom.

'Stocks!' announced Mr Chigley. 'Put these youngsters in the stocks, and vomit over *them*. That would stop it.' Old Mr Chigley, deaf bachelor and corn-seed merchant, was noted for his disconnected approach to the agenda.

Hubert's concern was the succession. Abernant was not renowned for its freethinkers. When proposals were made to twin the town, the principal candidate had been Bangor. Hubert prided himself on his vision, on his gift for entrepreneurial niches, on seeing the mark-up potential of foreign vegetables and meats that ended in i. His greed had class, and could have helped the town to leap from the fifties to the eighties, the decade in which they now languished.

Around him the talk had turned to charity, and the curse it is to profits. In a brief walk through the town, a shopper could choose between bringing succour to the cancerous, the blind, the elderly, the palsied, the terminally ill, and pets in need of treats. The epidemic of short leases had led to so many second-hand clothes shops that it was a wonder all the natives weren't naked. And now, as the malign march of the meters stemmed the flood of consumerist farmers, Oxfam had replaced the cobblers.

'There ought to be a charity shop for businessmen,' muttered the ironmonger, aware that his collections of individual nails were loss-makers, and would one day soon be hammered into a bankruptcy notice. 'We're a deserving cause.'

'If I put a begging bowl outside *my* shop, d'you reckon *I* would qualify for tax relief? Hell, no!' shouted Mr Armstrong. Surplus testosterone was an occupational hazard of running an off-licence.

Neither of those two for President, thought Hubert. He was also opposed to the absent owner of Celtic Militaria, who appeared increasingly seldom but had taken to wearing Nazi insignia, decorations that Hubert regarded as incompatible with the aims of mainstream commerce. Hubert had briefly favoured the youngish Mr Johnson, but decided his image of dynamism was primarily due to the stripes on his tracksuit, which he wore to promote his modern range of sportswear.

'Laid out like a casbah, those charity shops,' sniffed the baker, whose experience of things foreign was limited to Tenby.

It was agreed to encourage a boycott of Oxfam, and the meeting moved on to pizzas and their harmful cultural impact.

Hubert had once had a faction. He had swung votes, had tried to bring money into town. His big idea had been to run bullocks through the streets and turn Abernant into the Pamplona of Wales, but unlike Hemingway he had been thwarted by the RSPCA. He had also got his fellow members to back a sign on the bypass, publicising the lures of Abernant, but the town council could not agree on which lures these should be. Now without a faction and facing his wilderness years, he was keen that his successor continue in the Hubert way of thinking.

The meeting moved on from worries about fat Americans dribbling melted cheese in public to votes for the change of President. In a long life in a small town, Hubert had been at school with the chemist, watched local rugby with the baker, played a mean hand of poker with the haberdasher, undergone a vasectomy on the same day as the bookseller. Such familiarity was standard. Candidates needed no introduction, no manifestos, no list of achievements, and the only conflicts of interest that counted were sleeping with another member's wife.

Hubert read out all the names of the nominees, an oddly formal procedure in the drab, beer-stained bar. Privately, the ex-President favoured Mr Beavan the bookseller, believing that literacy gave the man a head start. Nor was he averse to Mr Bennett the baker, many of whose rolls showed originality and a desire to be market leader in dough. He did, though, have reservations about Mr Devonald of Dev's Dainties, who had little experience of the world outside of women's clothing.

Voting was by the simple raising of hands, with the work experience girl acting as teller. However, sight-lines were obscured by the random arrangement of bar tables, and several counts were subject to rancorous appeal. Further delay was caused by a confusion over proxy votes, a dispute over the majority required, and the deafness of Mr Chigley. In the end, it took five rounds and twenty-two minutes for the new President of the Chamber of Commerce to emerge.

It was a result that Hubert had little expected, the result he had least wanted.

4

'Bribery?' echoed Dafydd, the ex-postman.

'How d'you know it was bribery?' queried Clydog.

'A hunch,' said Hubert defensively.

'Do you want us to go undercover?' asked Dafydd with sarcasm.

Hubert did some glowering but ignored the jest. Secretly he regretted being so sceptical when Dafydd had claimed there were nudists in the valley. Now, any of his own revelations were buffeted by Dafydd's wilful doubts.

'I've never trusted the man. He's too unctuous. Always at funerals, being sorry.' Hubert glared the length of the delicatessen and across the high street at the shop of his nemesis.

His view was uninterrupted by customers. This was the gossip hour, that part of a wet afternoon when the public urge to buy overpriced foreign foods was at a low ebb, that moment when his companions Clydog and Dafydd would drift in to spread rumours. The three men's gossip had a wide catchment area, and they worked hard to keep their fingers on the pulse of adultery.

26

More often though, they would settle for sightings of strangers or news of a sheepdog gone feral.

Unusually for a delicatessen, the place had the feel of a crypt. Two steps down from the street, its flagstoned floor and exposed stonework gave Hubert a 5 per cent mark-up for atmosphere. Hemp sacks of cereals, sufficient for a siege, stood stacked against axe-scarred oak pillars, with the emphasis more on heritage than hygiene. The deeds and the low ceilings said sixteenth century, while the damp smells and ill-lit corners said proprietorial parsimony.

The trio were gathered in a recess at the rear: Hubert, so that he could puff his pipe unseen by health vigilantes, Clydog, so that he could wrestle with sticky chocolate fudge cake unseen by his eighty-two-year-old mother, and Dafydd, so that he could pretend to be conspiratorial.

In his dreams, Dafydd saw himself as a Welsh Deep Throat. He used to deliver the mail to the valley with time-out for tea and tête-à-têtes — until he came upon a P45 in his post. Sacked, single, and soon to be forty, he had put his life on hold to indulge in some bitterness and hard drinking, only to suddenly find fulfilment at Forget-Me-Nots, the florist's. Hired as a man intimate with postcodes — though a little gingery beard and a cracked reddish skin meant he was intimate with little else — Dafydd now drove the lanes with a van full of floral creations, the bearer of billets-doux in place of bills. He was happy in his new work. The lilies and roses of Interflora had gained him access to a secret world, a world of double lives, and every day he criss-crossed the valley like a sex detective charting the ley-lines of lust.

'So you can't prove that money changed hands?' persisted Clydog.

'Well, not money exactly, no,' muttered Hubert, wishing he had never spoken. He had let his animus for the butcher flood his brain with red mist, and he had overstated his case. Twenty years of looking across the high street at Mr Capstick, and hoping he would slice off his hand with his cleaver, had not helped Hubert's impartiality.

This was an instinctive and intense hostility, quite untouched by reason. Mr Capstick had never done any harm to Hubert. Indeed, had he done harm to Hubert, Hubert might have disliked him less. But in the butcher he saw a template for all those traits he found unforgivably mundane. He found his dullness offensive, his ordinariness provocative, his righteousness repugnant. The man wore a tie even in the heat of summer. For his honeymoon he had gone on a tour of cattle markets. On the wall of his shop hung a portrait of the Queen.

' 'Not money exactly . . . '?' repeated Clydog.

'I saw a black man today,' said Dafydd.

'Now there's a scoop for you, Clydog.'

'How do you mean, 'not money exactly'?'

Hubert was not eager to respond. What he suspected, but could not attest to, was that Mr Capstick had been unduly free with his specialist sausages. (The specialist sausages of the new president were a prized item: their herbal ingredients were a secret recipe passed down the male line of the Capstick family since 1852, according to the rustically painted legend behind his pre-war marble counter.) Hubert's hunch was that gratuitous sausages had greased the plates of swing-vote barbecues, filling whole freezers to gain favour. And were no doubt hand-rolled at the dead of night. But he was aware that such claims could be misconstrued as pettiness, the vengeance of a sore loser.

'So what was this black man up to?' asked Hubert, grateful for a digression.

'Well, nothing. It just seemed a bit odd. What would a black man be doing in the middle of the countryside?'

'You never had Royal Mail guidance on

that sort of thing?'

'He certainly wouldn't be visiting relatives. Not this side of the Cambrians.'

'I'm surprised you didn't try a citizen's arrest, Dafydd.'

'Said he was lost. Some story about looking for the rugby pitch.'

'From Kenya,' interposed Clydog. 'School exchange tour.'

'Oh,' said Dafydd. And was visibly disappointed to have his mystery solved so easily.

Clydog smiled with the smugness of experience, and then unveiled his own titbit of the day. 'I think our mayoress may be up to something.'

Hubert groaned. 'Again?' The news flash failed to fire his imagination. His mind was already elsewhere, pondering whether he should have slipped some Parma ham into plain brown envelopes, for distribution to the undecided. Or perhaps been more liberal with his Belgian chocolates.

'Does it involve scissors?' asked Dafydd, mindful of the woman's compulsion to cut tape in public.

'I'm not sure yet,' replied Clydog.

'Or is she still on about art in the abattoir?' (The mayoress was a devotee of *grands projets* but none — and here Abernant

30

differed from France — had ever made that strategic conceptual leap from breathy enthusiasm to core funding.)

'It's too early to tell,' replied Clydog, beginning to regret his impulsiveness.

Rhiannon, the paper's ailing switchboard operator, was the origin of his insights. The scoop consisted of the single fact that the mayoress had rung Miss Nightingale. All details of the conversation were unknown, except that it had lasted two minutes. The mayoress, sensitive to her status, preferred to bypass the scribbling class, and rarely was anything as vulgar as a briefing ever vouchsafed to Clydog.

'So, this 'thing' she may be up to . . . ?' asked Dafydd, increasingly puzzled.

'I can't say any more,' muttered Clydog, 'I wouldn't want to betray my sources.'

Hubert meanwhile had lost interest in Clydog and his secrets. Hubert had reverted to long-distance glaring, and was attempting to transmit his venom over some forty yards. Each glimpse of the unnaturally Daz-white apron of the butcher opposite confirmed him in his view that Mr Capstick was a man unsuited for the rigours of high office.

5

In another age, a beadle would have preceded Myfanwy Edwards along the wet Abernant pavement, clearing room for her mayoral bulk as she brought succour to her people. In the meritocratic eighties, it was just the size of her swaying bosom that helped her make headway. She was assisted by the lurid colour of her dress, which encouraged the weaker locals to shelter in shop doorways. This dress was not only lurid, but extra-large — Hubert, aware of her mayoral enthusiasm for charitable works, was given to loudly stating that, in the event of an appeal for the homeless, it would make an excellent bell-tent for a small family.

As the mayoress powered towards the public library, she was distracted by lute music. Or possibly flute music, as her artistic sensibilities were often a letter or two out. It came from a New Age person with a dog. He had positioned himself under the arch that led to the market hall, where there was a flowering of local craftwork every fourth Thursday afternoon, and his high notes echoed pleasingly against the Victorian stonework.

The dreadlocked teenager, upon seeing the large presence in purple, quickly focused on the more rococo and cash-rich end of the repertoire. His was an act that made art of beggary. Disappointingly, the dog did nothing. But he wore a sign saying 'THANKS', and by his owner's feet lay a collection of minor coins in a tobacco tin. Music was rare in the high street, certainly rarer than vomit, and the police were often slow to act.

The mayoress paused to listen, but did not mention she was a patron of the arts. Putting her busy life on hold, she let a look of musical appreciation spread across her face. This conveyed a sort of trance, a sort of direct line to the composer. (Whom she thought might be Mozart.) If she had a criticism of the performer, apart from his lifestyle, it was his lack of footwork. She liked music where the player moved his feet about, in a leprechaun sort of way, as it added certainty to the position of the rhythm. But, that apart, the mayoress welcomed the presence of a troubadour spirit, feeling that it added to the gaiety of Abernant.

This was not the opinion of the ironmonger, Mr Bufton, who attributed the drop in the morning's sales of four-inch screws to the presence of unwanted musicality. He had just emerged from his Aladdin's cave of esoteric hardware carrying a broom, intent on brushing dirt in the busker's direction, when he saw the mayoress, eyes half shut, and vibrating like a recently laid jelly.

'Ah, Mr Bufton!' she cried.

Mr Bufton was a timorous man, rarely venturing out of brown overalls, who had been in his fifties for as long as anyone could remember.

'Mrs Edwards,' he replied, with the formality he reserved for everyone except two close relatives.

'Lovely music, eh! Adds a spring to your step! And such initiative, too! Enterprising lad, don't you think!'

'Er, yes,' said Mr Bufton, redirecting the broom to sweep up some non-existent leaves that had caught his attention.

'Deserves to be rewarded!'

'Er, yes.'

'Unfortunately, I can't carry money when I'm wearing this dress. Would you be so kind as to give the young man some small change for me?'

And off Myfanwy Edwards swept, having done her bit for charity.

Mr Bufton had been worrying about bankruptcy for some decades, constantly troubled by the trend to sell things in packets, and so to subsidise yobs was low among his priorities. He had heard that New Age people were massing in the hills, ready to attack, and he thought it unwise to encourage them. But, on the other hand, the mayoress was not only a persuasive size, she also had a husband with a burgeoning interest in DIY. Reluctantly Mr Bufton began to fumble for change.

The mayoress continued on her way to the library. The alfresco music had sparked off her creative synapses, and now she was thinking street theatre. Not the agitprop variety, of course. But Myfanwy had recently seen a TV documentary about Ancient Greeks colourfully celebrating the fertility of their land, and she now had an idea for an Abernant version. Details were a little fuzzy, but she envisaged Young Farmers Clubs and hay-wains. Men and pitch-forks and rustic shirts. A sort of Harvest Festival, except more mobile, perhaps with lanterns. (But certainly with no facemasks of giant phalluses. The likes of Mr Bufton would not grasp the symbolic link between a phallus and a corn dolly.) She was considering whether to dress up some of the young farmers as furry animals, maybe in rabbit costumes, when she arrived at the giant glass doors of the library. And was for a second startled by her reflection.

The library was a hideous concrete

building whose iron innards leached rust stains resembling a urine discharge. Only during one decade had Abernant allowed the twentieth century to make its mark, and with fatal predictability the town had chosen the sixties. In a perverse celebration of local heritage, the reception currently contained an exhibition of black and white photos depicting the delightful, if impractical, old buildings that had been demolished so that the library could be built in their place.

'I'm looking for something on Old Abernantians,' the mayoress announced to the blonde library assistant. 'Famous ones,' she added, to narrow the search.

This addendum did little but pucker the young woman's face with grave doubt as she reluctantly put down her date-stamp. Then she led the way into the stacks.

Books in the Abernant library were not organised along conventional lines. The senior librarian was an archivist by training, and took a dim view of fiction. He considered readers of novels to be the frivolous element of his clientele, and accordingly placed this section in the far, ill-lit corner. What he valued, and put in pride of place, were serious works of research into the last 50 million years of mid-Wales. With heavy-duty binding.

The mayoress, forced to forsake her

all-conquering strides, followed the young woman at library pace as she guided her along the tall, glass-fronted mahogany book-cases that stood in dour rows nearby. Geological, topographical, archaeological, historical, botanical, their subject matter was embossed on thick subfusc spines, often in Latin. *Archaeologia Cambrensis (Supplements 1909–11)*. Here was the last redoubt of the Victorians.

And this tradition of amateur scholarship continued to the present day. The county seemed to overflow with obsessive recluses who produced definitive slim volumes on obscure local features, thus filling fine-mesh holes in the nation's knowledge. Thousands of micro-moths were caught and logged and their genitalia examined. Hundreds of dandelion sub-species were identified and related in roadside verges. A unique fossil was discovered on a rock ledge and its past life documented in detail. And the same fastidious attention was focused on vanished villages, on farm boundaries, on matters spiritual. Diocesan handbooks, long-forgotten sermons, church deeds and documents, all were found worthy of binding. No niche of Abernantania went unrecorded.

But Myfanwy was eager for a showier claim to fame, for trail-blazing of a funkier nature. She watched impatiently as the assistant ran her slow finger past the doctrines of *The Abernant Mandate* and the account of an émigré's travails in *From Wales to Mississippi*.

'Famous how exactly?' enquired the woman.

'Er . . . in a mid-Wales way,' said the mayoress rather uncertainly. 'But preferably dead.'

The assistant puckered her face some more, moved two paces, then pointed at a small maroon book. She fiddled through her keys and unlocked the glass cabinet.

'Well, this has got preachers, architects, naturalists, landowners, singers. And a couple of murderers — though I don't know whether they did it in a mid-Wales way.'

The mayoress took the book and glanced briefly through the list of contents, already finding the rare habitat of a library to be uncongenially cerebral.

'Yes, I think this'll do to be going on with. Thank you.'

The mayoress returned the book, and waited as the cabinet door was carefully closed again and carefully relocked. Then she followed the assistant back to the desk where the stamp was kept.

'About blo-o-ody time!' was the cry that accosted them.

The two women stopped, taken quite

aback, with no response to hand.

'About blo-o-ody time!' came the cry again, but now an octave deeper.

Angry men were rarely seen in Abernant, and never in the library. This was a land of patient, cud-chewing men.

But this stranger was from Birmingham, and had the air of a man who was permanently angry. He was a bulky six-footer, scarlet-faced under his black stubble, and with a close-cropped cannonball for a head. Although forty-plus, he dressed like a bouncer. He wore a black suit, shiny and a size too tight, giving a look of temper to a body that wanted to burst out. With the black suit came the black shirt, though whether as a statement of fashion or of menace was uncertain. And as the ill-judged *coup de grâce*, he had gone for a flashy silver tie. One suspected tattoos, but fortunately they were not on display.

Clearly not a man who liked to wait, he also had the movements of a man who did not like to stand still. Insistent on service, he stepped closer, unable to curb the body language of threat.

'I want to see your latest back copies of *The Mid-Walian*.'

6

'We never exactly specify the cause of the catastrophe, and the almost total destruction of the world,' said the suave young man, balancing the Meissen coffee-cup on his knees. 'We just hint at it being nuclear or biological. Some sort of accident, so you get more of a sense of man's folly. And of course, the survivors, the few survivors, have to cope with the consequences of that folly. In hostile, primitive circumstances. Not knowing whether they are going to live or die, or suffer the ravages of some terrible pestilence.'

His beautiful Italian companion smiled at him adoringly from the chesterfield. She had not yet spoken and it was unclear whether she understood English. Something about her said mistress.

'What is important is that the script creates an accurate feel of this post-Armageddon world, as well as a sense of the culture that has gone before and has been lost. Or is being destroyed by man's reversion to barbarism.'

The Commodore had not yet spoken either, but he understood sufficient English to feel in danger of a panic attack.

'Which is why your house is so perfect.'

'Perfect?' queried Dilys.

'In its hint of apocalypse,' explained the young man. 'And your tarpaulined roof will act as a visual masterstroke.'

This was not how Dilys saw her roof.

Or indeed her house. When she had received the reply from the film company, acknowledging her photographs, she had imagined her ancestral home was being chosen for some elegiac documentary, for a poetic tribute to the vanishing age of gentility.

But to be wanted as a setting for the end of the world . . . ?

This was not at all the social legacy desired by Dilys, and, not unnaturally, she began to bridle.

7

It was 11 a.m. and Miss Cecily Nightingale was drinking a cup of herbal tea. As she had done at 7 a.m. on her arrival at work. As she would do at 3 p.m. on her departure from work. Miss Nightingale was a proprietor of habit.

She had thirty-odd years of such habits, all developed since her father had died on the front steps of the paper that he owned and loved. He had slumped to the ground with a heart attack, brought on by the excitement of seeing a fire engine go past. It was, as the minister said at the funeral, how he would wish to have gone. Busy watching the local news being made. (Although, as the minister added, he would certainly want the fire to be speedily put out.)

The family had founded *The Mid-Walian* in the early nineteenth century, when awash with money from their mills along the Nant. Modest nonconformists, their simple aim had been a journal of record, benign and worthy. But over the decades, the business of corn changed and the world of water-mills ground into silence. All this while, though, the printing presses continued to clatter ever louder, and *The Mid-Walian* — still a media monopoly in the mountains — grew to be a milch-cow supreme. And the Nightingales nurtured their money-maker for more than a hundred years, and each generation took great pains to find a safe pair of hands for its stewardship . . . until a cardiac infarction abruptly pre-empted their procedures.

The laws of succession could not be called in aid. Primogeniture led to a drunk, and the other brother was half-man, half-horse. There were nephews, there were cousins, but the written word did not loom large in their lives, indeed was a constant impediment to their existence. So, in the all-male landscape of the fifties, it was the slight figure of Cecily that came to the proprietor's chair. Middle-aged, and new to the practice of work.

Miss Cecily Nightingale had won certificates for her neat handwriting at school. Her conscientious and reliable disposition had allowed her to take the school rabbit home during the holidays. In her attitude to litter she was old beyond her years. Her sense of propriety had made her prefect, then head prefect, and she regularly patrolled the grounds of her private school to put a halt to vandalism and girls kissing. Broadly speaking, she felt this was probably the range of qualities needed to run any institution.

But she had also loved her father, and her father had loved *The Mid-Walian*. Her earliest memory was a tour of the printer's, to see the drama of hot metal in action. And for his final twenty years, as an unwed daughter ministering to a widowed father's whims, she had subliminally been tutored in the paper's traditions. Suddenly, she was the inheritor of those traditions, almost the inheritor of a museum, of a business where time stood still. From here on, it would be her responsibility to safeguard the family future, to lead the paper into the post-war world. But already she had a vision.

She would save the paper by allowing nothing to change.

As elderly Miss Nightingale sipped her herbal tea in solitude, she wondered — not for the first time that troubled week — whether the infusion really did soothe the nerves.

Her Auberon, of course, was a constant trial. The gangly young nephew combined clumsiness and shyness in equal parts, and even as tea-boy he carried with him a threat of chaos. She initially had hopes the lad might be heir apparent, but catatonia and a stutter made management an unlikely career path. Her nepotism had aimed him toward photography, but cameras jammed at the touch of his fingers, even at the sight of his approach. And portraiture, as the mayoress had forcefully made clear to the editor, usually involves the whole face.

The mayoress, too, had been an irritant for Miss Nightingale lately. Even when she had been an ordinary citizen, the woman would behave as if attended by a personal Muse, but since given the seal of office, Myfanwy Edwards appeared to believe that she (and art) had a date with destiny. Whether it was grand opera or Plasticine moulds, corn circles or an Owain Glyndwr look-alike competition, the mayoress would move into Reithian mode. The telephonist had only to announce her name, and Miss Nightingale found herself fearing a proposal to reconstruct the Pyramids in Powys, or re-enact the Viking Conquests up the Nant. Her latest whim was some statue. Yet none of this was done in the name of art. It was done in the hope of baubles, royal baubles — or failing that, some sniggered, with the purpose of creating a region called Myfanwyland, to be visited all year round by coach parties. What irked Miss Nightingale most, though, was the woman's belief that *The Mid-Walian* should function as her private PR firm, converting her fantasies into reality.

But there was another, darker worry for Cicely that even sherry could not have dispelled. It was the arrival of the late twentieth century.

The Nightingales had become a rare breed, but a rare breed without protection. Few were the families who still owned newspapers, few were the newspapers still shaped by non-corporate hands. Something called economic forces — mysterious, invisible, malign, and living deep in the financial pages — was stalking the land, with the soft footfalls of a ravening wolf-pack.

Miss Nightingale had long taken pride, as had her father, and his father, in the profitability of *The Mid-Walian*. And profitable it remained. The paper held a rose-tinted mirror up to its readers and they responded with gratitude and loyalty — and a regular 20p. They even queued for the paper in the rain. But on a graph, the profit line was horizontal, and new-wave economists believed that profit lines should be vertical. So there was a school of thought in Abernant that the venerable *Mid-Walian* could make more money. That school of thought was her brothers'.

The views of Aidan and Theo, on any subject, major or minor, past or present, real or hypothetical, physical or metaphysical, were, by common consent, worthless. Except,

46

that is, in the context of the family trust. Where they were worth a majority vote.

The extended family rarely met, except for births, marriages, deaths and disagreement. Its members preferred to be dysfunctional in private. But rumours showed no such discretion. And it was at the 19th hole, after a Volvo owners' stroke play competition, that Cicely had first heard of her brothers' discontent (alleged). Never noted for their own editorial input, as she reflected tersely, her siblings had been heard to state — and in a slurred tone, she suspected — that 'sis and the paper should move with the times'. And that 'if she wouldn't, they would'. Because 'she was costing them money'.

This new interest in their finances was no doubt influenced by a drink habit and a horse habit rather than any grasp of the monetarist school of economics. But 'sis' could not be sure of their intent. Were her brothers referring to a shortage of scandal, to an excess of golf stories, to a lack of horoscopes, to the printing of photos that merged black and white into grey? And what is it they would do? Were they wanting to take on new staff? To get rid of old staff? To replace her as proprietor? Or something worse . . . ? She did not even know what credence to give to the rumours, as they appeared to have come via the driver of a flower delivery van. But what she did know was that she would never betray her father, nor willingly become the last Nightingale to preside over *The Mid-Walian*.

It was 11.05, and time to put her empty herbal-tea cup back on the tray.

8

'I'm not sure I want barbarism in any of the rooms,' said Dilys. 'Even with careful actors.'

Repeatedly she had promised a tour of the house, only to reknit her brows and return to the Dundee cake. Once, she had actually flexed her calves as if to rise . . . then unflexed them and enquired whether the cast could wear carpet slippers.

The producer retained his sympathetic smile, familiar with the way that hard-nosed negotiations masqueraded as the airing of sensibilities. In the distance, a third grandfather clock struck eleven, some twenty minutes after the first.

Philip was wondering whether to use the word *Zeitgeist*. He had used it a lot in his proposal to the network and it had gone down rather well. Cold War paranoia was hot right now and made for a good marketing tool. He had originally wanted to call his company *Zeitgeist* Productions, but this had set the bar too high for the spelling skills of his new graduate intake. So he had settled for The Now Company, which he felt conveyed urgency and a cutting edge agenda.

'In fact, I'm not sure I want actors indoors at all. We have a lot of porcelain. Couldn't they do their acting in the garden?'

Philip had not met gentry before, decayed or otherwise. Countryside was not really his thing, and the people in it not to his taste; everything he needed was in just one square mile, in West London's media land. Even what to wear for a rural meeting had been a mystery, and Carla, an apostle of fashion, had steered his slim figure from rough-hewn denim to elegant country casual. Too late, Philip had realised that to blend with the Powells he should have gone to a 1930s jumble sale. To blend with their furniture he should have gone to an 1830s jumble sale. A man of minimalist tastes, he had not previously sat in a room with a giant carved elephant — and a mahogany cabinet big enough for it to breed in.

'Think of us as family,' he replied. 'We respect your property like our own. And you get a free spring-clean when we leave.'

Carla raised her false eyelashes in discreet mockery, betraying an awareness of the vocabulary of dirt. She too was eager for the tour to start, if only to remove her trouser-suited Italian bottom from the dubious stains on the sofa. She was also disconcerted by the Commodore, who, though standing, appeared to be dead. Rigidly upright between the palm tree and the marble fireplace, left arm laid out awkwardly along the mantelpiece, weathered face focused on the far wall, this was the usual defensive posture he adopted for visitors. Fearful of incoming conversation, he perhaps felt the fronds gave him cover.

'And, of course, a generous insurance policy.' Philip ladled almost lascivious stress on each syllable of the word generous, allowing the listener to detect the lurking presence of the word fraud.

Forty years of bridge had given Dilys a face with emotional shutters — a luxury in view of the few emotions she possessed — and it was not possible to tell if the terms were tempting her. She chewed her cake slowly, as if counting its sultanas. She was, however, not thinking of morals or actors or cracked china, but calculating the laws of supply and demand. How many of her neighbouring gentry had leaky, dilapidated mansions? Offering a good venue for an apocalypse? And in need of funds? Alas, too many, Dilys thought, too many. Time perhaps, for the tour.

Philip meanwhile had said *Zeitgeist*, which was not a wise move. The Commodore's delicate mind was prone to overheat if he heard an unusual word (except for escutcheons, which were a life-long hobby of his). And this unusual word was a German word. Although the Commodore had not seen action overseas — or indeed action anywhere — he had long, unhappy memories of lying in a darkened room, worrying about the unnecessary noise caused by war. Now an old man, he found that all German words, whether *Zeitgeist* or *Blitzkrieg*, added significantly to his stress levels.

'Pills!' he said, brushing aside the fronds and bolting slowly for the door.

★　★　★

Gloom. If the old house had a descriptive noun it was gloom. Every shade of gloom. The gloom of a room with just one shutter open, the gloom of a room with a velvet curtain dangling loose from its pelmet, the gloom of a room with a chandelier reduced to its last three tiny bulbs, the gloom of a room where the wan morning light was overwhelmed by the dense shafts of airborne dust. Morning room, breakfast room, sitting room, anteroom, here the big beasts of the furniture jungle stood forlorn and hard to see: unpolished, mouldy, and cobwebbed. Here, writ large, was the tragedy of a land without domestics.

Unwarned, this once-grand house had anticipated the end of the world. Unscripted, the rooms had already created the mood for civilisation's last stand. Uncommissioned, the props for post-apocalypse were in place.

Philip congratulated himself on his find as he squeezed out of the small kitchen where jackdaw imprints marked the walls in some kind of post-modernist William Morris pattern. A brief passageway with bare plaster led back to the hall. He was an ideas man, and now he was envisioning his tattered band of survivors (ethnically and socially diverse, with some unresolved gender issues) shot in moody shade, hinting at a subtext of Hades, while outbursts of feral violence punctuated debate on the meaning of life.

* * *

'Oh, good gong, love the gong!'
  'Pardon?'
  'Oh yes, we can use a dinner gong.'
  'You can use . . . ?'
  'Early warning system, we can put it on the roof. Any sign of attack, they hit it.'
  To make his point, the visitor from TV hit the dinner gong. With force. At the other end of the hall, the old labrador shivered in shock, and pissed quietly on the Turkmenistan rug.

53

Philip was good at enthusiasm, especially with old people. Film production was all about charm.

'Would that be extra?' asked Dilys.

'Attack by whom?' asked the Commodore.

Philip was also good at diplomatic deafness, and so said nothing.

The house tour had reached the trout photo at the foot of the stairs, and had paused for *hommage*. The hall-stand made out of antlers, the outsize Oriental urn used for an ashtray, and the two stuffed spaniels under glass, had all been passed without comment. Philip himself felt it wise not to seem *over*-excited by these staples of country life, not to be too much a townie pushover, with safari-jacket pockets stuffed with dosh. Carla, though, already regretted she had left the breakfast room; once keen to come on location with her lover, she had not displayed a mature response to the bat droppings and the mouse.

Philip's most puzzling problem, however, was with the Commodore, whose attention was now wandering again, his troubled eyes gazing up the stairs. Philip had tried in vain to bond. He had tried charm, chit-chat, jokes, gossip about TV stars, all his usual winners. Sadly, he was not to know the password was fish. The old man lived in a very private world and allowed access to few visitors, even those in the glitzy business of roof repair money. His communications with Dilys herself were sparse and had all the warmth of Morse code. Not once had Philip observed a smile between them. He wondered how long their marriage had been so sour, and fell back on the received wisdom of his schooldays that the gentry only married for land.

'Would you like to see upstairs?' asked Dilys, as if the answer were in doubt.

'Very much,' replied Philip. His references to the screenplay, as yet incomplete, had outlined the turmoil of the survivors' lives. What he had illumined less was the never-ending need to keep alive the species, to rut and hump for posterity. On a wide-ranging and inventive scale. With little privacy. And a lot of nudity.

Dilys began to lead the way up to the landing, and the seven bedrooms promised in her letter. Philip paused to squint through the makeshift lens of his fingers, that fashionable trademark of film-makers. Here on these stairs he could picture hand-to-hand fighting as two rival bands of survivors struggled for possession of the property. Bloodied bodies tumbled downwards in his mind's eye. He captured the carnage in a slow Potemkin pan, and silently murmured 'cut'. Only then did he move to climb the modestly sweeping but unswept staircase, Carla keeping close by his side.

'Will there be jeeps?' demanded the Commodore. 'I don't want jeeps.'

'Jeeps . . . ? Why would there be jeeps?'

'Ruin the stairs, jeeps. I don't want jeeps.'

'No, there won't be jeeps.'

'My cousin let strangers in. They had jeeps.'

'I've got no jeeps.'

'Up the stairs, for bets. I don't want jeeps.'

'There are no jeeps in the script.'

'And they burnt the house down.'

'With jeeps?' asked Philip.

'1943,' said Dilys. 'Americans.'

'Will there be Americans?' demanded the Commodore.

'No. No, we've got no Americans, NO jeeps.'

The Commodore looked dubious.

'No fuel. Brave new world.' Philip smiled reassuringly.

The Commodore stayed silent, but left his mouth half-open in case he should wish to speak again.

The tour reached the first landing, and moved down a corridor where musty linoleum triggered memories of a genteel boarding house fallen on hard times. Long ago, the woodwork had been victim of the fashion for varnish, and after years of neglect a congealed brown darkened the air. Ancestors in flaking oils hung like an unknown guard of honour upon the walls.

'And four-posters?' enquired Philip. 'D'you have four-poster beds?'

'A couple,' replied Dilys. 'I'll show you the master bedroom.'

She stopped opposite a Ruritanian cavalry officer with a lance and a joke moustache and turned to the door on her right. Ahead, the corridor curved and brass wall lamps lit a shadowy way past more closed doors.

'We have a Chinese tapestry in here,' said Dilys, 'brought back by the colonial side of the family. A hundred and fifty years old, so I wouldn't want actors throwing darts at it.' Dilys tugged her cardigan tightly around herself and reached for the door handle.

But before anyone could enter, before Philip could even utter soothing words on the subject of darts, another door opened.

And an old lady in a white nightie appeared.

She moved like an unsteady ghost but was muttering like an unbalanced mortal.

'Oh, dear Lord, she's out!' cried Dilys.

The old lady slewed round, startled by the sound of voices, surprised at the sight of visitors. And after a moment's hesitation, she started towards them, a vague smile across her face. Big-boned for an apparition, she had unkempt grey hair and wore fluffy slippers. Her nightie was a couple of buttons short of respectable, she walked as though upon a pitching deck, and her hands were clutching a once-white ceramic bowl.

Dilys's face had till this moment been short of expressions, but on it now was a fast-moving choice of fury, confusion, embarrassment, even mortification. She pressed her palms to her cheeks as if to hide any further reactions from public view.

The Commodore stood transfixed, though this was not an unfamiliar posture.

Then Dilys cried, 'Get her back in!' And advanced upon her, but with noticeable caution, as though the old lady were a hand grenade in human form. Like an unwilling long-stop, the Commodore tentatively brought up the rear.

Philip and Carla watched as the old lady feinted, trying to side-step the attempt to capture her. But Dilys was alert to this and, being the more nimble of the two, blocked the way with a body swerve. The old lady swore incoherently and nearly stumbled in the ill-lit corridor. Behind Dilys, the Commodore ineffectually waved his arms, as sometimes works with sheep.

It was the first time Philip had seen the couple act with a common interest, but he had no idea what that might be. His initial theory he had rejected, for the woman was too old to be a walled-up love-child. Perhaps a reluctant member of a *ménage à trois*? Whom the years had left unlovely and unwanted? It was not even clear whether it was his duty to help round her up.

Carla gripped Philip tightly by the hand, her false nails making this a painful intimacy. As they looked on, the lady of the nightie tried a low, lunging move past Dilys, that in different circumstances might have resulted in a match-winning try, but here, on slippery linoleum, caused her to slide head first toward the wall. It was hard to judge whether she lost her grip on the bowl or chose to throw it at Dilys.

Josephine's aim was wayward, as had been her life, and several litres of highly alcoholic urine sprayed over Carla's soft cream sweater. Carla screamed, for cashmere stained easily. Dilys and the Commodore looked on aghast. And the owner of the urine began to giggle.

But Philip remained calm, as is the first rule of being a producer. He had just seen new plot possibilities, and was wondering what Josephine would cost as an extra.

He was also wondering whether the Commodore and his wife kept anybody else in the other bedrooms.

9

Clydog held up the reader's letter and sniffed it. It was the fourth reader's letter he had sniffed that morning. He was sniffing with a sleuth's nose, prompted by the instincts of a hack. He had fully read their contents, and something was awry.

Clydog knew well the writing habits of his readers. He knew them so well that when the readers failed to write, failed to respond to *The Mid-Walian* issues of the day, Clydog wrote the letters they would have written, had the thought but struck them. He would sign these letters Lloyd or Powell or Price, and source them somewhere hazy in the infinite acres of sheepdom. Thus adding to the vigorous cauldron of debate on the Letters Page.

Worming techniques, killer bracken, foreign sheep, women who smoke in the street, dangers of crossbred ducks: the preoccupations of readers were parochial yet perennial. Parking meters had been last year's hot topic, sometimes requiring a supplementary page. The Best Kept Village scandal had also been a good column filler, though the accusation that Llanbedr's vicar had deliberately littered his rival's cemetery was never conclusively proved. Currently, the post-bag was filled with talk of invasion, as parish after parish spread the wild rumour that waves of New Age travellers were within a day's march; the latest hysteria was that their disease-ridden wagons had on board a drug-crazed under-class intent on laying waste to the town.

But no-one had ever written a letter to *The Mid-Walian* about a poet.

Until a week before, that is — when a bemused Clydog had received 1,132 words of purple prose penned by the mayoress on the neglected life and works of one Ieuan Owen Owens, deceased. He being the quondam author of acrobatic word-play in several slim but seminal, evocative but subversive, avant-garde yet ageless volumes. Apparently. Proclaiming him the Dylan Thomas of Abernant, albeit unread for half a century, she had proposed his genius be immortalised by a statue.

Mayoral letters, even when daft and of dubious grammar, could not unfortunately be binned, and so her whim had passed into print.

A week had gone by — and a now baffled Clydog had received four other prolix paeans to the poet. All eulogised the man's metric mastery; all spoke in remarkably similar terms about his robust view of the human condition; and all wished to see him on a plinth. Abernant appeared to have an underground Ieuan fan club.

Clydog sniffed again. Different envelopes, different notepaper, different signatures, but all the letters had the same scent. Clydog was not an expert on perfume, though he had once dabbled with deodorant, but on the occasion of the parking meter riot his nose had been pushed into one of the fleshier parts of the mayoress. A woman with an unfavourable body mass index, she was prone to perspiration during ceremonial duties, and it had become her habit to be liberal with the distribution of *Ecstasy 69*. This was the scent that Clydog now recognised.

★   ★   ★

The mayoress readjusted the posture of the three teddy bears on her desk, for Tompy, Tufty, and Winky had wobbled off their bottoms during the many hours of her two-fingered pounding on the typewriter.

The letters sent, the world alerted, she had now composed a Proposal of Intent, its aim to inject some non-lethal culture into the council's veins. Abernant was a town that had no statue, not even a statuette. The eager archivist had searched all the records, and the only example found was of an inter-war Lloyd George, pointing. Possibly to the future. But after his death the town went Tory, and he had been turned into hardcore, to help extend the stockyards.

Choosing a subject that would 'convert the world of dreams into solid form' had greatly taxed the mayoress, whose previous finest hour had been upon a float, pretending to be somebody out of the Mabinogion. (In a toga and holding a trident, for reasons unknown.) The desiderata of the Arts Council were more rigorous. In particular, Myfanwy had struggled with their suggestion of a 'concept', she being uncertain how one took a chisel to a concept, or what shape it would be when finished. And besides, in her bones she knew the councillors would not be keen on concepts.

Which is why she had gone for flesh and blood, for an individual who 'best expressed the nature of their locality'. Mid-Wales being a rural area, she had briefly been tempted by Prof. Roy Groves, a name synonymous with lichen in the county, and whose studies of *verrucaria* had spread to Cardiff and beyond. But the artist in her won out. And so, after considering the Victorian architect who had designed the beautiful and historic — and now demolished — three-span stone bridge across the River Nant, and pondering over the town's one accomplished actress, whose career was tragically cut short by the loss of a leg when threshing, she had settled on Ieuan Owen Owens.

The mayoress had often felt that she herself could have become a poet had life turned out differently, and so was emotionally inclined to a monument in memory of a literary man.

Unfortunately, she had not managed to read any of his poetry, as Mr Beavan's second-hand bookshop had not yet tracked down an English translation of his work. But her maroon library book had referred to contemporary critical acclaim, and the librarian had located the back number of a poetry review in which the young writer was described as an iconoclast. With a provocative attitude to rhyme and passionate in a context of acerbic anti-pietism, whatever that was. It added cryptically that his good looks had been his downfall.

The prospect of resurrecting Abernant's long-lost poet had put the mayoress in one of her bouncy moods. Her love of the arts was second only to her desire to be honoured for her love of the arts, and she sensed recognition in the wind. Being one of the great and the good in a town of 8,000 had long got her nowhere, but soon her name would be known to the movers and shakers of Cardiff. The Welsh Arts Council was but a short leap to a royal garden party, the first staging-post to heaven. And with a statue to her credit, it could surely not be long before she reached her goal in life: headed notepaper with a little something from the Queen after her name.

Her Proposal now ready to print, she levered herself up from her revolving leather recliner and treated herself to six coffee creams. As she gazed out on the patio at her stone squirrels, her thoughts moved on to the councillors. She had lost many battles with the town council, who lacked her feel for the non-agricultural things in life, but this time she was untypically optimistic. This time, her plans contained the magic word beloved of all councils: free. She was not just proposing a statue of artistic value, but a statue of artistic value that would be funded by others. It was also a plus point that Ieuan Owen Owens was a good-looking artist, as no one likes a statue of an ugly person. *And* she had already thought of the perfect location.

Her proposal could yet become a landmark, a sculpture that would put Abernant on the tourist map. The mayoress had only one regret. Ideally, she would have liked the statue to be of herself.

10

I believe in meat, like my father before me.

Mr Capstick liked his opening line: first principles, continuity of values.

'I believe in meat, like my father before me.' The butcher tried the words aloud, swilled them around in his mouth, like a man tasting a good wine.

Meat and clean living, these are the building blocks of a successful business. The old virtues.

He had wondered whether a speech was appropriate, whether a declaration of principles would be welcomed by the other fifteen, not all of them morally serious. Or sober. But if he was to be a leader, his views on Abernant commerce needed to be known.

And the mortar round the building blocks is service, old-fashioned service. The bag carried to the car; the remembered allergy; the free poster of sheep cuts; the murmured God Bless; the extra bacon slice.

He made a note to lighten the mood here, with his aphorism that one customer lost and found is more valuable than the ninety-nine remaining regulars. He also briefly wondered whether to mention Mrs Capstick, but decided she was a given.

Then the draft went on to make much of his twenty-plus years of experience, his framed certificate as a master butcher, his *Est. 1852* sign that he repainted with gold lettering every second summer.

Fine wines mature with age, pheasants are the better for hanging, and so too must a business be here for the long haul. The fast buck is the quick death of reputation.

The butcher was tempted to allude to the errors of other shopkeepers' ways, but his victory vote had been paper thin.

Mr Capstick did, however, have a large hobby-horse or two that he wanted to exercise, and was glad to have at last found a forum. Over the years he had had urges to be a lay preacher, but had suppressed them because he was five foot four, a height which did not, he felt, adequately convey his gravitas. He had tried an alternative path by taking over as scoutmaster from the former vicar of St Brynnach's, who was currently sedated in a home for depressed Welsh clergy, but the butcher found the youth of Abernant resistant to any notion of civics, and more adept with sharp knives than he was.

He tore another sheet of lined writing paper from the pad, and dabbed the tip of the

HB pencil with his tongue. This was a habit inherited from his father, and now just a ceremonial reflex without meaning; although on some level he was puzzled as to why lead poisoning should be an essential prelude to writing, this was outweighed by his great attachment to tradition, whatever it might be. His other ritual was to write at an old roll-top desk which stood, its many minidrawers neatly labelled in capital letters, beside a standard lamp in the back room of his standard semi. From here he could watch the garden and be sure that nothing was growing in a disorderly manner.

The butcher wrote next of his perturbation at the growing anarchy of commerce. Torch batteries would turn up in the newsagent's, pot plants would turn up in the card shop, T-shirts would turn up at the petrol station. And sweets could turn up anywhere. The natural order of retailing (had irony been in his repertoire he would have called it the divine right of shop-keepers) was taking body blows from cowboy companies. Yet try as he might to invoke a general principle, his was a coded complaint. What really bugged him, what most fired his impotent ire, was that meat was turning up in the deli.

Mr Capstick regarded meat as the copyright, even the birthright, of a butcher — yet salami and prosciutto and chorizo were all now for sale in a glorified greengrocer's. He didn't know whether to be more upset by Hubert's lack of fair play or his lack of patriotism; Mr Capstick was against foreign foods, but then again he wanted the exclusive rights to sell them.

They had known each other — in the nodding sense — for some two decades, and Hubert's behaviour had consistently upset him. The man had a cavalier attitude to the vocation of shopkeeper. He thought nothing of disagreeing with customers, usually just for devilment. Often, though, it was because his Reduced To Clear shelf contained objects which were moving. (Thus confirming the butcher's view that a 'health food' shop was not a proper shop, and certainly not healthy.) Hubert was that most dangerous of threats to society, a man who didn't believe in rules and regulations. Or reputations. And he made jokes about it. With the best of wills, Mr Capstick could see nothing funny in telling the Commodore's sister that, if she was to qualify for a refund on his food, she would need not just a receipt but a death certificate.

He licked his HB pencil again. He had words to say on hygiene.

If pressed, Mr Capstick would probably contest the belief that cleanliness was next to godliness, and argue instead that it was a dead heat. He was keen on clean. He knew for a fact — because he watched — that Hubert was lax with a broom and remiss with a mop and wore a pullover whose hairs were a health hazard. He suspected that his glass surfaces would provide the fingerprint records of half the town. And he had heard talk of flagstones with cracks so deep they must hold two hundred years of germs. (No doubt living in a highly organised germ city, with germ suburbs and germ shopping malls.)

Then there was the pipe. Hubert's pipe. A malodorous prop, puffed with languid flair, its fumes rolled in fog-bank wreaths over the cheeses and the hand-patted butter, its nicotine contents hung in the air like a choke collar. And when not exhaling inside the shop, its owner would stand at the doorway to puff forth a pungent welcome, like a pre-war ad for Old Holborn. Hubert was puffing for freedom, for the right to his own brand of oxygen in his own style of shop.

Across the road, however, the butcher's life moved to the rhythms of bleach, in harmony with the needs for disinfectant. Yet he had never publicly voiced his deep disdain for the habits of his neighbour. Although a man of many firm principles, Mr Capstick preferred to move in mysterious and sanctimonious ways. So he had smiled his thin-lipped smile and busied himself, as ever, with the goal of perfect butchery.

And of late it was noted that Hubert the showman was keeping an unusually low profile. He had taken to lurking at the rear, the pipe-sucking done in the shadowy recesses, his smoke rising furtively behind the baguette stand. It was as if an alter ego was doing the puffing, and with lungs that lacked full-blooded bravado. For so long the *enfant terrible*, Hubert seemed to have had a dose of age.

Only the butcher knew why. Only the butcher knew of the visit by men in white coats. Only the butcher knew of the tip-off to Trading Standards. He salivated on his pencil.

A shop must be a fly-free zone; not a ceramic tile should go unwashed; not a marble top should go unscrubbed; not a germ should go unreported.

Yet the butcher had one more source of discontent, a secret grievance still to remedy.

Merriment. When Hubert gathered with his cronies to grin and to gossip, their laughter could be heard across the street. It was a frivolous laughter, at times uproarious and rowdy. It was a laughter that made a nonsense of responsible shopkeeping, a laughter that lapped around the butcher's shop-front, intent on mockery and disparagement.

But under new leadership, resolved Mr Capstick, the Chamber of Commerce would bring seriousness and rigour to the business of trade. Henceforth, their meetings would be laughter-lite. His election could yet become a landmark, an event that would put Abernant on the commercial map. The butcher had only one regret. Ideally, he would have liked to be mayor.

Summer

11

'Cecily Nightingale.'

The tone was peremptory, but the unsmiling receptionist who guarded *The Mid-Walian* did not immediately respond. Partly this was because she doubled as the telephonist, and was busy hearing about her sister's new outfit from Dev's Dainties; and partly because she was asthmatic and preferred to economise on the use of her voice, an approach not ideal for a position in communications. But it was also because of surprise, as in thirty years at the newspaper she had never, till now, heard anyone use the proprietor's first name.

'I want to see Cecily Nightingale.'

This time the tone was peremptory and cross. Rhiannon, a pudding-shaped woman, gazed abstractedly through the gap in the plywood partition. As an old hand on *The Mid-Walian* she had long ago learnt there was no such thing as urgency. She used to work in the classified ads department, where the concept of time owed much to the moon and the tides. There she had fully absorbed the company's old-world ethos, which held that to purchase space in the paper was a privilege, and the customer a supplicant. So news of summer fêtes often hit the presses in the autumn, and puppies for sale were sometimes fully grown before any buyer knew of their birth. Rhiannon could even recall a year when Valentine endearments were held over till March, and refunds denied.

'I *said* I want to see Cecily Nightingale.'

Rhiannon knew better than to weaken, and did not let on that she had heard. Besides, she found this an odd request. People who wished to see Miss Nightingale had appointments, and tended to look apprehensive. This man failed on both counts. And he had not polished his shoes.

Rhiannon was fortunate in having slightly hooded eyes, and so could carry out covert surveillance while continuing to focus on the merits of padded shoulders. Her yen when young had been a line of work where nosiness was a professional virtue, and now late middle age had left her with the body language of a thwarted spy. She noted disapprovingly that her subject had body hair on inappropriate places, growing wild and gypsy-like under his collar and cuffs. He also had a neck that was XL, with a bulldog bulge that suggested a business suit was not the neck's normal venue.

These, though, were merely incidental details of colour, and Rhiannon's wish was for the more solid nuggets of deep background. She had her theories on this person, and they ranged from green-ink letter writer to Mafia hit-man. But theories are easily come by; they constitute a poor second to the status of inside knowledge, which grants the kudos of being privy to secrets. When Rhiannon ran her undercover eyes over visitors to *The Mid-Walian* offices it was usually in the unsustained hope of a Welsh Watergate. It was also in the hope of love.

Rhiannon had never been married, nor received an offer of anything similar, nor even — as far as she could remember, and it was likely she would remember — been asked out to the pictures. She had always been the wrong shape for relationships. She had, apparently, even been a mismatch for the womb, and caused the midwife to pull a muscle. In her early years, she had found there to be little demand for a rhomboid teenager; in her later years, she had developed remorselessly into a woman without any known nooks or crannies. All curves in the family had gone to her sister, with whom Rhiannon shared a maisonette and a cat. Outwardly, her emotional life was now satisfied by her role as Match Secretary of the

Abernant Women's Bowling Green Team (though this was, in fact, a consolation post, offered when breathlessness had caused her balls to repeatedly fall short of the jack). But inwardly, deep down, she was consumed with physically impractical longings. She was yearning for Clydog.

For years, as she watched the world pass by her plywood partition, her pulse had quickened at the coming of the news gatherers' news gatherer, the man of a thousand secrets: Clydog the Knowledge. To her, Clydog resembled a kind of Factfinder General, an elder statesman of reportage. Yet though all-seeing and all-knowing, he was also avuncular and sedate and unmarried, *and* he rarely failed to doff his hat as he went on his stately way. He also bulked large in his tweeds and Rhiannon's subconscious had always warmed to aberrant body sizes. A man ill-suited to turnstiles was a kindred spirit, and, acting upon this affinity, she had for some time been attempting to bond.

Like a dog bringing bones for approval, Rhiannon would proffer him titbits for rewriting and hearsay for recycling. Being eager for status and kudos, she scanned the foyer like an early prototype of CCTV. Unfamiliar with the practice of passion, she believed the way to his heart was to be his source. In her daydreams, she was his operative in the field, his undercover agent in the foyer, even — and, on some level, she knew this was a stretch — his Mata Hari behind enemy lines.

'*Where is her office?*'

Rhiannon realised the man's stubble was now the wrong side of the partition. Her plans to elicit his life history were dead in the water. From the jut of his jaw, it also looked unwise to enquire about the nature of his business. Or indeed about anything. She had not even got a name to pass on to her newshound. Rhiannon sniffed furtively for deodorant, knowing the intelligence value of descriptive details, but the only odour was a hint of fried breakfast. Her attention was caught by a bead of sweat on the end of his nose, and, it being a cool day, she ascribed this to an inner volcanic violence.

'Top floor.'

As she watched Miss Nightingale's visitor turn and bound noisily up the broad eighteenth-century staircase, Rhiannon wondered what others knew of this meeting. Miss Nightingale was a private person, very proper, and not prone to see men with shaved heads or clashing ties. There had once been a man with perspiration stains under his armpits, but he had been a Land Agent, and it was August. The mystery visitor might be a salesman, but his technique seemed suited only to tank accessories. He might be a long-lost relative, but he had an implausible way of approaching the family bosom. The more Rhiannon applied her detective mind to the matter, the odder it seemed. Until an alarming theory began to form in her head . . .

★ ★ ★

The top floor had dispensed with décor: no carpet, no linoleum, and bare boards that were not even fashionably scrubbed, just bare. The corridor showed no signs of life and branched into brief cul-de-sacs ending in unmarked doors, which, had it been Paris, would have hidden an impoverished *bonne* or two. But here, whatever they hid stayed hidden, since it required a shoulder charge to overcome Miss Nightingale's locks. Meanwhile, nothing and no-one broke the dusty silence, not even the newsroom one floor below.

It was only when Eddie Trench reached the furthermost door of the labyrinth that he came upon a handle which responded to his rigorous rattling. Never a patient man, rarely a polite man, he found the *mañana* of mid-Wales a crime against capitalism and his short fuse was already alight at both ends. What he had seen so far of *The Mid-Walian* made a good case for management by firing squad. Eddie was a man who did deals, no messing, and after a two-hour drive he was not ready to ponce about on a landing. He dispensed with the niceties of knocking and pushed back the door.

★   ★   ★

Eddie blinked. He thought himself a hard man, not much given to blinking, but nonetheless he blinked several times. He had never been to the nineteenth century before.

At first, the half-light — from a distant bulb, unseen and anaemic — had revealed only the shadows of towering shapes, shapes that almost filled the room. But, as his eyes acclimatised, he realised it was not really a room at all but a sort of attic warehouse. Then, gradually, he was able to make out long rows of ceiling-high racks. And filling these racks were yellowing archives, stacked and filed according to categories of the arcane. Moving nearer, he saw not just long-forgotten editions of *The Mid-Walian*, but notepads, documents, catalogues, brochures, exercise books. The shelves themselves were made of metal honeycombed with holes, like adult Meccano, and in these endless holes hung endless hooks attached to endless photos and letters and cards and random scraps of paper.

Eddie Trench was a man not noted for intellectual curiosity, but he did know that the wonders of the past often had a high second-hand value and this gave him cause to pause. After a bit of squinting he began to browse.

'*Grasshopper Warbler, Reed Warbler, Sedge Warbler, Wood Warbler, Garden Warbler, Willow Warbler,*' started the list of bird species seen in the Nant Valley in 1933. Eddie chose not to read the entire inter-war record of local birdlife and put the sheaf of notes back on its hook. Further along the aisle, he came upon a special supplement commemorating the occasion when Edward VII had passed through mid-Wales, though urgent business had prevented him, it would appear, from actually stopping. Scattered beyond the supplement were sheets of faded blue notepaper listing esoteric potato recipes, and claiming to be Penderyn WI's wartime way to Beat the Hun By Healthy Eating.

At the end of the first aisle a flagging Eddie turned down a second aisle. Here the records were older, the light even dimmer. He strained to read that in 1883 several slates blew off the roof of the Guildhall and just missed hitting anyone. He did manage to read that in 1876 a remarkable landslide had occurred on the outskirts of Abernant, but a large mousy hole in columns two, three, and four left specifics to the imagination.

Eddie turned down (or was it up?) yet another aisle, wondering when last these records had received a visitor. It was as if this forgotten, mouldering store-room contained the remnants of a lost civilisation, meticulously filed in case of discovery by aliens. Ahead of him hung a chain of pallid rosettes, once pinned to prize bulls, now dangling from a water-pipe for no clear reason. Uncertain what constituted a rare social document, Eddie picked up a folder of rugby photos, corrugated by an ancient damp; faint pencil marks proclaimed the Championship Team of 1911. Sport was the nearest he had to a hobby, and he knew nerdy things about games of the past. He flicked through the first photographs, immaturely amused by the sight of hard men in knee-length shorts and mutton-chop whiskers.

'Do you take herbal tea?'

The voice floated from the far end of the aisle. Eddie struggled to focus. Here lay the source of the light, a bare bulb above a desk, with a small attic window beyond. Seated amid this indoor twilight was a tiny female figure, her features hard to determine.

'Oh . . . er . . . ' He hurriedly replaced the photographs.

'Or perhaps you're not a herbal-tea man?'

Fuck. Five seconds and he felt on the back foot.

'I'm not thirsty, thanks.' But he was. His own world had lifts; four flights of her stairs at a macho run had not been wise. The sweat was barely dry, his heart only just back to normal.

As he approached her paper-strewn desk, she stood up, immaculately cardiganned, and held out a firm, filigree-boned hand.

He reached across. 'I'm Eddie — '

'Trench. I know. My brothers have spoken of you.' These were words that begged for elaboration, and the silence she let ensue as they sat was exquisitely pointed.

' . . . Right. Er, good. So, presumably you know something about the game-plan.'

'Is that a modern phrase?'

' . . . Er, I guess so. Means development strategy, restructuring, that kind of thing.'

'Because I play golf, and I'd not heard it before.'

'Uh-huh. They believe, your brothers, that modernising the paper is — '

'Do you play golf, Mr Trench?'

'Er, no. No, I don't.'

'Very good for the upper body.'

'Yeah. Yeah, I suppose it would be.' For an instant, he caught himself wondering if her remark were meant to be disparaging. He found it difficult to read the little old lady, not least because she was wearing a green eye-shade. This was once the headgear of choice for hard-bitten newsmen in Hollywood movies, and the sight disconcerted him. 'Anyway,' he continued, opting for what was his idea of sweet reasonableness, 'they've come to me for my know-how. I've got papers right across the Midlands, local papers, have done for years, built 'em up from scratch. Got a bit of an empire now — Trench Newspaper Holdings Incorporated. You've probably heard of 'em.'

'No.'

'Very big in Birmingham.'

'I've heard of Birmingham,' she said helpfully.

'Er, yeah . . . yeah, I'm sure you have . . . Now, my newspapers — '

'Nothing but trouble, Birmingham.'

'Trouble?'

'Building reservoirs in mid-Wales, wrecking the Welsh countryside.'

'Yeah, yeah, I see, very sad.'

'Perhaps you could run a campaign in your newspapers? Try and have the reservoirs taken away?'

'Er, yes, further down the line perhaps.'

Plan A was for him to be the fourth partner and to oversee *The Mid-Walian*, laying much emphasis on sex and violence and grabby headlines, but still allowing Miss Nightingale some of her input. Eddie was starting to have doubts about Plan A.

'Now, my newspapers aim to give the punter what he wants. That's golden rule number one. And what your average joe wants is a paper that's easy on the eye, has a fair dose — pardon the pun — of scandal and crumpet, and is a bit of a laugh. That's the way to make the serious money, my dear. It may mean a few changes to this place, but we'll soon get your *Mid-Walian* into a different league.' He gave what he hoped was an encouraging curl of the lips.

'So, Cecily, when people round here buy your paper, what is it you reckon they want to read about most?'

Miss Nightingale did not hesitate. 'Funerals.'

'*Funerals!*' He stared into her eye-shade. 'What sort of funerals?'

'Dead people.' She was tempted to add 'mainly', just out of mischief, but instead she continued, 'Ordinary dead people, ordinary lives being celebrated. We publish the messages on the flowers, the numbers of the hymns, the names of the mourners. A whole page sometimes.'

'These dead people . . . ' Eddie began, trying to get to grips with this information.

'And all much appreciated. Sometimes the family buy two copies.'

Eddie struggled with the concept. 'We have dead people in our papers too, but we like them to be stabbed or shot.'

'And what else do you have in your papers? In this different league of yours?' The words were neutral, but the tone was genteelly laced with broken glass.

'Well, for a kick-off, my papers don't do 'ordinary'. They do 'out-of-this-world', or 'bizarre', or 'gob-smacking'. Or the editor gets sacked!' He tried a laugh, unwisely as it was not a lovable trait. 'And we mainline on exposés. The usual suspects — naughty councillors, randy vicars, bent bank managers. But your *Mid-Walian*, it doesn't seem to print any 'high-impact' stories.'

'We have Country Weeds You Can Eat,' said Miss Nightingale, and enjoyed his discomposure. 'Now that's a very popular feature. Especially in the summer. Recipes appeal to every generation, don't you think?' She smiled sweetly — fifty-two years of private yoga had taught her the gifts of serenity, which she found invaluable when wanting to outwit.

Struggling to connect, Eddie went on, 'And the other thing a successful paper needs is gimmicks. Day One of my contract, there'd be astrology. Astrology and scratch cards. And real-life confessions of the locals!'

Miss Nightingale adopted a weary and consciously condescending air. 'I doubt that any of our readership — '

'And Page 3 girls, of course.'

Miss Nightingale briefly lost the power of speech.

'I can see it now!' exclaimed Eddie Trench. ' 'Miss Topless of Abernant!' That'll get Farmer Giles double-parking his tractor at the newsagent's.' He smirked. 'Or is it Farmer Geraint?'

For almost the first time in her life Cecily Nightingale abandoned her belief in the supremacy of sweet reason. The experience of decades had taught her that readers of *The Mid-Walian* liked their paper to be a prelude to the niceness of heaven. But in Eddie she had found a man immune to the self-evident truths of life, blind to the realities of the rural world. He was clearly someone who would never understand that farmers turned to page 3 to learn about the dangers of sheep dip. And who would never be persuaded that the readers' need for sex and violence could be satisfied by the Nature Notes.

Miss Nightingale leaned forward, resting her forearms on the mound of readers' letters to which she was replying in person and in detail, and forced herself to focus on Eddie Trench's stubble. She felt a quizzical look would best suit the occasion.

'And all this is called a 'game-plan', you say?'

He nodded.

'And it means your 'development strategy' for the paper?'

'Spot on. You're getting the idea!'

'Hmmm. You do overlook a few basic points however.'

'Fire away!'

'I would refuse to publish it. The reporters would refuse to write it. The printers would refuse to print it. And the readers would refuse to read it . . . Though the dustmen might agree to bin it. Would any of that be a problem?'

Eddie, who had limited experience of little old ladies, wondered whether long hours alone in the half-light had driven her mad. He had offered her the chance to move on from the journalistic Dark Ages, and had been rejected. He had shown her how to mint money from the scratch-card world of tabloids, and had been spurned. The two-hour drive had been wasted. He pushed back his chair. It would be best to leave. Best to hightail it out of the archival murk, and return to the land of neon.

Miss Nightingale watched him feel his way out along the dusty racks, and could not repress a small victory smile when she heard the door slam behind him. All in all, her own game-plan had gone rather well.

★　★　★

The door shut, Eddie Trench stomped along the bare landing, clattered angrily down the stairs, and decided it was time for Plan B.

12

'Guess what — Dr Frost is queer!' announced Dafydd.

His passenger stared glumly through the windscreen at the warm summer rain and said nothing.

'Certainly wouldn't be asking *him* to examine me if I had genital warts.' And added quickly, in clarification, 'Not that I have.'

The road up the valley was starting its climb and Dafydd had to raise his voice above the rackety diesel of the florist's van.

'No-one ever suspects men in suits, do they? Not of being a bum-bandit. Mind you, thirty years of marriage and not even his wife knows. In fact, no-one knows it!'

Dafydd paused again in the hope of questions and astonishment, but only a low moan was forthcoming, prompted by the mention of marriage.

'Red rose, it was. Single red rose. Now that is *not* the way you welcome a new doctor to the practice, is it?' He took his eyes off the road to seek confirmation from Gareth, who was sat slumped and shrivelled inside his mouldy Barbour. 'Not a *male* doctor. Right?'

Dafydd had only been in possession of these facts for about an hour. Ideally he would like to have passed the news on to someone more receptive than Gareth, whose social circle was limited to hill sheep. But Gareth was the first person he had come across on his rural round.

'Bet that didn't come up at the interview! 'How d'you feel about sex with the senior partner? Three times a week after meals?''

He glanced across again, to see if Gareth enjoyed this jest, but only body odour and wood smoke emanated from the passenger seat.

'Pity the greetings envelope was so well stuck down!' Dafydd added, and gave a dirty laugh.

This was the perfect pretext for ribald suggestions, but after barely a mile he had to concede that uproariousness was not the mood of the moment. So Dafydd fell silent and concentrated on the bends. He had driven this winding route for twenty years as a postman and knew it well. Beyond the pine trees on the hillside ahead he could already see the tarpaulined roof of his destination, though most of the church below was no longer a landmark, the nave no more than knee-high, since the night of the flood. Dafydd was eager to reach the estate. In his van he had a delivery for the Powells that promised to be his second big story of the day.

Nonetheless, had he been receiving psychiatric assistance, like Gareth, there is a good chance that Dafydd would have made less of the gay doc shock scandal earlier that morning. Although his behaviour seldom betrayed it, although his consciousness had little knowledge of it, although he would indignantly have denied it, his sexuality was threatened by the colour of his van. Accustomed for many years to the dark manly red of the Royal Mail, he found the pink pastel shades and the stencilled flowery things on his bonnet often created a need to overcompensate in male company. At times, deep down, he felt like a mobile hairdresser, and from this came the urge to put clear blue water between him and poofs. He was much relieved the job did not include a uniform.

Gareth's trauma, however, was more serious than the paintwork on a Ford Escort. He had returned from town one day to find the bank manager's head between his wife's thighs. Although this was a service the bank manager supplied to many of his overdrawn female customers, Gareth had taken it badly — and ignored the normal complaints procedure. His attempt to close the joint account with a shotgun had incurred penalty points, and only the needs of his sheep had kept him from jail. And so Gareth found himself living alone, barred by bail from most of town, and banned from driving. But his probation had still to be completed and any antisocial move could yet mean the clink of handcuffs.

'Just short of the ridge'll do me,' he muttered.

Dafydd often found him walking the lanes, not always in the straightest of lines, and would return him to his farmyard. Such charitable acts were against the rules of flower delivery but Dafydd was a rebel. The valley bus now only ran on a weekly whim and to be carless was to live in exile. To also be wifeless on the lonely hills was to live in limbo.

'Divorce come through yet?'

Gareth did not reply. He had never been a conversationalist.

Dafydd had got to know him — as much as anyone knew him — through the delivery of bills. (It was sadly significant that Gareth would rarely be sent anything in a white envelope.) He was a runty man, who would be waiting at the farm gate in the dawn light, kicking his tractor wheels for entertainment. Abnormally for runts, he was the whole litter, an only child whose marriage had been but a blip in long years of bleak bachelorhood. On sighting the postman, he would nod, and the two men would share a silence. Usually while rain fell softly.

Dafydd reached the bend where the vet's wife had driven straight on and killed a horse in 1967. He applied some cadence braking.

'I have problems with anger,' said Gareth.

'Pardon?' said Dafydd.

'According to my probation officer. 'Bob'. He says I express it inappropriately.'

'Is this about shooting the moles?'

'I don't shoot them any more. The police took away my gun.'

'Oh, that's right. So, this anger you have problems with . . . '

'I've got to channel it, Bob says.'

'Channel it where?'

'I'm not sure yet. Because I've got stuff to work through.'

'Stuff . . . ?'

Gareth nodded earnestly.

'What sort of stuff?'

Gareth's brow furrowed into deep lines, and he gave much thought to the answer. Then he slowly shook his head. And retreated into his Barbour.

Dafydd let the revs drop as they came within sight of the grand old gates rotting at the entrance to the Powells' long driveway.

Rhododendrons, many of them higher than the van, sprawled in late summer disarray across the edges of the gravel drive as it curved languidly towards the mansion's portico.

Dafydd had never delivered flowers here before. In the house's heyday, flowers had no doubt arrived by the armful, by the shedful, in flamboyant bouquets of gratitude, acknowledging a six-hour dinner or a weekend's pheasant-filled hospitality. Even Dilys' time in quangoland had been cause for gatherings of the worthy, milling mirthlessly for an evening of charitable chat. But the times of late had been quieter, and a discreet card of thanks or a follow-up phone call served as modern tokens of appreciation. No-one lavished gestures on the reclusive commodore or his very proper sister.

Which made the dozen red roses all the more puzzling.

What sort of man, wondered Dafydd, was sending such a romantic offering to the old spinster? Why did the note contain such heartfelt thanks? What was meant by these 'eagerly anticipated' future meetings? And what was this unavoidable delay for which the man was so profusely, so suavely, apologising?

The crunching of the gravel acted as an early warning system and the Commodore's sister reached the front door before Dafydd could even set the ancient bell system in motion. During his postman years Dafydd had brought her sundry packages, usually from colonial-style stores, and the one unchanging feature of this elderly ice maiden was her composure. But today she seemed distracted, disconcerted even. And the courtesies bordered on the perfunctory. Then, as Dafydd handed over the flowers from Forget-Me-Nots, he had an instinct of something awry with her impeccable, albeit outdated, dress sense. All looked to be in order, ready for parade, but somehow there was some detail that was wrong, that was out of place. And then the strange thought struck him that, although she had come from indoors, Miss Powell appeared to be damp.

It was not for him to comment though, and he briskly returned to his nancy van (where Gareth now sat clutching his cap in his hand, having been unable to resist the feudal doffing reflex). As the Queen Anne front door shuffled shut, Dafydd watched the starchy spinster sniffing at her bouquet of flowers. Her face was in shadow, her expression obscured. And Dafydd was only left with more questions. Was her strait-laced heart pounding with passion? Or was sixty-plus too old for a maiden aunt to blossom? And who on earth was this fancy man called Philip?

13

The mayoress was also driving up the valley that morning. She rarely visited the country-side, preferring the cosmopolitan buzz of Abernant. Already she was finding it difficult to follow the easy-to-follow directions that had been given her.

It had been a tiring and tiresome few months on the sculpture front. Organising the councillors all to vote the same way, for the purposes of art, had proved a bit like herding sheep with a dead dog. Few were actually opposed to a free sculpture, but most were puzzled as to its practical purpose. What did it do? Why was it needed? And wouldn't birds crap on it? Although no-one admitted as much, theirs was the apathy that came from a project without any perks or greasing of palms. How did one get a backhander from a statue? And then there was the statue itself. There appeared, for instance, to now be a military lobby in Abernant. They argued — well, not exactly *argued*, this being a local council, but they stated very repetitively — that it should be of a general on a horse. Second choice was to create a tableau of distinguished councillors, but the deadlock over which worthies would become The Burghers of Abernant contained enough vitriol for another Hundred Years War. There was also the inevitable proposal of a farmyard animal, local in appearance. Closely followed by the wish for a royal personage. Waving. The only clear consensus was that the statue should not have holes in it.

It was this absence of an organised faction that allowed Myfanwy's protégé poet to prevail. Despite his supposed status as the Dylan Thomas of mid-Wales, Ieuan's poetry remained a mystery. Several of the older councillors claimed to recall him, and they spoke disparagingly of the untidiness of his house. Adding that he wore eccentric clothes. But facts were few and time was short.

It is perhaps indicative of Abernant's unworldliness in the arena of the arts that a vote was passed to authorise a sculpture without anyone spotting the somewhat central need for a sculptor.

Step forward the mayoress, proclaiming herself in charge of Sculptor Selection. This seemed a bold initiative. Potters were two a penny — every tourist likes an odd-shaped plate — but sculptors were a rarer life form. The rules required the artist be indigenous, but budget cutbacks at the county art college had left its courses with little more than coloured paper and scissors. Also, historically, the town's Labour Exchange was not known for its queues of jobbing sculptors. So, put bluntly, the Welsh hills were not alive to the sound of chisels. The mayoress, like most who occupy the local limelight, was cordially resented by her underling councillors, and they held high hopes for her failure.

They had not reckoned on Roderigo Williams.

The man had a bass voice and a big brown beard. He was nearly six feet including the heels, and wore a lumberjack shirt winter and summer. Had he been English he might have worn a loose neckerchief and looked a bit florid. Instead, being allegedly local, he wore a Celtic cross and looked a bit raddled. He also had hands you would not like around your throat.

The summer before, the mayoress had gone through her salon phase. She had wanted to be a cultural melting pot, and put out the word that wine and cheese awaited artists and intellectuals every second Thursday between two and four. Unfortunately, the same six people turned up every fortnight: a potter who made egg-cups with frogs on, a divorced museum attendant who pressed wild flowers, a lapsed yoga teacher, a husband and wife who performed dog impersonations, and a folk singer. The only break in this routine had come on the day when a hairy man with big hands had turned up.

Roderigo Williams had not been drawn by the culture or the conversation or the cheese. He had heard about the two hours of free wine. And he was in the mood for an argument.

Myfanwy was quickly impressed. Her new find was difficult, truculent, and temperamental — everything that artistic types are meant to be. He even spilt drink down his shirt. And tried to grope the folk singer.

The unexpected guest had a weather-beaten look, though of a colour that suggested foreign weather, which gave him a whiff of mystery. His presence in the area had gone little noticed, yet he spoke of an impending local commission for fifteen Greek goddesses in marble — the whim, he claimed, of an eccentric, possibly mad, millionaire in the hills. Such allusions peppered Roderigo's speech, and the impression grew that he was a 'colourful character'. His accent had the hallmarks of Welsh, but the name Roderigo led Myfanwy to the insight that he had a hidden, more exotic past. She tried to subtly probe in her booming middle-class way, but by 3.59 all she knew was that he had drained her Blue Nun dry. Then, with a belch, and a dismissive hand gesture, he announced that Art called. And was gone, without leaving so much as his card.

★ ★ ★

A year later, and now the mayoress was out looking for '*a muddy track*' just beyond '*a lone pine*' just past '*a dangerous bend*'. Roderigo Williams rented a cottage — so she had been told — somewhere on the Commodore's dysfunctional estate.

Faced with so much that was green and wet, Myfanwy was soon at a loss. The B-road up the valley had many bends, and since all were rendered dangerous by her mayoral disdain for braking, Myfanwy needed more specifics. To her right was river mist; to her left was bracken. A few miles out of town, and she pulled on to a squelching verge to go over the sketchy clues to Roderigo's whereabouts — marked by an X, and reached by a dotted line.

The only hint of habitation was an isolated bungalow hidden behind a beech hedge. She thought of knocking for assistance, but could see no sign of life. She did not know it, but the owner was also hidden, his smartly dressed body behind a curtain. He had recognised the car, and did not wish to help. The last time they had met had been in kinder, grander days, when he lived in town and bestrode the civic stage. For this was the home of disgraced Mr Blake, the manager so very publicly dismissed for the unusual banking practice of placing deposits in his customers. He still remembered her pious condemnations — and also found her too fat a damsel to rescue from distress — and had resolved (or so he thought) that their paths would never cross again. But he was puzzled by this sighting, and wondered where she could be going.

After a minute or two, the torrential rain began to ease. Unwinding the window, the mayoress made out a lone pine not far distant and lurched off once more.

Successfully past the pine, she turned on to the muddy track just beyond. This undulated across a cow-patted field, a nearby row of alder marking the course of the river, and for the first time Myfanwy had doubts about bringing the mayoral Daimler.

She tried to focus her mind on her imminent act of patronage. The dark skies were at last beginning to fracture, and not far off she could see the outline of the cottage tucked bucolically amidst bushes. A large and ramshackle lean-to, knitted together with brambles, clung to its near wall, the contents spilling on to a makeshift courtyard. Which, in turn, gave way to half an acre of thistly pasture that declined bumpily to the banks of the Nant. A carved wooden sign by the rusting farm-gate read 'Maeshyffryd', but monolingual Myfanwy was immune to the ironies of its translation: 'delightful field'.

Suddenly the late summer sun gave birth to a rainbow. In a moment as rare as the perfect storm, its myriad colours arced to ground some fifty yards ahead of her. She was briefly transfixed by the glow. And then bemused. The bright golden haze was not on the meadow, but suffusing the figure of a one-armed Christ.

He stood lopsidedly on the courtyard, with what Myfanwy took to be an understandably pained expression. The mayoress peered through the Daimler's mist-smeared windscreen, and almost forgot to brake at the gate. She knew that, traditionally, over the centuries, Jesus had been depicted in many different forms and guises, but always, as far as she was aware, in possession of both arms. It had until now been her clear understanding that Christianity was a two-armed religion. Indeed, this was an essential for crucifixion. Unease came over her at the prospect of provocative blasphemy — blasphemy did not go down big with the councillors, nor any ratepayers of her acquaintance.

Beyond the half-size wooden Christ stood a row of outsize female torsos, their plaster casts impaled on poles and stretching into the thistles. Although herself the owner of an outsize female torso, the mayoress again struggled with the meaning. Meanwhile, all around her, driftwood had been hacked into abstract shapes, or left to rot aesthetically. And scattered nearby, the innards of a phone box lay next to an upended bath tub, one of many casual juxtapositions on the courtyard, a setting in sharp contrast to the soft toys of Myfanwy's own home life.

The morning's storm pattered to a halt, snuffing out the rainbow's exotic light. The mayoress decided it was time to step from her car, though the mud did militate against a grand entrance. As did her sandals.

At the same moment Roderigo stepped out of his atelier lean-to, having heard the sound of slush. A man with no phone, he was not forewarned, but the arrival of a Daimler and an opera-sized woman in a puce and lime open-neck sack promised to add interest to his day. He watched her hop from tuft to tuft, not wishing to spoil the spectacle by offering assistance. Besides, he had recognised her immediately, and still remembered the taste of her cut-price wine.

'Roderigo!'

Roderigo grunted. But he smelt money in the air, and chose his grade of grunt with care.

The mayoress leapt at last to dry land; she held out her hand, but Roderigo raised a warning palm to reveal days of ingrained dirt, so they took the handshake as a given. And briefly stood like waltzers in waiting.

'So this is your studio! Where it all happens! And such a setting to be creative in!' Myfanwy gushed. She tried to peer over his shoulder at the lean-to.

He made no attempt to move his shoulder.

'And how are the goddesses coming along?'

The answer was immediately in his eyes. 'All mouth, that millionaire. Saw the price of marble, and bottled it. Ploughed his money into ostriches, last I heard. And then buggered off.'

'Aaah, such a precarious existence, the arts,' she said, with unappreciated empathy. 'And are you managing to keep busy?'

'Always keep bloody busy! Offers coming out my ears, woman.'

'Of course. I meant — '

'Out my ears. That's why I'm filling up the field. Got a big job on in Cardiff.'

'Cardiff? What, the castle?'

'Well, near to it, yes. So I suppose you're stuffed on the poet?' He snorted with pleasure. 'Bit of a basket case, that idea.'

For an instant, Myfanwy thought she saw a woman's face at the cottage window, wearing strange make-up and staring at her.

'Nonsense,' she responded. 'Put Abernant on the map, this statue. Be a landmark. *And* make the sculptor's name.'

'My name's already made, thank you.'

'Oh no, I meant — '

'Can't imagine a dead poet would add much to my oeuvre.'

'Be with full artistic freedom.'

'D'you think I ever accept less?'

'Guaranteed money. Arts Council.'

'Probably a pittance then.' But after a moment he weakened. 'Better take a pew.' And, somewhat to her surprise, he gestured to a pew.

It stood in the lee of the lean-to, and after a small wipe she was sat looking towards the river.

'Salvage,' he commented.

'Salvage?'

'From the river. You'd be amazed what floats down from that church.'

'Oh . . . ' said the mayoress. 'Oh, the *church*! Of course.' And she sighed with relief as he gave Jesus a kick.

'Even had a corpse. Or most of one. Useful for a life class. Except you'd have to sketch from half a mile away because of the damn smell.'

Myfanwy gazed upstream, but could see nothing but a distant tarpaulined roof. An occasional tree was faintly reddening, jumping the gun for autumn.

'Lovely spot,' she said. 'I suppose this is where you sit when you wait for your Muse to call.'

'Do I, bollocks! See you know sod all about art. Me, I'm like Tchaikovsky.'

'Tchaikovsky?'

'Russian composer. Nineteenth — '

'Yes I know who Tchaikovsky is!' she said hastily, mortified by the misunderstanding.

'He had an admirer, said what you said. 'Madam, I sit at my desk at nine every morning,' he replied, 'waiting for my Muse to come. If she isn't here by five past, I start without the bloody woman.''

The mayoress felt the patron/client relationship was not going well, and decided to mention money again.

Roderigo, meanwhile, had begun to whittle wood. 'So what sort of poet is he?'

'Iconoclastic. Avant-garde. Irreverent.'

'Yes, but what's he write about?'

'Er, I'm not exactly sure.'

'Why, are you daft?'

'I — I haven't been able to find an English version yet.'

'Oh. So he writes in Welsh?'

She nodded.

He pondered. Iconoclastic. Avant-garde. Irreverent. These were attributes which perfectly summarised how Roderigo regarded himself. It would almost be a self-portrait. And he'd be on a plinth.

'Elenid might have a Welsh copy. She reads Welsh.'

'Elenid?'

'My latest woman. But she can't come out at the moment. She's in touch with the other side.'

'The other side of what?'

'No, she's a spiritualist.'

'Oh, I'm sorry. I mean, I didn't realise . . . '

'What's your deadline?'

'A few months, I guess. But when d'you finish your big Cardiff commission?'

He made a wavy gesture with his hand. The meaning was not clear. It was not meant to be clear. He liked to shroud his work in mystery, especially when that work was for an Indian restaurant, down by the derelict docks, where bas-reliefs of big-breasted women were much in demand.

'An artist's life is about priorities,' declared

109

Roderigo. 'Why don't I give it a bit of thought, and get back to you?'

It was apparent her audience was over. The mayoress stood up, a damp patch on her bottom. But she was not downhearted. She had at last realised who she saw in the rough-hewn and moody Roderigo. Heathcliff.

Her hunch was that he probably had gypsy blood, from ancestors with a wild, free-wheeling temperament. And a passionate temper. She understood for the first time how Emily Brontë must have felt. She wondered how she might learn the mysteries of his exotic past.

14

'Blackmail?' echoed Dafydd.

'How d'you know it's blackmail?' asked Hubert.

'A source,' said Clydog defensively. 'And their theory seems to fit the facts.'

'Yes, but why would anyone blackmail her?'

'Hubert has got a point,' said Dafydd. 'I mean, what sort of dark secret could Miss Nightingale ever have?'

'Something bad to do with golf?' offered Hubert, struggling with a straight face. 'Secretly replaced a lost ball on the 18th? She could have her plus-fours removed for that.'

'It was a reliable source,' said Clydog, even more defensively. 'Said a very big aggressive man came to see her. Unannounced. Very threatening. And sweaty.'

'It is possible to sweat and not demand money with menaces,' Hubert observed. 'After all, you're sweating. And you're not blackmailing anybody.'

'Big, aggressive, and he didn't give his name. What's that tell you?'

'She had a rude visitor.'

'And he left looking very angry.'

'But not carrying a bundle of used fivers wrapped in old newspaper?' queried Dafydd.

Clydog bridled. 'At least I don't believe the Commodore's sister has a toy-boy.'

Hubert sucked thoughtfully on his pipe. 'This big, aggressive man — '

'From Birmingham.'

'From Birmingham. Does he do contract killings?' asked Hubert. 'Because I've got a job for him. I want Crapstick blown away.'

He moved briefly to the counter to wrap some macaroons for an old lady with a Pekinese.

'Another meeting of the Chamber of Commerce last night,' explained Dafydd. 'Instinct tells me there was a difference of opinion.'

'Hubert sometimes has a difference of opinion with me and I haven't even spoken,' said Clydog wistfully.

Hubert was soon back from the counter, and bearing a wedge of sticky chocolate fudge cake for Clydog. 'Here! Rub this on you.'

Clydog looked longingly at it . . . and then declined. 'No, not today, thanks.'

'That's a first!'

'I thought you had a strategy to outwit the butcher,' said Dafydd. 'What was it you said . . . ? 'With superior brainpower and political cunning'?'

'The man's mad,' declared Hubert.

The other two sensed this was not his last word on the subject of Mr Capstick, and parked their own conversation in a siding.

'He's drawn up an agenda. The Seven Steps to Happy Customers. And he wants no drinking or smoking in the meetings. And he wants the meeting room moved. And he wants to start the evening with a prayer. And a fingernail inspection.'

He was rewarded by looks of surprise.

'OK, I made that one up. But I'm sure it's a long-term goal. He'll have us all come with a hygiene certificate from a nurse.'

'Where's he want the meeting room moved to?' asked Clydog, feeling a page 8 paragraph coming on.

'A church hall. Don't think he's fussed which church. It's just to get us away from the beer so none of us takes the piss out of him. And to give the town the 'correct' business image. He's very keen on image. He's planning a cleanliness campaign. Wants Abernant to be called 'The New-Pin Town of Mid-Wales'' Hubert grimaced. 'Sign like that on the bypass, that'll really draw in the trade!'

'So I'm a Customer,' said Dafydd, 'Make me Happy.'

'He's very keen on smiling at them. I think he practises smiling on the lavatory. Though

113

God knows why, because he's a miserable sod. 'A smile a Day Keeps Losses at Bay.' That's one of his. One of many. I keep expecting him to give us cushions with happy thoughts cross-stitched on to them.' Hubert paused for his venom to recharge, and then said, 'He shouldn't be a butcher, he should be a butler. He's got the sort of tongue that reaches those parts that never get dusted.'

'Resign then.'

Hubert was briefly silent, though it was hard to say if he were letting that thought cross his mind. 'Did you know there's even a patron saint of butchers? Saint Bleeding Bartholomew! Died in Armenia, flayed alive and beheaded. Though whether he was then roasted to a succulent pink is not known.'

'How did you learn all that?' asked Clydog.

'His feast day just 'happened' to be when we held the meeting! So Crapstick came complete with a prayer.'

Before he could elucidate, the old lady with the Pekinese came back in, and complained the macaroons were not to her dog's taste. Hubert sighed wearily, and made his way over to the counter again.

Clydog turned to Dafydd and said worriedly, 'So if it isn't blackmail, what is it?'

'Have you libelled anybody?'

Clydog looked so aghast that Dafydd said,

'Sorry. Stupid question.'

But no answers seemed to fully make sense to Clydog, and he had been puzzling for several days. Possibly Rhiannon's facts were a little wayward. The woman did sometimes show signs of melodrama; a Gorgon of a gate-keeper, she was a rather sad and needy creature whom he would have avoided had there been a back entrance. But something in her story was disturbing and laid low his spirits.

'All part of the service, madam. I just hope Mitzi likes waffles.' Hubert's baritone rumbled across from the shop doorway, then he re-appeared round an oak pillar, pulling a face.

'Would that be Step Two to Happy Customers?' enquired Dafydd.

'Yes indeed, sucking up to dogs, essential part of successful retailing. Here, Clydog, I've got you a treat. Bark once for yes, twice for no.' And Hubert handed over a Mississippi Mud Pie, the royal standard in Clydog's list of confectionery treats.

'No, I don't think so,' said Clydog, handing it back.

'No? Are you sickening for something?'

'Well, I've felt better.' He wiped a florid hankie across a florid face. 'I seem to puff on the flat now.'

'You don't look great. You wouldn't be my colour of choice,' said Hubert.

Clydog glanced across at the mirror in the office, and saw an ageing, sweating, pot-bellied man with the complexion of a sun-dried tomato.

'No. No, I think I might drop into the surgery.'

'Good idea.'

'Pay Dr Frost a visit.'

'Aaah,' said Dafydd, at last seeing his chance to make an impact upon the conversation. 'I'm not so sure that's wise.'

15

The phone was ringing somewhere deep in the house.

Old and Bakelite, its faraway tones had the dim echo of a lost cause. The closed doors in the shadows of the entrance hall muffled the source and subdued the sound. For some moments, his cadaverous head on one side, the Commodore had stood and considered the evidence that the house might have an incoming call. Then, reluctantly, he made his way to the front reception room.

The telephone was not immediately visible. Indeed, not much was immediately visible under the plastic sheeting that Dilys had bought from Mr Bufton the ironmonger. Initially, it had been a precautionary measure, as had the buckets. But gradually the rainwater from the roof had explored more and more of the Queen Anne intricacies in the architecture. The water had taken particular interest in the bay, and had dribbled down behind the folded-back shutters, causing the walls' ancient paintwork to form into brittle curlicues.

Then the water had got bolder, sensing an

absence of builders. It had started to drip from one or two cornices, quietly, politely, but with a methodical rhythm known to cause madness. Then it had ventured along the joists, to drip through the ceiling at unforeseen junctures. Its area of command and control gradually expanded and soon the bay had to be evacuated. Before the month was out, all territory at the far end of the room was only nominally in the hands of the Powells, and recent sorties had reported the spread of mould.

Always the grandest of the rooms (once the local gentry's venue for musical *soirées*), its furniture had now retrenched, and tried to regroup in the dry. But the Achilles' heel of a ceiling is the light fitting, and a vanguard of elite raindrops were soon descending the wires. Unsure when or where the attack would come next, the Commodore had kitted out the hard-back chairs in old waterproofs, and a defunct Barbour lay tightly spread across the pouffe. The chesterfield, source of discontent for Carla's bottom, was now only divested of its plastic on truly sunny days. Although Dilys and her brother would still occasionally pass the evening in the front reception room, lost in nostalgic silence, their melancholy presence was akin to King and Queen Canute on a night out.

The subterranean ringing continued to taunt, and the Commodore moved tentatively through the room like a man in search of a fish. Twice he pounced upon plastic excrescences, only to bring forth a plate of cake crumbs and a forgotten Meissen coffee-pot. His hearing no longer was A1, and he heard the sound of the phone on the fuzziest of frequencies. Confused, the old man paused, and looked around the room for visual clues. It was another wet day, and each direction the Commodore faced he found himself gazing through indoor sea-mist. He moved toward the mantelpiece, where the palm tree glistened as if freshly sprayed, for he had a memory of a phone-like object next to the candlesticks. Stepping carefully around Dilys' potted ferns, he stretched out to a bulge beneath the sheeting.

★ ★ ★

Philip Courtauld replaced the receiver and gently removed his wife's Persian cat from his chest.

'No joy?' asked Jane.

'It's like ringing the far side of the moon.' He reached down from the sofa for his wine glass. 'Only with worse static.'

'Well, you've got nothing to tell them.'

119

'Ah, but that's the time to tell them sweet nothings.' He smiled at her, with the confident charm which had once disarmed her, which now she so distrusted.

'And they'll wait, these Welsh? While you raise the rest of the money?'

'Oh, waiting's good, waiting's helpful. Be shit weather soon. Then it'll look like survival time for real! And we'll have actual snow and a cast going blue.'

He was an unlikely creator of a drama that dealt with society *in extremis*. He had suffered few knock-backs in life, apart from a 2:2 in Media Studies and a mother who left home when he was twenty-four. Although only moderately heeled himself, he was married to a designer made rich from the foibles of fashion, and they lived in a hi-tech house with original things on the walls.

'I've decided to call it 'Aftershocks'.'

'And if you don't get given the money?'

He pondered — or did he pretend to ponder? — this possibility.

'Oh, it's a sexy subject. Just a few budget details to be sorted. Give it time.'

'Time and a script.'

Another smile, a touch more circumspect. 'It just needs a polish.'

Jane said nothing. The pilot script was at the chrysalis stage, having trouble with pupation. Philip had a track record, but in promotional videos, training videos, videos that peaked after fifteen minutes. Plot and characterisation was a foreign land, and he was still learning the language.

'Anyway,' he added, 'it's the pitch that counts. And I'm good at pitching.'

'Yes,' said Jane, who had returned to the pages of her wok magazine, 'you're very good at pitching.'

Philip's only creative uncertainty was the ending. Should two survivors be left, to walk off hand in hand, into an unnaturally glowing sunset? Or just the one? Seen sideways, with a silhouetted hint of early pregnancy? Not for the first time, he tried to visualise the scene and the camera angles. Despite his denials, he too felt frustration at the project's delay.

His mind went back to the absent Powells. He toyed again with the telephone.

'The old dears might be in the garden, I suppose. Country people don't seem to move very fast.'

'Even when *you're* phoning?' This time, his wife did not look up.

'You've not met them, Jane. Glitzy call from London, they'll love it!' he insisted. 'Bit more schmoozing, and they'll even want to be extras!'

Philip was, as usual, strong on the

dynamism. Since setting up his indie company — that standard macho act of all his mates in media — he had really got into the go-getting, for self-made men were in tune with the times. He took a sip of wine and dialled again.

★ ★ ★

'Who?' asked the Commodore.

'Philip,' said Philip again.

'Philip who?' asked the Commodore.

'The man from the TV. Who's going to make your house a star.'

'The man from where?'

'TV.'

'We don't have a TV,' said the Commodore.

'No. From The Now Company.'

'From the now what?'

'Er, can I speak to your wife?'

'My wife?'

'Yes.'

'My *wife?*'

'Yes.'

'My wife is mad.'

'Sorry? Your wife is . . . ?'

'Who are you?' demanded the Commodore.

'I'm Philip. We talked about jeeps.'

'I don't want jeeps.'

'No, there won't be any jeeps.'

A voice was heard off. A female voice, chastising. Followed by a muffled struggle with the phone.

'Hallo?' said Dilys. 'Who's speaking?'

'Philip,' said Philip, with diluted dynamism. 'And, um, how are you?'

'I do apologise. He's not good with phones.'

'Is he not?'

'Now semaphore, he used to enjoy semaphore. No speaking, you see, and no close contact.'

'R-right.'

'They're all dead now, of course. His friends who knew semaphore.'

'Oh. That's sad. Did you get my flowers?'

'Yes, thank you. I've put them in water.'

'Oh good.'

'We have a lot of water just lately.'

'Oh good. I've rung to explain about the slight delay. It's actually *good* news. It's because we've got a star. A big star.'

'Too much water.'

'But, of course, as you'll realise, big stars are very busy people. And not free at the drop of a hat. But the minute that our star is — '

'We need more tarpaulin.'

'More what?'

'Tarpaulin, for the roof. We need a cheque.'

'Oh, I'm not sure that tarpaulin is an appropriate item for me to — '

'You said it was a visual masterstroke.'

'Aaah. Yes. *Tarpaulin!* Yes, I'll, er, I'll try and chase the accounts department.'

'Would you chase your legal department at the same time?'

'Why's that?'

'No-one has sent us a contract yet.'

'My goodness, haven't they? Oh, I'll rap knuckles over that! That's very sloppy. Very unprofessional. Incidentally, seeing as we're on the subject of money, how would the pair of you like to be ... *extras?* See how television works! Mix with the stars!'

'We've got black mould as well.'

'Y-yes. You'd become famous, captured for posterity! Exciting, eh? A rare chance to be part of the magic of film!'

'And the cornice is rotting.'

' ... Maybe have your name on the credits?'

16

Gareth Richards didn't like offices. He'd been in a lot of offices lately. Often up narrow, poky stairs. As a hill-sheep farmer, he was ill at ease when not near a hedge. As a tetchy loner, he was short on the skills of conversation. As a cuckold, he wanted to be left to himself.

Gareth clutched the jokey coffee mug, and shifted his bottom about in the beat-up leather armchair. This was seemingly supplied for homeliness, for client-friendliness, but, like the tacky back room it stood in, the loosely stuffed seat was merely the public face of underfunding. His probation officer sat opposite him in a second beat-up leather armchair to ensure that subliminal signals of a non-hierarchical nature were sent out. The only other objects were a desk, a plastic chair and a file-filled alcove, yet already two looked like a crowd in the crudely partitioned office.

'So, how are your leisure interests coming along?' asked Bob breezily.

Despite Bob's best efforts, Gareth did not feel reciprocally breezy. Bob belonged to the dress-down school of probationary theory, and to make his clients feel unthreatened he rarely strayed from denim. Gareth, however, belonged to the dress-up class of criminal, and to indicate respect he came wearing a tie with his Barbour. The current political dialectics of rehabilitation eluded him, and to add to his discomfort was the age of his confidant. Gareth's opinions were not even known to his Maker; to be asked personal questions by a younger man — a man in his thirties! — was an act that felt faintly indecent.

'I've done some more hedging.'

' . . . Good.'

'Thought I'd try for some competitions. Get to meet other hedgers.'

'Good. Good.'

This was not the hobby Bob had hoped for. Lack of socialisation had been a mitigating factor in court, and he had hoped to introduce the novelty of friendship into Gareth's life.

Bob waited, but his client did not elaborate, nor instance any further social breakthroughs.

'And in yourself, would you say you are feeling more cheerful?' Yet as Bob gazed at the bleak midwinter that was Gareth's face, he felt his own will to live was in doubt.

'Difficult to tell.'

Bob often found it hard to dispel a sense of disappointment at his client's lack of criminal disposition. When news had first reached the office that a man had burst into the bank with a shotgun, loudly registering a complaint about the manager's unauthorised use of his penis, Bob's spirits had been greatly lifted by the hope that more interesting crime was finally reaching the town. A client list of minor vandals, lager louts and public pissers was doing little for his career path, or for his *joie de vivre*. So the prospect of a cavalier, larger-than-life criminal, with a taste for public mayhem, had briefly brought a spring to his step.

Bob suppressed a sigh, and looked down at the list of other mitigating factors for Gareth that had gone before the court: relationship issues; rural isolation issues; mental health issues; alcohol issues.

'Have you thought any more about what you can bring to a relationship?'

' . . . What, like feelings?'

'Well, yes. Emotional sensitivity would be an example.'

Gareth thought for a long time, picking away at a patch on the arm of his seat. Twice he started to speak, then thought better of it.

'I'm not very good at feelings. I'm outdoors such a lot.' He narrowed his eyes, as if trying to remember a feeling he had had recently. In fact, he had just noticed that he could make out the tip of the mountains over the roof of the house opposite.

Bob wondered whether to introduce the subject of his own failed marriage, to make the farmer feel more at home, but fortunately realised that adultery was probably not a bridge-building topic. So instead, he leaned forward, reducing the emotional space between them.

'Do you remember my explaining the purpose of my being here with you?' he asked in his most professionally caring tones.

'To advise, assist, and befriend.'

'That's right, yes! To advise, assist and befriend.' Cue smile.

'You can be honest about anything with me, Gareth. Is there anything particular that you'd like to talk about?'

'The bank manager.'

'Apart from the bank manager.'

Outside on the stairs there was a distant clattering of feet, followed briefly by the sound of cheerful voices. Somewhere another interview was going on in the old house, now brutally converted into an annexe for the caring arm of the law.

'Shall we look, perhaps, at how you feel you fit into society?'

'How I fit into society?' he repeated, as if

he feared he were in the wrong class.

'Well, for instance, do you feel you have any grounds for grievances?'

'With society?' Gareth looked blank.

'Well, 'society' is, I suppose, just one's way of saying other people.'

'Oh.'

'Any thoughts on that, on society?'

'The bastards don't care about me, so I don't care about them.'

'Uh-huh. And are there a lot of bastards out there?'

'Reckon so. That's why it's the best place to be, on the hills. Or in the pub.'

'Are you still drinking?'

'Not since the pub closed. And since the bastards banned me from driving.'

'Do you think that was fair?'

'Have an occasional can at home, of course. Take my mind off it all.'

'All what, Gareth?'

'Being arrested. Hounded. Having no gun.'

'You did leave the bank with a hole in it.'

'Can't take my own sheep to market. Can't go to market without being pointed at.'

'Do you ever think about why? about why this has happened?'

'Then when I come home, the fire's out.'

'And who do you blame for all this?'

'The bank manager.'

17

The sinecure given to young Auberon required him to take the odd photo, usually of a funeral cortège, and to service his aunt Cecily with herbal tea. On the hour every four hours. Although Auberon learnt little of modern journalism, he did master the rigours of punctuality, taught by a woman whose routine had an immutability rare for the times.

Which is why her absence from her room at 11 a.m. on Tuesday 17th September was the cause of such shock.

Enquiries established that at 10.37 a.m. the proprietor had hurried coatless through the lobby and out of the building, scarcely acknowledging Rhiannon the receptionist, who had made a note of her departure time, her demeanour, and the speed of her walk (though holding back the most sensitive details as an exclusive for the ears of her idol).

Miss Nightingale owned an old snub-nosed Rover 100, that well-bred car of county folk with class enough for understatement, and if Clydog had been standing upon the Nant bridge instead of doing twelve deep-breathing exercises in the *Mid-Walian* washrooms, he would have seen his employer turn left and right and take the road that led to the golf course.

It was, of course, a road that she knew well. It was the road she drove when carrying the Nightingale Cup to her competition; it was the road she drove when playing for the county; it was the road she drove when practising her putting after work. It was, however, not a road she had ever before driven for a mid-morning whisky.

The car park was, as so often, fuller than expected, occupied by middle management with alibis. A light drizzle was falling on her reserved parking space under a rare row of elms. In both directions, a proliferation of white lines and wooden notices marked out the bays of the privileged with a vehemence that would not have disgraced the military.

The one-storey golf club had been built with little flair. With external resemblance to a mock-Edwardian motel, its décor was a visual version of Muzak. Plus rules. It was a place of more rules than a penitentiary, and they lined the walls even unto the toilet. The building's redemption was its views of the world beyond, of the switchback tree-lined course and the mountains.

Miss Nightingale moved across the floral-carpeted Howells Memorial Lounge to her favourite window seat, set beside the plate glass that looked out over the first tee. Her younger self gazed down from the far wall, the Wall of Fame where Kodak had captured captains past and present in sweatered postures of triumph. Edgar the barman was not yet in bow-tie mode, was still twenty-six minutes from officially smiling, but he had a history of deference to former scratch players and silently acceded to an out-of-hours malt.

She sat sipping it slowly for several moments, soothing herself with the sight of an overweight executive hooking his ball into the bushes. Then, with a trembling lip, she laid the letter upon the glass-topped table.

She had been a little late to open the post that morning, as the editor had wished to know the paper's policy on paganism, and whether to give coverage to police reports of unexplained dancing in the woods. It was well gone nine before her pewter paper knife was set to work. Miss Nightingale always made neat piles of her envelopes, decided by colour and size, and the small, white, faintly official envelope had not ranked high in the grading. So her eye had run unsuspectingly down its contents, and only by the last paragraph did her brain fully realise what it had read.

Never before had her brothers, venal and weak though they were, delivered their thoughts on paper, in words chosen by a solicitor.

★　★　★

Cecily Nightingale was not a woman given to self-pity, but, gazing out through the drizzle that played such havoc with one's grip, she briefly identified with Mrs Hartford-Stanley, whose scorched remains on the twelfth had caused her to depart this life with an unfinished round. Cecily too now felt her future stolen. She had for long assumed her lasting legacy would be *The Mid-Walian*, its eighteen pages true to her ideals, and a tribute to her constancy. Now, her decades of dedication were to be aborted by a bolt from the blue. A forced sale to a stranger would be her final curtain.

Emotions new to her normal crisp thinking could not be dissuaded from the mêlée in her mind. Was it, she wondered, the fraternal betrayal that hurt her the most? Or was it the victory of the baddie, Mr Eddie Trench? Or maybe the crass surrender to the shallow values of the decade? Or the breaking of an unspoken promise to her father? Or simply the ending of a noble family tradition?

She had only read the letter the once, hoping that denial would leave the world unchanged. But slowly, as she watched the pairs and foursomes trudge off into the mist, the discipline of her schooldays re-asserted itself and she examined the wording more closely.

She and the old regime had six months left to serve. The fine print of corporate bloodlust had still to be determined, the thirty pieces of silver still to be tested with the teeth. The text spoke effortlessly of 'modernisation' and 'change', the buzz-words of men with buzz-saws, duplicitously intent on massacre. The readers were to become consumers and the shareholders were to become rich. And news was to become product. But beneath the talk of takeover, the subtext was colonisation. The unique and idiosyncratic attitudes of *The Mid-Walian* would be ceding sovereignty to identikit journalism, a landscape where one news fits all — and a man from the middle of England makes a mint.

She feared for her staff. Few had the facility for lurid language; none had the flair for writing smutty captions beneath a Miss Abernant. The letter's phrasing spoke of 'challenges', that stalking-horse of redundancy, and offered scant comfort for faint hearts or weak hearts. Lawyers who knew

134

nothing of her loyal workers would be shaping their fates with dots and commas. Already there were hints at 'packages', which was not encouraging since this was now a term with terrorist overtones, usually leading to the panicky evacuation of public buildings. Not normally an indecisive woman, Cecily Nightingale was to haver long and hard over how all this news should best be broken.

Then there was a sop, a taunt. The figure of 10 per cent was dangled as a postscript, and should this miracle increase in circulation be achieved, the dotted line would be torn up, and nothing signed upon it. This 10 per cent was to act as something called 'a deal-breaker'. *The Mid-Walian* would witter on. And Mr Trench would retrench.

All parties knew this to be a chimera, none better than the proprietor, who by now would have offered to be a page 3 pin-up herself, had research figures found this a promising solution.

Miss Nightingale slowly ran her finger down the condensation on the window, finding a feeble metaphor in the gloomy grey of the weather. The unjust prospect of her many years' work being wasted, of the family name being scattered to the winds on her watch, was hitting her hard. She did not wish to end unknown and forgotten. Although she could no longer see the twelfth hole through the mist, she still remembered how the tragic Mrs Hartford-Stanley had been denied even a modest memorial stone upon her final fairway, the Committee having declared any such tribute an obstruction to play.

18

Mr Lionel Blake, *bête noire* and bank manager, fancied a walk. He was not normally the walking sort, fearful that nature might interfere with his highly developed dress sense. But this was a walk with an ulterior motive, and besides, being a sacked bank manager left time on his hands.

Not that Lionel was unduly downhearted. Had the public scandal been too upsetting, he would not have kept the press cuttings. (And put them in a scrap book.) As he would say to those friends who still spoke to him, to be the pensionable side of fifty and described by a tabloid as the 'Lothario of Loans' had done wonders for his pulling power. He did regret the furtive photo taken through the beech hedge, which had shown none of his tan and little of his charm. But, on balance, serial adultery had not been a fatal career move.

He now gave financial advice independently, and found his reputation to be an asset with the randier investor. Even as 'Love Rat' in the *Western Mail* he had found the kudos sufficient to generate fan-mail and several phone numbers. Though 'Wanker Banker' had a downside. What he did miss from his previous life was wood panelling, since this gave gravitas to his propositions.

For his walk he had eased his tightly creased slacks into green Wellingtons — a colour picked up in the tones of his silk scarf, artfully looped under the silvery-grey hair that had recently advanced a raffish inch towards his collar — and now he paused to wonder whether a robust cane was *de trop*. He was at heart an urban animal and a good judge of the stripes of a suit, whereas rural casual, with its tolerance of mud, was a slightly alien art. Lionel decided, rightly, that a twirly-type stick had the hint of a fop, and was not essential for the crossing of a few flattish fields. Each time he left the house — or entered it, or viewed it from any angle — he regretted its purchase. The divorce had put paid to his double frontage, to his curved verandah, to his walk-in cloakroom. He had traded down, and even the encouragement of ivy had yet to give character to his sixties bungalow. Lionel was an 'original features' type of man, but Artex had no known classical period. Ideally, he would not have moved out of Abernant, would not have chosen semi-seclusion, but whispers and winkers on every second corner had led him to opt for a lower profile. He regretted that his new home mocked him with the name Sunny Bank.

He left through the back door, across the token patio and past the barbecue stand, then on to where a right of way ran by the rear hedge. His route lay beside the copse, and up along the river. He could easily have driven the mile or so, but he wanted his arrival to look casual, unplanned, a man passing by.

He had passed by quite often in recent weeks. Initially, he had just gone to recce the river, for he had long been vaguely attracted to fishing, or, more exactly, to the image of fishing, or, more exactly still, to the image of casting. The rhythmic flexing of the muscles, the imperious arching of the back, the muscular thrusting of the arms and pelvis, the magisterial control of a demon from the deep, this was sexual poetry in motion, an action any woman would love to watch. However, he found the river's only angler was the Commodore, whose technique stirred few erogenous zones, and dampened even the desire to tarry. And so it was one day, after slipping discreetly away downstream, that Lionel had come across Roderigo, who was chamfering a nipple.

The bank manager had since been back some half-dozen times to visit his nearest neighbour. Ostensibly they had little in common. One man was well-bred, the other ill-bred; one was consensual, the other confrontational; one lived by application of his brain, the other by sweat of his brow. Yet, at heart, each had a similar self-image. Each saw himself as some kind of outlaw, as someone swimming against the tides of convention. Each nurtured a private image of an anti-hero, maybe even a martyr. And each saw himself as a sex symbol.

But conversation, sparky and welcome though it was, fell short of the full motive for the five-field walk. Roderigo had a lady friend.

The lady friend was seldom in evidence, as he and Roderigo would usually sit amidst the artistic detritus of his studio. Sometimes, given sun, they would sit outside on half-sculpted logs, and he would catch an occasional glimpse of her through a window of the cottage. One time she had brought out beers, and had stayed briefly to smile. She had an angular, theatrically made-up face, and her home-sewn dress was lavishly adorned with gold brocade. Roderigo said this was because Elenid believed that in a former life she had been Nefertiti.

Lionel, who had not previously got his leg over an Egyptian princess from 1300BC, had resolved to make her fuller acquaintance. And the sight of Roderigo's pick-up truck heading in the direction of town had stirred him to fancy a walk.

Only as he strolled across the final field and heard hammering did he realise that he had made an error, and that blokey talk was again likely to be the afternoon's staple.

'You need a hobby, Lionel!' cried a cigarette-cracked voice. 'Something to stop you poncing round the fields like the Lord of the Manor!' This was what Roderigo regarded as robust humour.

'Just checking on my peasants.'

'Commodore was doing that earlier.' The hammering stopped, and Roderigo stepped from the shadows, stretching his arms. 'He's a strange old git, that one. I think he was trying to put my rent up, but it's so hard to tell with him. Never quite enough words to make a sentence.'

'You're right, though, he was trying to put your rent up.'

'How d'you know?'

'Because I used to handle his account and — '

'Don't tell me you shagged his sister?'

'And all that land, those farms? He's tens of thousands in the red. Amazing. Owes almost as much as the rest of the valley put together!'

'Well, he got no joy from me. I did the penniless artist routine.'

'That didn't need much acting.'

'You wait, I'm about to become a household name. Did you ever learn how the old guy blew so much? Has he got a secret vice?'

'Nothing that imaginative. Just a brain that stopped in 1943 and a wife who drinks gin for the county.'

'Poor bugger. I wonder when he last smiled?'

'It'll be fish-related. So, how are you planning to become a household name, Roderigo? Got a dramatic death lined up?'

'Just yours. You know this mystery poet hoo-hah? All over the local rag?'

'Hard to miss.'

'Well, I'm to do the statue.'

'You?'

'Yes, me. Arts Council whittled it down from some thirty candidates apparently.'

'My gosh! Impressive! No more Indian tits for you then.'

'No more free Indian meals either.'

'Will it be life-size, this statue?'

'Be fucking huge!'

'I've never heard of this Ieuan Owen Owens.'

'No-one's ever heard of Ieaun Owen

Owens. Except Myfanwy Edwards.'

'That's tricky.'

'That's perfect. Artistic licence in spades. Mind you, I need to read up on him. That's where Elenid's gone. To collect his collected works, in the original.'

'What, from Emrys Beavan? Bookseller to the fairies?'

'I don't know. I've never been in his shop.'

'Full of Celtic mystery. Witchcraft for beginners; the mystic powers of trees; King Arthur and his corn circles, that sort of thing.'

'I know Elenid buys a lot in there, she says he's very learned.'

'Perhaps he is in Welsh. Always struck me as very stupid in English. I was in the Chamber of Commerce with him. Before the fall.'

'Should have asked you to go instead, get a reduction! And see if you can walk the high street yet, without being stoned to death.'

'Oh, it's got more subtle. It's death by pursed lips now.'

'That's your small town bourgeoisie,' Roderigo said authoritatively. 'Broom-up-the-arse lot.'

Lionel nodded in agreement, glad he had not worn the cravat.

'And ripe for a kicking.'

Lionel nodded again.

'But then that's the power of art,' said Roderigo. And added, after a pause for what passed as thought, 'That's the power of art.'

'Of which you are an articulate exponent,' replied Lionel.

'You know what I mean. Dickhead! Challenging the way things are. Not accepting reality. Having a different vision.'

They were by now both seated on logs, facing away from the low, late afternoon sun, and looking down the line of giant bosoms on spikes that stretched toward the river. Roderigo had produced a couple of beers.

'I get up people's noses,' said Roderigo. 'Because I don't accept their rules. I make my own rules. That's what an artist does.'

'That's what I tried to do as a bank manager,' said Lionel ruefully.

'You were in the wrong line of work. You're a free spirit.'

Secretly, Lionel wanted to be a free spirit with a pension so he said nothing.

'I hate that fucking town,' said Roderigo. 'And I hate the people in it. Two-faced, po-faced, prissy bunch of bores. All dull, grey people; in their own dull, grey world. Walking around like there was a by-law banning pleasure. They wouldn't know how to show emotion if you wired them up to a bomb! I mean, imagine — the highlight of their year is an *agricultural show*! A tent of vegetables, a game of skittles, and mud. Says all you need to know, doesn't it?

'Anyone with an ounce of gumption leaves this place as soon as they can crawl. Only coming back to die.'

This was intended as the killer blow of his peroration, but the silence that followed was suddenly pregnant with an awareness that neither person present had managed to depart the Abernant area.

★   ★   ★

'Eyes,' said the bank manager. 'Always look them in the eyes.'

'Yeah?'

'Women love that. Guaranteed.'

'Oh right.'

'The eyes are the key to their soul. And all other parts!'

'Useful to know. Perhaps I ought to talk to Elenid. She's never mentioned eyes . . . Mind you,' mulled Roderigo, 'there's a lot about Elenid that's a mystery.'

Lionel Blake took another beer from the crate. 'Like what she was doing in Egypt 3,000 years ago?'

'Oh, that's well documented.'

145

'It is?'

'Oh yes. She researches her past lives very thoroughly.'

'Sorry, did you say lives?'

'Oh, she wasn't just Nefertiti.'

'She wasn't?'

'No. No, she has been all sorts — well, all sorts of Egyptian princesses — down the centuries. She's got all the details.'

Mr Blake felt a sudden need to reassess his lust levels. He had always considered himself adept at pillow talk, at the sweet whisperings of *amour*, but the challenge of seducing a woman who might believe she was lying in sand next to pyramids demanded a technique that was perhaps beyond him.

'Have you been anybody?' he asked Roderigo, a little nervously. 'I mean, like in the past.'

'Me? No. Not my thing. Never liked history.'

'Oh,' said Lionel, both relieved by his reply and bemused by its insouciance.

'She can find out who *you*'ve been if you like.'

'Can she?' He failed to disguise his alarm. It was not an alarm at who he might have been, though he was pretty damn certain he had never previously been anybody else, but an alarm that he was amongst lunatics.

146

'Oh yes. It'll take a few sessions, but if you let her dig deep enough she'll ferret out the clues. A good friend of ours turned out to have been a Roman centurion. Not far from here, as it happens.'

'But it didn't make *The Mid-Walian*?' Lionel felt an urge to maintain his integrity by the employment of light irony.

'I don't think she'd want it to make *The Mid-Walian*. She says newspapers always trivialise the subject.'

Lionel was wondering how critically to pitch his riposte when a violent thudding drew the pair's attention to the pick-up surfing the ruts of the track in the neighbouring field. The conversation died as they watched and waited.

Elenid raced in and spun to a hand-braked halt with a mechanical mastery that belonged to the twentieth century; as she climbed out of the smoking pick-up, the bank manager struggled to make sense of what he saw. And what he saw — indeed, what he had seen before, but had somehow blanked from his mind — was a slight, sweet-natured woman in her early thirties, overly prone to henna. Dressed in gold-bedecked black, she gave no sign that a pick-up was a comedown for a multiple princess.

'Hallo, Lionel.' She kissed him lightly on

the cheek, leaning in to him with the warmth of a naturally tactile friend. He could smell the powder from her thick make-up, unfashionably white and a touch too close to the clown end of the spectrum.

'Have I been gone long?' she asked Roderigo, as if devolving responsibility for her absence. Lionel watched her smile at her man with a feyness that he found hard not to distrust.

Then Elenid swung around, and teasingly waved a small plastic bag in the air. Lionel had a suspicion, based on nothing but years of lechery, that she was naked beneath her dress. Although she appeared petite, there was serious breast movement to be considered, while the rest of her born-free body language seemed to say that she was too unworldly to remember knickers.

'Twelve pounds fifty.' She held up a medium-size paperback, with a cover in dull green and brown stripes. The tone was disapproval, and perhaps surprise, that any poetry book should be so costly. 'And you're not the only one to have ordered a copy.'

'I assume we're not talking bestseller here?' said Lionel, instinctively suave.

'Emrys said half a dozen have just come in. And he's trying to get hold of some second-hand copies in English.'

'Has it got a picture of Owens?' was Roderigo's instant thought on seeing the book.

'No. No, it doesn't,' replied Elenid.

'Oh damn! Damn, damn.'

'But the poems do give a clue to his character,' she said, playfully holding them just beyond his grasp.

'You've looked at them?' asked Roderigo.

'Over a quick coffee,' she replied, and smiled at the two men.

'Well . . . ?'

'Well,' she murmured, 'they're actually rather raunchy.' She looked around for a log. 'Shall I translate . . . ?'

19

At almost the same moment, the butcher was sitting down alone on a cold marble slab, out of sight at the rear of his shop, and starting to unwrap his own copy of the poems. Mr Beavan had delivered it personally, discreetly, just before closing time — causing Mr Capstick to shut the shop at 5.29 and leave the eagle-eyed Hubert greatly puzzled.

His intention had been to read the poems at home, but then he had thought of Mrs Capstick. It was rare he read literature in her presence. (Or read anything in her presence.) (Or read anything anywhere else.) But although the couple kept their interchanges to a minimum, usually on domestic matters and the death of pets, he was worried lest she ask details of what he was reading. And according to letters the mayoress had sent to *The Mid-Walian*, what he was reading was iconoclastic, avant-garde, and irreverent — just the sort of thing to damage a marriage.

Yet he felt it his duty to read the Owens output, and so be a better arbiter in the matter of the statue. He had already raised his siren voice at the Chamber of Commerce, warning that their customer base would not take kindly to seeing poets on pedestals. But he needed to know more details; already he feared the Dylan Thomas comparison could lead to more public vomit.

He thumbed the index, pausing at Erotica. He shivered, for the six beef carcasses on hooks kept the temperature uncomfortably low. He adjusted his position on the slab, and tried to decide whether the professional approach would be to take notes. He read a line at random. *She that has sweated in my sweat.* He looked away from the rest of the poem. What, he wondered, would be these notes that he took?

He skimmed the list of topics. Brothels; voyeurism; adultery; boating; adultery as a life force; a buzzard; adultery as a duty; Brechfa Wells; God: Mr Capstick could get no grasp on the man's soul. And meanwhile, as he sat enclosed by cold, white-tiled walls, lit by unfeeling neon, there was an ache in his own fireproof soul. Although the shock and disgust he had expected was dutifully seeping through him, another emotion was loose somewhere deep within.

He turned to the preface, an account of early lust and Marxism that had led to later lust and drinking. It was everything he feared from the arts: a celebration of how debauchery was transmuted by the rigour of metre into life-enhancing tosh. As a man of many morals, it irked him greatly that when an 'artist' pursued depravity he was classified as bohemian, a character, and given a get-out-of-jail card. And yet all the while, as Mr Capstick leafed through this life of versified perversity, and mentally catalogued the sexual infractions, the private ache that stayed below the radar would not leave him.

Alone with six cow carcasses and his thoughts, he was struggling with the chill of loneliness. He did not recognise it, nor entertain it, but this was the loneliness of a marriage in decay, shown now in sharp relief. The butcher had begun married life as a man embarrassed by sexuality, then, as inhibition compounded inhibition, he had become embarrassed by sensuality, and then, before long, he was avoiding all form of physical contact, until ultimately he was evading even the mention of anything bodily. Embarrassment had grown to phobia. The union had become disjunction. Mr Capstick was here, and Mrs Capstick was there, for the words and themes of Ieuan Owen Owens must not be jointly heard: these touched on topics too intimate and too pertinent and too long repressed to be given air.

As the butcher readied himself to finally read some sample poems, he stood up to revivify a leg gone numb, and the poetry book fell to the floor. When he bent to retrieve it, his eye was caught by the lines *Because one woman's true to me/ I must be true to two or three*. Distracted by distaste, his head bumped into the rump of a Friesian. He grasped the clammy, bloody carcass to slow its swinging, and was quietly grateful for the reassuring world of butchery.

Then he reached for his biro to underscore the offensive lines. Somehow he had expected limericks, where the last line would rhyme with *duck*. Instead, it was goatish rutting that was to provide his censor's ammunition. He pressed hard upon the page, once, twice, but nothing appeared. He tried a third time, and only then did he realise that the biro's ink had congealed in the cold.

20

'So,' said Elenid, closing the book with a grin and a flourish, 'have you got his essence?'

Roderigo, a stranger to the non-visual arts, said, 'Bleeding weirdo.'

Lionel, who loved to hear a woman talk dirty, even when the words rhymed, said, 'Perhaps we could hear the one about the Paris whore-house again?'

Roderigo threw more wood on the bonfire.

'I see him hewn from rough stone,' spake the sculptor.

'It'd certainly keep the cost down,' said the bank manager.

'I'd love to have met him,' said Elenid. 'He sounded a lot of fun.'

'You like the artistic type, do you?' enquired Lionel.

'Oh yes. And I've never fucked a poet.'

Lionel felt his blood likely to clot.

'He died at forty-nine, if the mayoress is right,' said Roderigo, thinking of his art. 'Don't know what from. Dick failure, probably.'

Lionel was still transfixed by Elenid. 'What about painters?' he asked her, hotly hoping for further revelatory details.

'Me and painters? Would that be oil or water?' Elenid responded, leaving almost no word free of innuendo. 'Tell me, do *you* dabble?'

'Oh, indoors and out,' he shot back, never losing eye contact.

'Should I make him young or old?' worried Roderigo. 'What's a good age for a poet?'

They each considered the matter.

'He could be young and beautiful,' said Lionel.

'Or old and interesting,' said the former Nefertiti.

Lionel sensed he was leaning against the open door of her libido.

'And I guess the bugger needs to be doing something poetic,' Roderigo went on. 'What sort of things do poets do? Anyone seen a statue of a poet lately?'

All three drew a blank. And gazed at the fire.

Lionel Blake felt it was about time for the return walk. Mission more or less accomplished. He had sent out sexual signals since her arrival, and they had been beamed back with little need for decoding. Still remaining — but for another time and place — was to sort out the logistics of lust. However, as of now, he felt an hour and a half of bohemianism was quite enough. The bank manager was not a fan of wood smoke, or sitting on things that weren't chairs, and poetry — no matter how sexy — gave a far lesser thrill than finance.

Lionel gazed one last time upon Elenid, and wondered if her breasts were the inspiration for the bas-relief that was destined to enliven curries in Cardiff.

'You like the dress?' she asked.

'Er, yes. Yes, indeed, gold's a favourite colour of mine.'

'Hark, a banker speaks!' If mockery were intended, it was made painless by her playfulness.

'And, I'm afraid, a banker leaves.' Lionel tried to give his smile some sexual subtext, and started to ease his slacked bottom up from the log.

'Perhaps he could be holding a book?' muttered Roderigo, still wrestling with the demons of creativity.

'And maybe a quill pen?' suggested Lionel, flicking lichen from his thighs as he stood.

For Lionel, the arts were not an area of expertise or interest; what Roderigo — or any sculptor — created with his hammer and chisel was a matter of little importance. Even had the man been busy on the statue of David, Lionel would probably have felt the marble to be more use as executive worktops.

'You need a model,' said Elenid.

'A model?' repeated Roderigo.

'To help get the statue right.'

'I know what a model's for,' he snapped. 'And there's no chance. Not on the money they're paying.'

'Why not ask Lionel?'

'Lionel?'

Lionel wished he had got his bottom off the log more quickly.

'Lionel's free.'

'No, I could never — ' began Lionel.

'And he's the right age,' she added.

'No, I — '

'And he looks like a sonnet would come naturally,' she went on.

'Yes, he has got some good bone structure,' mused Roderigo.

'No, sculpture's not my sort of — '

'And the same sex drive,' added Roderigo.

'What? No. No, no way am I going to pose for a public statue.'

'Why not? Don't be a spoilsport,' urged Elenid. 'It'd be fun.'

'Yes,' said Roderigo. 'You'd be an icon.'

Lionel tried to laugh, but struggled as vanity was his weak spot. 'No, I think not. I'm not the posing type.'

'Oh, go on,' bullied Roderigo. 'Put two

fingers up to everybody! Say no to the wimpy world of banking!'

Lionel looked unhappily at the pair of faces. Hers was laughing, teasing, his was challenging, mocking. Together, they were trying to bounce him to act against his will, to ignore his better judgment. He wanted to be strong, decisive, and resist them . . . And yet a little bit of him liked the idea of a Mr Blake for posterity. And the chance to see more — in every sense — of Elenid.

He hesitated, uncertain what to do.

21

Rupert was getting rather old for sex. Some of his legs were wobbly, his hair was loose, and his breath smelt. And he found the modern bitch too fickle and demanding. Nowadays his limited hope of excitement came from pheasants, as they were dead on arrival and easier to get a grip of.

So the Commodore was surprised when, en route to the river, he saw his old gun dog about to go AWOL. Rupert had abandoned the path across the field and was making a slow bee-line for the woods. Deaf to the Commodore's entreaties, and oblivious to the shuffling cattle, the dog plodded tenaciously onward, like a drunk who has heard Last Orders.

The Commodore set off in equally slow pursuit, one geriatric in parody of another. This was not exercise that he welcomed, but it was preferable to life at home. Every day now he left the house to escape the sound of tarpaulin flapping in the wind, and to free his mind from the fear of the coming invasion. He worried there would soon be no more fish in the river, so often did he seek solace in its pools.

The labrador entered the woods, his object of interest still unseen, though an occasional bark could now be heard. The noise echoed through the ivied oak trees, raucous amidst the restful rustling of the breeze. This was secret land, prime estate land that, under the Commodore's regime of bewildered neglect, had fully defaulted to nature. The dog sniffed his way along a badger track that ran through the overgrown undergrowth, and, creakily outpacing his master, Rupert was soon sending wood pigeons up in a flap.

The old man lost sight of his dog as the surplus greenery slowed his path, but then, on rounding a line of ancient beeches, he saw Rupert at the edge of a clearing, deep in doggy conversation.

It was at first unclear whether this was a post-coital exchange — conducted after the briefest of mountings — because the scene ahead was not the normal canine encounter, but something more surreal. And rarely found in mating.

The other dog wore a sign saying 'THANKS'.

(The dog was also male, though with Rupert's failing eyesight, that sort of error was plausible.)

The easily puzzled Commodore was baffled as to why a whippet, and apparently a rare literate whippet, should be found upon his land — only to realise, as he reached the clearing, that there was even more mystery afoot. Rupert had stumbled on a sort of doggy heaven. Half a dozen assorted mongrels were roaming the grass, none of them with collars. All of them were scrapping and yapping free of human constraint. As were several small and scruffy children.

Old Indian films came to the Commodore's mind. Ahead, he could see several tepees and a bonfire of logs, whose smoke was rising sluggishly up through the foliage. There was even a horse tethered to a tree-stump. Less Indian was the collection of near-derelict camper-vans, an old ambulance, a fifties coach and some type of steam engine. A forgotten forestry track, which dated from the days when the woodland made money, was now a morass of mud, testament to this eccentric traffic.

No adults were in sight, but a line of washing linked two bushes, and from somewhere came singing, the words tenuously linked to a guitar.

The Commodore felt he probably ought to take action, but had no idea at all what action that might be. Or how he might take it. What threw him most — though even his subconscious might have struggled to explain

161

this — was the absence of a front door to knock on. He was a man dependent on formalities, and without a front door he was uncertain how best to make a complaint — whatever that complaint might be, and therein lay more uncertainly.

He was hazy about laws. He knew that, as someone with a family crest, these were on his side; indeed, the Chief Constable had told him that, should he ever drive with a few malts too many, a blind eye would be turned. But the law of trespass was tricky, he had learnt that from his father. What he wanted, what he supposed he wanted, was for them — whoever 'they' were — to go away. But, being a man of many dark fears, the Commodore suspected this could mean hand-to-hand combat.

'Nice old dog.'

A white youth with dreadlocks stood beside him — a cultural complexity beyond all fathoming, as were the hand-ripped jeans.

'He's a killer,' said the Commodore.

'Doesn't look it,' said the youth.

Rupert lay down. It had been a long walkies.

Adrian stroked the labrador and blew into his nose. 'Must be his day off.'

The Commodore watched him distrustfully, noting a dead rabbit in his left hand. He had little knowledge of youth, even the normal sort, as his wife had never been sober long enough to have a baby. Not that he regretted being childless, as he did not see the need for people under forty. The young, he often felt, were the enemy within, an aperçu based on their behaviour at hunt balls. But the sight of a yob at close quarters, and possibly breeding nearby, made him long for the life of a hermit.

'Nice bit of wood, this,' said the youth. 'I'm Adrian.'

'It's my wood,' said the Commodore, trying out a hint of assertion.

The youth laughed. 'Outmoded thinking, mate.'

' . . . What?'

'Concept of ownership, outmoded thinking.'

The Commodore stared at him blankly.

'Not *your* wood, *everybody*'s wood.' His fleece-clad arm waved to take in a wide assortment of trees.

'Er, no. My father — '

'It's nothing to do with your father.' He spoke as if to a backward child. 'Property is theft, mate.'

Dimly, the Commodore was becoming aware that the fail-safe refrain of ages, 'Get Off My Land!' had hit some sort of philosophical obstacle. It made him doubt whether now was the right moment to lay claim to the rabbit.

'Yes, but I own the wood,' he said.

'No. Only within a corrupt capitalist structure.'

The Commodore had not expected this rejoinder, and fell silent as he assimilated the new information. Then said, 'Yes, but I own it.'

The youth laughed, though not in an unpleasant revolutionary way.

'Not any more.'

The Commodore was stumped. He knew this couldn't be correct — he had documents — but was perplexed as to why reason, obvious and infallible middle-class reason, had achieved so little effect. He gazed down at the youth, who had now got Rupert to roll on his back, and wished he had something more fearsome than a fishing rod.

Uncertain what he should do next, the old man looked over towards the encampment. A pretty young woman in a smock was humming to herself as she hung out more washing. A multicoloured hand-woven rug lay draped across one of the tepees. A hammock was swinging nearby, tom-tom drums on the grass to one side. A saucepan of water was boiling on a primitive barbecue. Sunlight lay in shifting patterns across the ground, glinting on the windows of the untaxed transport.

'We're anarchists,' said Adrian, in answer to a question not asked.

'Oh . . . ' said the Commodore. 'Are you the leader?'

'It's from the Greek,' said Adrian, somewhat surprisingly.

'"Leader-less."'

'Oh,' said the Commodore again. It had been a mystifying morning.

He could think of nothing, short of casting a spell, that would remove this strange time-warp world from his land. It was time to retreat. Time to return to the normality of the gentry. He urged a reluctant Rupert to his feet, the dog sorry to surrender this hidden harem. Then the Commodore focused on the young, cider-stained anarchist, and tried to look the part of a landowning Powell, mindful of the men whose disdainful portraits dominated the corridors of his life.

'Gamekeeper,' he muttered at him. 'I've got a gamekeeper.'

It was a less than effective threat. Indeed, the state of his stricken finances meant that he had not got a gamekeeper. But he let the thought of gunshot linger in the air as he turned away, keen to escape this unkempt camp-site for vagabonds, and set off through the wood.

... And yet, as he and Rupert plodded back toward the river, he constantly thought of the home that awaited him, and part of him wished that he too could hide away in a tepee.

22

'How about a nice liqueur with your coffee?' pressed the mayoress, gesturing at her walnut-wood drinks cabinet on wheels.

Mr Pritchard was now very worried. He had been suspicious when the *homard bisque* arrived. He had been quite worried by the *boeuf en croûte*. He had been definitely worried by the *fondant à l'orange*. Altogether, with the Chardonnay, this was more than 'just a bite to eat'. More than just a casual invite.

'Not at lunchtime, thank you,' he said cautiously. 'Better not.'

Surely her intention could not be sex? Not an afternoon of adultery on the *chaise longue?* In his four years as Chief Planning Officer he had till now merited only a ceremonial wave. Nervous, he sought refuge in his coffee.

Myfanwy sized him up. He was a trim man — she could have fitted two of him into her dress — and she knew, from his small talk, that he did thirty-five press-ups a day. Personal fitness enabled him to run the half-marathon every year, which he did because he believed it would make him more interesting. He had grown his pencil moustache — and all the cacti — for the same reason. Edwin Pritchard believed there to be a wrongly held, but widespread, view that people in planning were dull, even though he himself wore cowboy boots at the weekend. It was this hidden inner man that Myfanwy was now trying to locate. Was Edwin, she pondered, the type to take risks? Had he the nerve to throw caution to the winds? For, small though the planning officer was, he alone could offer her the one thing that she passionately wanted.

'This is a . . . a delicate matter,' murmured Myfanwy.

'Oh,' said Mr Pritchard, feeling himself colour.

'And I think it needs to be a secret that stays just between the two of us.'

Suddenly, he found himself wanting to mention his erectile dysfunction. Although this condition had cast a long, albeit wilting, shadow over his sporadic attempts to be a Romeo, and although it was the medical alibi that he secretly blamed for his failure to marry, he was now thinking, for probably the first time in his life, that an unreliable penis could be his salvation. Sex with the mayoress was a forbidden fruit he had no wish to nibble. Not just would her lust be a logistical nightmare — even though he liked to think himself open-minded on the subject of sexual positions — but Mr Pritchard's fantasies were fluffy affairs in which no mayoral figures were present. The most debauched recesses of his mind favoured the centrefolds of *Playboy*, circa *1965*, and they kept him very content. But when he summoned up an image of the mayoress *au naturel*, a heavy-duty dominatrix stepped forth from the shadows, her gross flesh testing a black leather corset to bursting point, her squidgy hands waving handcuffs and a whip at him. In this fevered vision, he could even foresee hot wax being dripped on to his ailing privates.

'The War Memorial site,' she said softly to him.

'I beg your pardon?'

'Has to be the perfect location for it.'

The Chief Planning Officer looked at her in confusion and alarm.

'For what exactly?'

'For the statue. Of Ieuan Owen Owens.'

There followed a moment's silence.

'I wonder if I might have that liqueur?' he said.

As she wheeled the trolley over, he wearily prepared his powers of resistance for another struggle, now on the planning front.

The War Memorial site was a sensitive subject. No-one had ever been able to explain the failure of any local citizenry to die in the Great War. For over half a century, this had been a mystery to historians and a civic embarrassment to councillors. There was no shortage of heroism or medals, just a failure to actually die. Statistically, Abernant — then a smaller town — had been due at least six dead, with a memorial appropriate to their sacrifice. The absence of such a monument in the main square had not reflected well on the town, making it appear a place deficient in patriotism.

The arrival of the Second World War had offered the chance to remedy this situation. Obviously no-one wished for the death of any Abernantian, but there was discreet civic relief when, thanks to Hitler, the require-ments for a war memorial were finally met. A roll of honour could at last be carved. And the public could now have a place to pay their respects. But — perhaps as a consequence of the twenty-five-year wait — the post-war planners had then overcompensated, and had set aside, in gravel, a disproportionately large part of the square. When the modest granite cross and plaque had been officially estab-lished, there was space left for several more wars.

It was this niche, at the heart of town, that the mayoress now wanted to claim for the arts.

'A brandy perhaps?' she suggested.

'And a mint for the breath.'

He wondered how best to tell her no. Historical precedent, architectural proportions, sightlines, perspectives, use of public space, Mr Pritchard was not short of reasons to resist. He was a cautious town planner, preferring to follow trends, not set them. Some twenty years after the rest of the nation, he was dabbling with pedestrianisation. And looking tentatively upon an inner ring road.

'It's not Italy,' he said. 'You can't just put statues up.'

'Oh, Edwin,' she replied coquettishly, 'I think you underestimate your power.'

It was misjudged flattery. Mr Pritchard did not underestimate his power, but the power he cherished was the power to stop things. He did not unduly mind what things these were — a nonwooden door, the wrong shade of yellow, the wrong size of sign-writing, a heterogeneous skylight, an ill-judged gate, an unapproved caravan, a house numeral in a vulgar font, a surplus centimetre on a window, PVC on anything except a woman — because for him the power of veto was a

171

clerical aphrodisiac, and the combination of fine print and a conservation area was the closest he got to orgasm during office hours (or after).

'I'm just a public servant. I have no power.'

The mayoress made a doubting gesture with her hand, but did not press the point as she had other gambits in reserve. Like blackmail.

'And anyway,' he added, 'it's not a question of power.' Mr Pritchard sipped his drink. 'It's a question of procedures. And propriety.'

And pomposity, she thought. 'And personal judgment,' she said.

If he spotted a barb, he showed no sign. 'And, of course, I work in the physical world, so I leave a legacy. An imprint.'

The mayoress knew several of his imprints. They were the cause of sniggers, and on at least one occasion a small mocking crowd had gathered. And had seen some £7,000 of public money bite the dust, a legacy that had not impressed the ratepayers.

This was because a new vogue word had appeared in government circulars. And if the Chief Planning Officer had a weakness, it was new vogue words. On official stationery. It being the lot of politicians to fight a losing battle with their mother tongue, these words usually had the clarity of imported fog. This season's hot hit word, the hair-trigger for grants and bigwig visits and career climaxes, was 'heritage'. Heritage was the history loved by costumiers and PR companies, a history without fibre or facts, history puréed until it had the smooth and silky blandness to suit the most dyspeptic tourist stomach. Mr Pritchard's error had been to erect a heritage bus-shelter.

High profile in the high street, this object celebrated the properties of sheet glass as encased in an elaborate iron frame of tastefully muted rococo, seemingly ordered out of a brochure from George II. Historic yet timeless, ancient yet modern, rooted in both now and then, its style told observers that the structure belonged to a forgotten but classic epoch, possibly only found in C.S. Lewis's wardrobe. However, it took up a little more space than a non-heritage bus-shelter, indeed it jutted slightly into the newly narrowed road, itself adapted as Mr Pritchard's token gesture to another new vogue word: pedestrianisation.

As a result, the first bus to arrive knocked it down, in a shower of compacted glass.

'And the physical environment,' continued the Chief Planning Officer, 'is very important to the citizen. He needs to be offered aesthetic stimuli, but within a user-friendly setting. And my role, as guardian of public taste, is to ensure that his leisure experience is not too challenging.'

'And this citizen, he would be challenged by a statue?'

Mr Pritchard, who was out of the Arts Council loop, had not received any new vogue words on statues. And quickly responded, 'What if everyone wanted to put up a statue?'

The mayoress chose not to engage with this line of argument. She comforted herself with the story told her by the fire chief. The onward march of the *faux* cobbles and mini-chicane, designed by the planners to deter heavy traffic and bring safety to the high street, had proved an unusually rigorous initiative. The first vehicle to be deterred by the calming measures was the town's fire engine, its wheels wedged firm between neo-Georgian bollards. The crew reacted by posing for photos, while the engine's response to the 999 call was a protracted and very stationary wail. Remedial pedestrianisation was effected a week later.

Although no heads rolled in the planning office, at least one neck had, she heard, been vigorously loosened.

Mr Pritchard waxed on, reaching for another brandy. 'The trouble with art, it's always subjective. Quite unsuitable for the centre of a town, where everybody would see it.'

The mayoress, whose own grasp of the arts bordered on the capricious, restrained herself from comment.

'And the first rule of planning,' continued the Chief Planning Officer, 'is to never put up anything in sight of a newspaper office!'

Still she said nothing, but took note that he was sensitive to publicity. The mayoress knew little of her guest's character — which she lumped under the heading of men in suits — and found it useful to let him talk. In particular, she encouraged him to talk about the inner ring road.

The inner ring road had been in the planning stage for thirty-five years. There had been seven known variants of the route, and another three were believed to be hidden in a vault. In the beginning, the town had been of so limited a size that construction of the road would have involved the razing of all known buildings, and had caused the cost-benefit analysis to not be encouraging. But, over time, the market town had grown from tiny to small, and twice every week the wall-to-wall cattle trucks filled the air with diesel and mooing. Calls for action had become harder for the planners to ignore, and an Eighth

Known Variant had been crafted by Mr Pritchard.

'Because,' he explained, like a man with an invisible script, 'I see my role as a planner to be forward-looking.' He paused. Then added, 'Not backward-looking,' in case the direction was still unclear. Nonetheless, the Chief Planning Officer gave the impression of a man who, ideally, would like to keep both eyes closed, and not move in either direction.

Any proposed road was likely to be controversial, particularly among those who objected to wrecking balls swinging through their property. Not since the parking meter riots had civic sensibilities been so ruffled, and The Mid-Walian had even received letters with rude words. No paving stone would be left unturned when scrutiny of the road began.

But as yet no one knew its route. In an unexpected turn of events, the town hall had put a 'Postponed' sign outside the public exhibition of Mr Pritchard's inner ring road. Two years' work with a wide range of coloured pens remained hidden from view. And there had, so far, been no official comment.

'Fine-tuning,' he said, when pressed by the mayoress.

'Tuning of what?' she enquired.

'Oh, a few spelling mistakes and a couple of smudges!' He laughed, a little loudly.

'Yes, Welsh street names can be a bugger, can't they?' said Myfanwy with apparent sympathy.

'Indeed they can!' Mr Pritchard laughed again.

Myfanwy waited for this unnatural enthusiasm for laughter to die away. And then spoke rather quietly.

'I've seen a copy of your route.'

She watched him go pale. She found it rather satisfying.

'Oh.'

Mr Pritchard seemed to have speech problems. Eventually he said, 'It was an oversight.'

'Quite a big oversight.' She poured herself a Baileys. 'As oversights go.'

'Yes, well . . . '

'Are you not good with maps?'

'I-I had a lot to juggle. It's not easy, so many things in the way of that road. Didn't leave much room for manoeuvre.'

'Even so . . . *Twelve* of their prime parking spaces relocated. The cattle market won't be happy.'

'I'm reworking it . . . trying to, er, rejig that whole section.'

'I imagine it could be difficult, painting the

white lines for those parking spaces.' The mayoress paused, and took a long slow sip of her Baileys.

'Well, I — '

'Given that you've placed them all in the river.'

Mr Pritchard swallowed hard. 'The photocopy was black and white. Hard to spot the river. Easy mistake.'

'Expensive mistake, though. Could be embarrassing . . . if it became public. 'A pound to park your car six feet deep in the Nant!' Not very career-enhancing.'

Mr Pritchard reached for the brandy bottle.

'What sort of size is this statue?'

23

'Transferred?' echoed Hubert and Dafydd.

Clydog nodded.

'You might be *transferred*?' repeated Dafydd, as if needing a sign in neon.

'Like a football star?' asked Hubert.

'Like an unwanted dose of the clap,' replied Clydog, quite out of character.

Hubert and Dafydd exchanged looks.

'I need a cake,' said Clydog. 'Even if it's the death of me.'

Hubert handed him something dark and disgusting and treacly.

'How can you be transferred?' demanded Dafydd. 'The old lady's only got one paper.'

'The old lady soon won't have any papers,' replied Clydog, looking sorrowful and sounding angry. 'She's being bought out. And I'm being — '

'*The Mid-Walian*'s being taken over?' interrupted Hubert.

'Yes, and I'm being — '

'Taken over by who?' interrupted Dafydd.

'By — ' began Clydog.

'I bet I know!' interrupted Hubert.

'He's — ' began Clydog.

'It's that rude sweaty bloke!' interrupted Hubert. 'Isn't it?'

'Yes, and he's — ' began Clydog.

'What rude sweaty bloke?' interrupted Dafydd.

'Big, bald, from Birmingham,' said Hubert. 'Right, Clydog?'

'Right, and he's — ' began Clydog again.

'So much for your blackmail theory then!' teased Hubert. 'Call yourself a journalist!'

'Not for much longer,' replied Clydog. 'Not in mid-Wales.'

A sudden silence fell over the delicatessen. Shock hung in the air, eventually broken by the sound of heavy chewing.

'Oh, Clydog, I'm sorry,' said Hubert.

'Yes, really sorry,' said Dafydd.

Then they hesitated, unsure how to decently steer the conversation from the minor human drama of Clydog to the top-grade outrage of *The Mid-Walian*'s capture by marauders from Brum.

'Said he wants new blood,' continued Clydog. 'Miss Nightingale, she argued for a special package, to try and protect her best staff. It seems that newspaper chains like to offer this twelve-month exchange scheme. And swap employees.'

'So you get to work somewhere else for a year?' said Hubert.

'Yes.'

'Could be good,' said Dafydd encouragingly.

'Where would it be?' asked Hubert.

'Chicago.'

Another sudden silence fell over the delicatessen. Clydog did some more chewing. This new — and quality — piece of information slowly sank in.

'There wasn't a second choice? Like Llantwit Major?' enquired Hubert.

Clydog did not respond.

'So, it's an early bath!' said Dafydd, in his best stab at compassion. 'Well, at least it should be a hefty hand-out for you.'

'Yes, and you'll probably qualify for a blue plaque,' said Hubert tenderly. ' "Last of the great pencil-suckers." '

'We'll get Myfanwy to give you the freedom of the borough. And a photograph with the goat.'

'It would be with the crime squad,' said Clydog.

'What would?'

'The job. You'd get to ride in bullet-proof cars. With armed police.'

Hubert looked at him, uncertain of his point.

'Twos and blues. Shootings, stabbings, contract killings. Sirens always going.'

'And so . . . ?'

'Downtown Chicago, that's Al Capone territory. Gangland. That'd be my crime beat.'

There was a quite unfamiliar tone to Clydog's voice. Just for a second, Hubert had thought it was enthusiasm.

'I'd get to see America's dark underbelly,' announced Clydog.

This was not a remark that either Hubert or Dafydd had ever expected to hear, and each paused in the hope that the other might offer his thoughts first. It was Hubert who eventually broke the silence.

'Why would you want to do that?' he asked.

'Have you not read any Ed McBain?' replied Clydog.

If Clydog could be said to have a hobby, it was detective novels. He read them on dark winter evenings; and on sunny summer evenings; and on evenings in the other two remaining seasons. While his aged mother slept, or grumbled, in the armchair opposite, he would work his way through assorted slaying and blood-soaked criminals. Too breathless to be a gumshoe, too timid to be a cop, from seven to ten-thirty he would leave Abernant for a parallel universe. Now he saw his chance to live the dream.

'So if you'd read any Terry Pratchett, would you take a job in Discworld?' responded Hubert.

'I've never been to America,' explained Clydog.

'You've never been to London,' said Dafydd. 'Why not work up to Chicago in easy stages, perhaps a couple of day trips to Llanelli, see how it goes?'

'Because I fancy a little bit of excitement before I finally peg out — things like hearing the sound of gunfire, or seeing a corpse on the sidewalk, or meeting a perp.'

This was new conversational territory for the delicatessen. It crossed Hubert's mind that Clydog was suffering from stress. It crossed Dafydd's mind that the gay doctor had put him on the wrong medication. For as long as they had known Clydog, he had never surprised them, nor shown initiative. He had the same genetic make-up as a hefted sheep: unable to go more than a thousand yards from home (unless rustled). For his own good, they both felt the need to dissuade him.

'You won't get cocoa in Chicago.'

'It's illegal to walk at your speed.'

'In mid-Wales, you see,' said a dogged Clydog, 'your typical crime is a tractor without lights. But over there, if I'm on the crime desk, I could be covering all sorts. Shoot-outs in night-clubs. Kidnappings. Cadillacs full of gangsters' molls. Senators full of bullets. And I'd be out

riding with the twos and blues, lights flashing.'

'Clydog, the first sight of a man on a
meat-hook, you'd throw up your breakfast.'

'And the cops would never take you out on
patrol. You're too fat for a flak jacket.'

'I can look after myself. I once stopped a
runaway heifer.'

'By accident.'

Clydog was not in the mood to listen,
either to them or to the irregular beat of his
heart. Ironically, Eddie Trench thought he'd
made him an offer he could not accept.
Instead, he had opened a door that Clydog
would never have knocked on. Although
Clydog had lacked the imagination for a
mid-life crisis, he did possess an occasional
alter ego, which wanted to do things that a
wheezy weary mummy's boy did not dare,
and which lived in the pages of fiction.

'What worries me,' said Hubert, 'is who
they'll swap you for.'

'Miss the gossip, will you?' said Clydog.

'Well, there's that. But I'd have to find a
supplier for bagels.'

'So how long have we got?' asked Dafydd.
'Before you go puffing down these mean streets?'

Clydog shrugged, trying to hide a disappointment that his big adventure had not
been taken more seriously. He had felt the

same on the three occasions that he had applied to be editor. The interviewing panel had quietly joked amongst themselves, as if the man before them had wandered in by error, and self-evidently lacked the qualities they were seeking. Why this should be, he did not know.

He looked across at Dafydd. 'Probably a couple of months before the takeover. Miss Nightingale won a last-minute stay of execution, to see if we can improve the sales figures.'

'Is that very likely?'

'Wouldn't have thought so,' replied Clydog. 'Though I reckon there's some big scandal brewing at the council. They've pulled the plans for this new road.

'Now my instincts — and forty years as a reporter has given me pretty good instincts — tell me that the head of planning has been caught taking bribes so as not to demolish something. Probably the old cinema. And that would produce a *lot* of interest. A *lot* of newspaper sales.'

'Or Dafydd and I could do a drive-by shooting,' suggested Hubert. 'Always helps circulation in America, so I understand.'

24

Gareth's hands were going numb as he struggled in the cold and the rain and the growing dark, his left leg calf-deep in the rushing waters of the steep-sided dingle, his stomach pressed against the brambles and the bracken, and his forearm bearing down on the backside of an ungrateful sheep, a sheep that constantly kicked in panic as the farmer, wrestling with the rusty fence-wire wound round her haunches, made desperate attempts to disentangle the barbs from the greasy and matted fleece which hung thick with gobs of dung.

By the time Gareth freed the animal, which he had only found after a three-hour search, all light had gone from the day. He was a dozen steep fields from home and he plodded back down through the mud as if on autopilot.

Time was when he would have left his boots outside, but all trappings of domesticity had gone from his life. Even the welcoming porch light no longer worked. And the kitchen only had a cold pork pie.

As every night, he emptied half a scuttle of

anthracite into the still-warm Rayburn and slumped down in the worn armchair beside it, diverting only for a pack of beers from the fridge. He could have gone across the farmyard to the centrally heated bungalow of his elderly parents, and had meat and two vegetables, preceded by soup and rounded off with some form of fruit pie, most likely apple. But they had been right about his wife. Provincial and prejudiced and purblind, they had been right in their distrust of women from foreign parts, like Ireland, where red hair is trouble and long legs lead to loose sex.

Gareth had hated their protectiveness, and now he hated their pity.

Now the only company he kept was Jessie. This he kept a secret, for fear his fellow farmers think he had gone soft. The place for working dogs was barns, or perhaps — if the home had children — a roughly wrought kennel. But Jessie, the staple black-and-white collie of the borders, had moved from the hay in the barn to a basket by the Rayburn.

Gareth rubbed her vigorously with a blanket.

'A few weeks, and I'll get my licence back,' he promised her. 'Then you can ride in the Land Rover again.'

Jessie looked pleased.

This was the time of day he dreaded. No

sheep to distract him, no wife to comfort him, no home life to envelop him. He was not a reader, he was not a telly watcher, and his only sport was skittles, played just at summer shows. Alone in the remote farmhouse, nothing happened except in his head. And the thoughts went round and around.

'If only I'd learned the salsa,' he said.

He stroked Jessie's ears, and the dog nuzzled him in encouragement.

'She wanted me to learn the salsa. Said it would be good for us. Dancing.'

With his free hand, he tipped back the first of the cans, and guzzled. He had rarely used a glass since Moira had left.

'Lot of touching, in dancing. She said we didn't touch enough. Said I wasn't good at touching.'

Gareth gazed at the ring-pull.

'It's not easy to know what to touch, with a woman.'

As he reflected on this, he instinctively ran his hand along his dog's neck, oblivious to the canine satisfaction he was providing.

'And I never liked to ask.'

He stared at the National Farmers' Union calendar on the dimly lit wall opposite, all its days for the coming month still blank. He squinted, unsure of the make of October's tractor.

'Bob says I should have gone to a marriage guidance person. Or some such bollocks . . . though I sometimes wonder if I should have.'

Jessie, who had heard it all before, silently arched her neck, inviting another rub. And was successful.

Man and dog had a strong bond. At his lowest ebb, facing jail, his wife gone, her adultery public and comic, Gareth had contemplated various means of ending it all. What had helped dissuade him was the knowledge that the dog's previous owner, another lonely farmer, had gone the same route, and hanged himself from a beam. It had somehow seemed unfair on the dog, traumatic even, to have it suffer a second dead owner. It would be poor reward for working hard, for being loyal. So he had carried on living.

Gareth half-closed his eyes, and tried, with limited success, to imagine the mysteries of marriage guidance.

'But then, I reckon nothing would have stopped that bastard bank manager.'

Wherever Gareth started from, even if he started from his days as a toddler, he ended up at the bank manager.

'He targeted her. He bought raffle tickets off her; he made jokes; he showed her his Rolex watch.'

His cashmere sweaters had also been a big hit, but this was one of the few details that Gareth had not uncovered. His loss had left him obsessive. Moira was his one fleeting shot at women, and he held out little hope of fluking another. So now he reran his past, and endlessly raged at the man who had starred in it.

'He's a smooth-talking bastard. He said he knew Donegal, and it was a lie. Probably said he could do salsa. He'd lie about anything . . . And he wore perfume. He worked for a bank and he wore perfume! And they didn't see fit to sack him. The man's a pervert. My wife stood no chance.'

Jessie squealed as anger led her owner to rub too hard.

'He did it in our bed. Five bedrooms of his own to do it in, and he did it in ours. And he kept his socks on. When I walked in on them, he still had his socks on. Red socks. And it wasn't just normal sex. Not proper sex. It was . . . it was the sort of sex that . . . '

Gareth's eyes welled up, and he fell silent, unable to share the shame of those shocking bedroom images, even with his dog.

25

''The beautiful woman has come.''

'Pardon?' said the bank manager, trying not to lose his pose.

'Nefertiti. That's what her name means,' explained Elenid.

'Oh,' said the bank manager, wishing that she was in his field of vision, and would talk less about Ancient Egypt.

'I was known as God's Wife. I had a neck like a swan. And I wore a tall blue crown.'

Lionel's outstretched arms were beginning to ache from the weight of the poetry book in his hands.

'And a Nubian wig, with a diadem. Whilst over my body was just a simple robe tied with a red sash.'

He also felt that he'd still not managed to capture the look of a man 'immersed in the white heat of creativity'.

'I was the high priestess of a new religion. Every day I would worship the sun god. Aten. And for this I had to maintain a state of perpetual arousal.'

Lionel, who had long regretted having to stand on a tree stump, now felt himself wobble.

'Fuck, fuck, fuck, fuck, fuck!' cried Roderigo. And tore up another sheet of paper.

★ ★ ★

'The guy'd never wear a cravat,' insisted Roderigo. 'He's a poet, not a poser.'

'OK, let's ditch the cravat. Let's go open neck.'

'And I don't like the book.'

'Perhaps just a pen?'

'What, holding it? In case a rhyme came by?'

'He could suck it.'

'Yeah — and make him look like he'd got a cigar.'

'Not if it had a nib.'

'I'm not doing a fucking nib. This is a mood piece.'

'Then I'm not sure what the mood is.'

'Well, it's certainly not bloody Wordsworth. You look like you're counting clouds.'

'Perhaps he should be sitting at a desk?'

'Perhaps *you* want to sit at a desk. Idle sod! No way is he sitting at a desk! It'd look like he was taking a bloody exam!'

'It was just a suggestion.'

'I want emotion, raw emotion. Tortured soul stuff.'

'I'm not sure I can do tortured soul stuff.'

'Well, imagine I'm going to hit you with the axe.'

★ ★ ★

'Is this better?'

'No.'

'How about this?'

'No.'

'This?'

'No.'

'I've not got any more expressions,' said Lionel.

★ ★ ★

'Stand on the ground, but foot up on the log, elbow on the knee, hand on the chin, and a wild look in your eyes.'

Lionel repositioned himself, and Roderigo walked round and round him, searching for the angle that captured the spark that created the spirit that provided the inspiration that would trigger his creative processes. Elenid stood a few feet away, smiling and shimmering; her off-the-shoulder, almost off-the-bust, dress was in gold velvet, and its tones changed when she moved, which she often did for effect.

'Should I stare into the distance?'

'OK, but not as if you saw three ships come sailing in on fucking Christmas Morning.'

Roderigo stepped back, and looked at him again. 'Muss his hair up.'

Elenid ran her fingers through Lionel's hair, effecting a transition from distinguished to tousled, but somewhat short of unruly.

Roderigo stepped further back.

'And he would never have a crease in his trousers. He'd never have an iron.'

'I'm not having my trousers rumpled,' warned Lionel.

Roderigo harrumphed a bit, but let the idea go. He moved his easel for a fresh angle, and Lionel did his best to summon up some mental torment, as requested. Toulouse-Lautrec, but taller and Welsh, was one of many contradictory notes he had been given.

He focused on some of the *objets trouvés* lying around in the entrance of the lean-to. A china cat, a cart-wheel, an old ceramic sign for Gitanes, half a dozen odd-shaped bottles, a Singer sewing-machine, something wooden with drawers, a bicycle pump, a sign to Carmarthen. None of them was much protected from the rain and he wondered at their purpose. Were they chosen for drawing practice, or there for resale value in hard times?

'I was sculpted by the great Thutmose,' said Elenid. 'My limestone bust was one of the wonders of the ancient world. I had thicker lips in those days though, deep, crimson lips.'

Lionel had noticed the lips earlier, and wondered if and when he might get to kiss them. To be pouted at when posing was to be a victim of bondage without ropes, a rare and kinky sophistication. This assumed, of course, that he had not misread her — and reading her was hard, given her claim to be over 3,000 years old. Was this an act or did she believe it? Was she having fun or being driven by a drug-induced destiny? And should he mock or should he play along? It was the quality of her research that disconcerted him, that made him wonder if she was perhaps a little bit Ancient Egyptian.

'More intense!' barked Roderigo. 'More intense.'

Lionel tried to oblige, but his forte was persiflage, his genre was drawing-room comedy. He tried to stiffen some sinews, and recall some of the more unpleasant aspects of the disciplinary procedures employed by his bank. And he tried to rerun those customer service moments which lent themselves to erotic verse.

'I made love to Moses, you know,' said Elenid.

The jutting jaw weakened, and he felt his posture suffer. True or not, this was a high benchmark to aim at.

'Fuck, fuck, fuck . . . ' began Roderigo, and he ripped another sheet from his drawing pad. 'Lionel, you still look too bloody bourgeois! Like a wanker, not a lecher! You're meant to struggle with your soul, you're changing the history of poetry. You're telling the world to sod off. Oh, let's take a break.'

And Roderigo stomped away into the field.

★ ★ ★

Standing beside the river, his hands thrust into the pockets of his jeans, Roderigo knew what the problem was, the real cause of his sculptor's block. Deep down, he couldn't give a toss about the poet.

He threw in a couple of Pooh sticks, and mulled some more. By taking on the commission, he decided, he had compromised his artistic integrity. And thus could find no relationship with the subject matter. And hence no vision. This, he knew, was historically a common error among artists, when too eager to please a patron.

He watched his sticks stubbornly refuse to move, and if anything edge slightly backwards.

Roderigo blamed the mayoress. He had no time for the small-scale and the piddling. He was an artist who favoured the bold, the dramatic, the flamboyant. What he'd really like to do, what he'd always wanted to do — apart from big-nippled outsize breasts — was a god or two. He was particularly keen on Neptune, whom he used to draw as a child. He loved the arrogance of the pose, the thrust of the trident, the contemptuous swelling of the belly. And he was drawn to his life as a hell raiser, for this was a turbulent god who was mean and moody, and got to lay all the goddesses.

The larger of the two sticks had become waterlogged and looked likely to sink.

If there was any pleasure that Roderigo could gain from the day, it was to see Lionel's confusion. Previously, the man's sexual thrills came from the subtleties of subterfuge, from lust behind the arras. He moved in the shadows, made assignations, and thrived on adulterous deceit. But at Maeshyffryd the rules of play were different, and the social fig leaves were discarded. The liaisons of Elenid were on the public record, for the public pleasure, and Lionel had yet to grasp, yet to conceive, that his flirting could be other than furtive, that its consequence would be other than trouble. And Roderigo loved to watch him wriggle.

He bombed the surviving stick with a stone, and observed the ripples spread. And then, as he gazed down into the reddy-brown water, it slowly dawned that his idea for a sea-god need not be dead.

★　★　★

'On the table?' said Lionel, doubtfully.

Roderigo nodded. 'Change of plan.'

Lionel removed his loafers and clambered on to the round, battered dining-table in the cottage's only downstairs room. The ceiling was low and he had to avoid the cloth light-shade. Cosy but poky, the room looked set to hold a bring-and-buy sale for bohemians.

'Now sit. Like you would on grass.'

Lionel sat, a little like a man at a Glyndebourne picnic.

'On one haunch, legs a little open.'

Lionel shifted his position until he was leaning back, resting on one arm and half a backside, his body facing them.

'Relax more. Well, relax physically, but look as though you rule the world. Or want to. You're an arrogant sod.'

Some forms of arrogance did not come too hard to Mr Blake, but world domination was a struggle.

Roderigo and Elenid looked carefully at the

bank manager squatting on their table.

'Better,' said Roderigo, thinking it wise not to tell the bank manager that he was now a sea-god. 'How's that feel for you?'

'Good. Yes, good.' Lionel moved his thighs about a bit. 'Sort of languidly insolent.'

'Great, we can build on that.' Privately, Roderigo regretted the lack of a trident, but reckoned he now had an image he could work with.

'My character could be thinking about a poem,' said Lionel helpfully.

'He could.'

'What sort of poem do you reckon?'

'Oh, it should be anti-something. Definitely anti-something. He's an anti-man.'

'An anti-man?'

'Anti-authority, anti-convention, anti-tradition, anti-religion, anti-everything!'

'But sexy like rebels are,' added Elenid. She whispered in Roderigo's ear, and he gave her a big, encouraging smile.

'You know what would be perfect? Be really in character?' said Elenid, with the authority of one who had studied the poetry in detail.

'What?' asked Lionel.

'I think he should be anti-clothes.'

It took Lionel a few seconds to realise what had just been suggested.

'What . . . not as in naked?'

'No, no!' said Roderigo reassuringly.

'Oh good.'

'No, as in nude.'

The bank manager laughed dismissively. 'Never! Not on a plinth!'

'Hallmark of all great statues. You could be the David of Abernant.'

'Bugger that!' said the bank manager, determined his cavalry twills should stay firmly in place.

He looked from one to the other, only to grow uneasy when he saw both faces beaming with encouragement.

'Forget it! No. My personality's coming from my clothes,' he insisted.

'No need to worry about Elenid. She's seen no end of cocks.'

'From almost every century,' confirmed Elenid.

'I'm not worried about Elenid,' he replied. But instinctively Lionel adjusted his pose, loinwise, his concerns having now shifted from public embarrassment to private arousal. He suddenly felt very vulnerable upon the table, which was not an easy place to crawl off.

'I'm sure it'll make a lovely feature,' said Elenid, adding with a sweetly malicious smile, 'If rumour is anything to go by.'

Lionel was a libertine of the old school, and the sexual politics of post-modernist couples left him floundering. Besides, seductive remarks were a man's job, even if he were crouched below a lampshade.

'Doesn't mean I want to go flaunting myself in public,' he said somewhat feebly. He looked across to her lover, hoping for some kind of support.

But Roderigo had little to say. Except, 'Who's to know? No-one.'

Roderigo was starting to feel inspired by his new, and possibly unique, concept for a civic memorial — a poet and a sea-god in one.

Autumn

26

Adrian gave a discreet nod of his flute as the old ambulance trundled past his pitch by the market hall and turned up a side street. Ramsey, his dog, was less discreet and barked twice, causing his THANKS sign to become lopsided.

Without missing a beat of his Gershwin, the town's only busker glanced up at the clock above the ironmonger's. His dreadlocks briefly hung at an angle, stiff from lack of cleansing water. The 87p lying in the tobacco tin at his feet was not a critique of his music, which did credit to his public school tutors, but a commentary on his choice of crusty as a lifestyle. The mud-caked boots, the hand-ripped jeans, the scrumpy-stained shirt, the shapeless shaggy fleece, all marked him down as a threat to polite society, of which there was a lot in Abernant. And no amount of dazzling roulades could compensate.

For several minutes more, Adrian bounced his music off the vaulted stone above him, the flute jerking skyward, the *joie de vivre* of his riffs mocking the plodding gloom of the passers-by. In the early days, he had toyed with the idea of a notice, its words to elicit sympathy, existential and financial, for his lot. Favourite was 'unloved son of a bishop'. Most crap was '3 wives, 2 dogs, and a macaw to support'. But such a notice made him feel a mendicant, and he wanted to be a troubadour. At least until varsity began.

He glanced up at the clock again, and allowed himself a brief but florid coda. He then reached for his rucksack, which was leaning — with malice aforethought — against Mr Bufton's ironmongery. It was a rucksack of globe-trotting size, but quite empty. Although not a cold day, he dug out a pair of gloves from its side pocket and pulled them on. The flute securely stowed, he put the lead back on Ramsey, a wistful-looking whippet unaware of his role as pimp. Then, head down, Adrian set off quietly along the high street with his dog.

The old rusting ambulance had parked down the side street in a little-used disabled bay. From its rear doors had emerged three New Age travellers, impeccably dishevelled and seemingly supplied by a casting agency. All were young and hairy and male and looked unhappy with the structure of society. None of them spoke. They walked down the narrow street a little like outlaws in a Western, but with the poor posture that comes from wigwam life. They knew their way, they had their plan, and after a couple of streets were within sight of their goal. KwikSave.

It was the town's only supermarket, achieved by demolition of a much-loved Quaker meeting house. The supermarket, however, had the advantage of being a new vogue word, and Mr Pritchard had instinctively reached for a bulldozer. The KwikSave building had the same relationship to good design as the KwikSave name had to correct spelling. It had three aisles and very bright lights and a lot of things in bulk.

The New Agers pushed open its plate-glass doors and walked three abreast down the first aisle at a steady pace. Mid-afternoon in mid-Wales is a low point for the retail experience, and there was only a handful of shoppers available to be disapproving and mutter social criticism. At the end of the aisle the three men wheeled right, went to the end, and turned up the last aisle.

Here stood the freezer cabinets. Like men who had recced a bank, the first of them went to the packaged pies, the second to the cartons of cake, the third to the tubs of ice cream. With admirable synchronicity — which belied the public view that such people lack discipline — they flung back the lids.

They looked from left to right.

They saw the aisle was empty.

They replaced the lids.

And waited. Several minutes passed. The scene remained the same, no-one else in sight. The trio grew restive, and passed a bottle of water to and fro. But never shuffled far from the cabinets. Eventually, they heard the sound of footsteps. A shop assistant rounded the end of the aisle. And the three men flung back the lids again.

As one, they unzipped their flies. Standing back, they pulled out their cocks, and each sprayed an arc of urine over the store's best bargains.

It was not a long, comprehensive piss, more in the realm of a short, sharp anti-capitalist spurt. Just enough to leave a light yellow moisture over all the target foods, and dent the week's profits.

But none was in the mood to be a martyr. As a somewhat delayed cry went up from the shop assistant, who had received no staff training in guerrilla urine, the three men regrouped their penises and clattered towards the exit at a fast trot. Before security could be alerted, all three were out of the door and on the way back to their ambulance.

Meanwhile, at the rear of the premises, the long nose of Ramsey had just come into view near the loading bay. Although not the normal place for his walkies, here were foody smells new to a dog of the dropping-out classes and this made him keen to sniff round the backside of KwikSave. Adrian, however, tugged gently on his lead and the whippet retreated, and joined him out of sight behind a wall.

Adrian kissed the dog's nose, and tickled his tummy, and whispered 'Ramsey' in his ear. To any onlooker, it was that most disarming of scenes, that guarantee of British probity: dog lover at play with his pet. In truth, Ramsey was surprised by such affection at this time of day, but said nothing and responded with licks. (There was much that the whippet did not understand about their relationship, not least that he had been named after an archbishop, thus providing his youthful atheist owner with constant pleasure when calling him to heel.) This unexpected moment of fun and frolics lasted longer than seemed natural, and had reached a point where Ramsey would have secretly welcomed a ball, when his owner's ears pricked up.

'Filthy dirty bastards!'

'Should all be shot!'

Sounds of anger and outrage began to fill the air. Clunking doors with heavy rubber skirts swung back and forth, and orders were shouted. Someone jumped from the loading bay. Then came the unmistakeable rumble of a wheelie bin, and Adrian punched the air.

The plan had worked. Meal after meal was being dragged out, and not just the goodies that had suffered a direct hit. The laws of PR had trumped the laws of hygiene, and urine by association was enough to condemn a steak pie. The entire contents of all three freezers were being voided, down to the last and deepest raspberry ripple. The criminal waste of capitalism was triumphant.

Adrian waited until the loading yard had grown silent and empty again. Then he ceased the loving and the patting, took off his large, empty rucksack, and hurried towards the wheelie bin — pausing only to signal to a hidden posse of outlaws in a camper-van.

'Din-dins, Ramsey!' he cried. 'Din-dins!'

27

'Jeez! Helluva lot of tarpaulin!' exclaimed the location manager.

He let his Jaguar slowly freewheel past the rhododendrons while he gazed for the first time upon Chateau Powell, and noted with satisfaction that its once fine features had obligingly begun a photogenic decline. In a few winters' time it would be able to audition for the role of ruin.

'End of the world doesn't come cheap,' rued Philip, still hazy as to how he had so often found himself handing over money to *prevent* repairs.

'Bit of subsidence would be nice, with a couple of hefty cracks,' mused the location manager, whose name was Greg ... or Kevin, or Alphonso, or Quentin, for he was a flexible man, and ready to be whoever or whatever it took to schmooze an owner.

'I can do you a rotting cornice, according to the latest complaint,' said Philip, who had now appointed himself director as well as producer and writer. 'Oh, and some black mould.'

'You're a class act.' Greg slipped the Jaguar

back into first, and continued down the long gravel drive, the tyres picking up a thick mat of sodden brown leaves that muted the sound of their progress. And bore witness to the laying-off of the gardener. On a fine day, the silhouette of the Queen Anne house had a touch of fairy tale. But it was a grey day, like the day before, and the day to come, and even nature had lost interest in the world.

The 4.8 litre Jaguar came to an unhurried halt by the pillared porch. A few yards further on, the terrace began its descent to the remnants of a croquet lawn, where in happier, more feudal days there had been garden fêtes and bubbly lemonade. And down beyond these untended gardens, beyond the medieval yew hedge, lay the rubble of St Brynnach's, the family church, where even the dead Powells no longer lay in hallowed memory.

Philip was first out of the car, his script and files in a funky folder, his mood instantly tuned to the PR wavelength of upbeat. The rain, a very similar rain to the rain of his last visit, was waiting to greet him. This time, he pulled on a brand new Barbour, its sheen as yet untroubled by the rigours of life in West London.

The location manager emerged with a studied slowness, and stood scrutinising the building's façade with what appeared to be scholarship. Fellow professionals would recognise this as a man deciding what to hammer where — and how best to deny it.

Then a rear door of the car opened, and a foreign-looking blonde in a fur coat stepped on to the gravel, and moved lovingly to Philip's side. And had her bottom patted.

Philip led the way into the imposing porch, grasped an iron handle on the end of a long wire, and tugged hard. Far away, as in the best of Gothic horror, a clapper could be faintly heard hitting a bell.

It prompted the protracted shuffling of feet, then the long clank of a bolt, and then the melodramatic rattle of a chain. Philip had forewarned his companions of the cadaverous Commodore with the parsimonious approach to speech. And he had alerted them to the hard-to-charm Dilys. What he had not expected was to be greeted by the mad-haired woman from the attic. Looking like Mrs Igor.

What gave force to this shock was his script, draft eleven. To his politico-thriller with sex romps Philip had now added Mrs Igor as ghost, confirming that his grasp of genre was far from strong. An unlikely extra, she flitted through the plot — and several walls — with a banshee abandon, the result of being bricked up for many years. Ideal for cranking up the drama's tension, her character was also gifted with powers to foresee each of the survivors' futures, which, for the purposes of the teenage demographic, were universally bloody and rather noisy. Adept at adopting the narcissism of writers, Philip had come to believe in her fictional existence — which did not stretch to opening heavy doors and saying hallo.

Behind Mrs Igor, the greyness of the day had infiltrated the house, and the murk of the entrance hall could almost be classified as fog. It was only mid-afternoon, and the much-prized fish at the end of the stairs was scarcely visible.

The old lady smiled coyly at them, clutching her winceyette nightdress to her loose bosom like a teenage coquette. She beckoned them in, offering slurred words of welcome. Philip revised his original theory that she needed help to escape, possibly from a bizarre rural bondage scene. With an elaborately courteous wave of her arm, she gestured across the hall to the front reception room, then set off on the journey towards it. Although her walk had the unsteadiness of a high-wire act, she moved as one whose body still aspired to breeding and comportment, albeit now doomed to parody.

She paused to balance herself by the giant

Oriental urn with the cracked Chinamen, and smiled again, apparently at the pleasure of company. Or perhaps she thought gentlemen callers were sure to bring gin. Uncertain what to say, or maybe how to say it, she shifted her glance from one to the other. As if out of nostalgia for a pampered past, she ran an admiring hand down the fur coat of Philip's companion.

'Josephine!' cried Dilys shrilly, entering hall right, and carrying an oil-lamp.

Josephine looked like a dog that done wrong. Except this time she offered no resistance. As Dilys took her brusquely by the arm, she gave a little farewell wave to her new friends and allowed herself to be led off down the hall. Almost out of sight in the deep shadows, Dilys directed the woman called Josephine into an anteroom, and a key was heard to turn in a lock.

'My brother's wife is not well,' said Dilys succinctly upon her return, a statement that left Philip to reassemble the family tree and to wonder how many times he had caused her gratuitous offence. 'It's the damp.'

★   ★   ★

The front reception room was not how Philip remembered it. The Commodore was still there, still rigidly upright by the palm tree (though it was now nearly leafless, unaccustomed to life in a rain forest); the furniture was still there (though now huddled in a sort of circle, as if expecting a surprise attack from Indians); and the Meissen coffee-pot was still there (though now the mould made coffee-drinking an unwise venture). What was new was the plastic sheeting, the array of buckets, and the fruiting fungus.

'See — the set's already been dressed,' Philip whispered to the location manager, with a smirk.

There was a certain reluctance to sit, even when Mr Bufton's industrial strength plastic had been peeled from their seats and laid temporarily over the elephant. Philip seemed to specialise in women who were picky about where they put their bottom, and Ulrika — willing though she was to experiment in other ways — would only let her fur come into contact with the arm of the chesterfield. From where, nonetheless, she gazed adoringly, and — exhibiting the second characteristic of Philip's lady friends — mutely.

The others made the best of the rest of the lumpy Victorian furniture — apart from the Commodore, who was a stand-alone man. Making the best of the social gathering was less easy. The air was damp, like a faint wet fuzz on the face. Sections of floorboard had warped; part of the plaster was growing a grizzled black beard; a king-size stepladder rested against the piano. All the scene lacked was builders. And Dilys. Who had frostily gone in search of afternoon tea.

The Commodore made no attempt at small talk, nor talk of any other size. He just stared straight ahead, like a man on parade in fear of jankers. His face was rigid, emphasising a scary bone structure found in horror movies, and raising the nightmare that he needed a million volts to be kick-started.

'Six episodes!' cried Philip, holding up a pilot script of *After-shocks*. 'Late evening. Channel 4. Possible repeat. Starring Sharon Bellacuzzi!' He hoped the recognition factor might take hold, but neither eyelid flickered. 'Your house could become a landmark! Be on postcards. You could soon be seeing coach parties up your valley!'

He paused to take questions.

'My bed's wet,' said the Commodore.

In any other company, Philip might have advised adult diapers and gone for the laugh. But he had grown wary of the Commodore, and feared lest he raise the subject of jeeps again.

'And this is the man who will help me

make magic in your lovely home,' replied Philip, with a deferential gesture toward his location manager.

Greg raised a right arm in brotherly greeting. 'Brochfael,' he said. 'After the sixth-century Powys prince.'

The Commodore showed no signs of bonding. Nor interest in magic. Even an introduction to Ulrika had no noticeable effect on his vital signs. Philip tried the human touch.

'And how's your dog?' he enquired. 'Is Rupert still retrieving?'

For the first time, the old man fixed him in his sights.

'Dog's got a cough,' said the Commodore. 'And watery shit.'

Ulrika reached across to take her man's hand, feeling the need for a squeeze.

'I'm sorry to hear that,' said the empathetic Brochfael. 'I used to have a coughing dog.'

A dead leaf fell off the palm tree, joining a small brown pile of deceased leaves, curled in crunchy rigor by the fireplace.

On all sides, the oils of men in uniform looked down upon them.

The familiar feeling of a conversational cul-de-sac descended.

★ ★ ★

The afternoon tea-cups were passed carefully from hand to hand, with Dilys acting as a guarantor of gentility. But this time the china had no well-bred markings. There was no sign of cake nor napkin. No mention of Lapsang Souchong.

'Just saying how lovely to see you both again!' lied Philip cheerily, trying to ignore the sound of regular dripping in the bucket by his leg. 'And how have you been?'

Dilys turned up the wick in her oil lamp. All three followed her angry upward stare at the ceiling's central light, and saw where the abseiling raindrops had come to blows with the electrics, and charred the wires and seared the plaster. And plunged the old house into lasting night.

Philip had journeyed to Wales as the buoyant bearer of glad tidings. His opening words were to have been 'Great news! Green lights all round!' There was even a bottle of Bollinger in the pheasant pocket of his Barbour. Now he had to use the charm that was failing on his wife.

'I'm sorry if the delay has caused any inconvenience,' he said.

'It was easier in the Blitz,' snapped Dilys, leaving open the question of how the Luftwaffe had misrouted to mid-Wales.

Brochfael decided to sit this apology out.

He could count fifteen bulbs in the one chandelier alone, and the grovelling needed was beyond his pay grade.

'Aah, the Blitz!' said Ulrika, pleased to have heard a word she thought she knew.

'Oh God! The Blitz!' cried the Commodore — and was overcome by the need to bolt from the room. Saying as little in farewell as he had in greeting.

'I have had weather in every room,' said Dilys, widening the cause of her complaint. 'My brother now has to sleep downstairs,' she added accusingly. 'As does his wife.'

Strange how life imitates art, thought Philip. Key among his plot points for post-Armaggedon was the increasing shortage of usable bedrooms, and the unlikely couplings which that led to. But he felt this interesting fact unlikely to pacify.

'I'm sure that I speak for everyone at The Now Company when I say how much we regret — '

'£47.32 on candles alone.'

' . . . any inconvenience — '

'£62.43 on extra buckets.'

' . . . that has been — '

'And £99.99 on a tepee.'

'A tepee?'

'I have kept all the receipts.'

Philip smiled weakly. Three hours from

London, and he was in a cultural black hole, a hole as weird and deep as any that Alice had climbed down. In this strange place were people whose hearts did not beat faster at the thought of stars in their home. Here there were people who experienced no thrill at the glamour of making a television series. Here were people who did not own — nor even want — a television. A state of mind beyond all known experience.

★   ★   ★

Greg and Philip stood beside the brick dovecot folly, which the doves had long left, and looked across the old walled garden. The late afternoon mist came in squalls, blurring their view of the now ragged espaliers. Everywhere, the weeds had engaged the vegetables in a fight to the death, and the only likely meal on the menu was nettle soup. Greg took some more photos, and glanced back at the house.

'You could sell tickets for that tour,' he said. 'Gormenghast for Beginners. Be a little gold mine.'

Philip did not respond. He was trying to think of imaginative filmic uses for a thistly tennis court and a derelict dovecot.

'A little gold mine,' Greg repeated, working

quickly against the fading light. His attention had turned to the elaborate Victorian greenhouse, once heated and home to the fashionable pineapple, now only an evocative glassless shell. He constantly wondered about the labour costs, as he had it in mind to buy an estate one day.

'A pig roast!' said Philip. Then he looked around and waved his love to Ulrika, who was watching him from a distance, her footwear allergic to country surfaces.

'A pig roast?'

'Let's say the valley is overrun with wild boar, extra-large because of radiation. If we get the cast to tear chunks of meat off with their bare hands, that'd be a great scene. Sordid and medieval, just right!'

Greg was uncertain where they would obtain deformed local boar, but said nothing. For the file, he took a few shots of the small pet cemetery. Under a weeping willow, more than a hundred years of dogs, mostly named after Roman emperors, were having a final quiet lie-down. With a carved, occasionally poetic, parting tribute to their work with grouse and children.

Then the two men crossed to where the giant rhododendrons were crowding out the drive, advancing like a slow and shaggy breed of triffid. It was the last location of the day, the last setting that the grounds had to offer.

Greg wiped the mist from his lens. 'What a place to grow up in! Run wild in.'

'Go mad in.'

'I played croquet once,' said Greg. A propos of nothing obvious.

They walked back to the car, where Ulrika greeted her lover with the affection due to a returning traveller.

A few damp leaves lay spread-eagled on the windscreen, as if nature had been fly-posting the meaning of autumn. A late rook flapped home to its tree by the river. On the far hillside, the first farmhouse of the night had put on its outside light.

Philip opened the car door to depart, but almost at once a complaining cry was heard.

Greg looked to the house beyond.

'I think the old lady wants to speak to you again.'

28

'Secret admirer, Dafydd?' teased Amanda, the prettier of the two women in Forget-Me-Nots.

If Dafydd blushed, it was hard to tell because much of his face had the look of streaky bacon, and the colour crimson had colonised his cheeks. He blamed this on his years as a postman, as though getting in and out the van in all weathers caused industrial injury on the scale of a miner's emphysema. He put little emphasis on the role that alcohol might have played. Yet, in truth, he had been overly pink even as a child, when he answered (or, more often, failed to answer) to the playground call of 'Carrot Head'.

Dedicated to Dafydd, the six yellow roses were the last of the Interflora orders for the morning's delivery round. Interleaved with greenery, and swishly packaged by the shop, his flowers came with the words 'Love' and 'Anon'.

'Playing away, is she?' Amanda enquired, and June, wrapper of the cellophane, laughed.

Dafydd was secretly pleased to receive this attention, for both these women were the sort

224

he found attractive, being between the first flush of youth and the final flush of the menopause, but he offered no comment in reply. It was the second time this month that the anonymous source had sent him roses, and he preferred to milk the mystery.

He closed the back door of his camp van, which now held some dozen deliveries. Mostly they were the bread and butter of births and deaths, though even these strengthened his status as a man with both ears to the ground. But also aboard, as so often, there was hint of a dirty dalliance or two, bringing him hope of grist for the gossip mill. As he got behind the wheel he was already thinking of how best to address the deli.

It was the social high-point of his week, that empty hour when the three men would gather to mull on life's latest. They had clocked up years together, same time, same place. It had begun as chance encounters, as the happenstance of shopping, as refuge from the rain. Some days it was an outing for the ego, some days it was an exercise in envy, some days it was an escape from solitude. Gradually it had become an act of competitive communion. A moment of time-out from the world.

And yet these whiled-away afternoons in

the forgotten dust of the deli also stirred an ill-defined unease in Dafydd, a lingering melancholy which he tried not to analyse.

He was born in Abernant, as were Hubert and Clydog, though they were older, with gossip that went back to the war. He had never been a child with ambition, for to have ambition was not a family tradition. To be a postman, with a route as regular as the orbiting moon, had been his heady idea of fulfilment. The downside of his life was with the ladies, for there had never been much call for ginger in Wales. And though pensioners found him always chatty and helpful with the milk and willing to clip a hedge it was not a charm which worked well upon young, unmarried women. Indeed, none of these three men of the world had worked out the opposite sex. Clydog's hat was the most that he had removed in the presence of a woman. And although a dream of romance still remained, Clydog was waiting first for his mother to die; he placed his best hopes of allure on having her house. Hubert alone had managed to marry, with plans for a deli dynasty, but it was a childless, charmless affair, more mercantile than marital. Husband and wife only appeared in public behind the counter, and then to bicker over prices.

But if the arcs of these three love lives fell

squib-like to the earth, the arcs of their career paths described no better pattern. Hubert's plans to puff his pipe in other shops had remained just that, a pipe-dream. His imperial designs to expand to Brechfa Wells and beyond never quite left the drawing board. His aim to bestride local politics like a Victorian magnate had given way to a malignant mischief-making. Clydog yet hoped for an American renaissance, but the role of duty scribe and WI amanuensis was not the calling he had privately, youthfully, aspired to. His was the journalism of Groundhog Day, and after forty years the element of surprise was fading. As for Dafydd, he would maybe have taken pride in a gold watch given for a lifetime of well-performed postal duties, but twentieth-century capitalism had proved too unreasonable. So the salary cheque had ceased, the seniority pips were lost. And while flower delivery had its secret satisfactions, it lacked the same status, and provided no holiday pay.

The three men were not likely companions, not drawn by shared interests or hobbies. For it is a cruel rural truth that the smaller the community, the less is the chance of choosing your friends. All that truly united them was the passing of time. And time was the fear that lurked in the shadows of Dafydd's little-used mind. Time, and the life that was passing him by. Ten years more and the three of them would be sat upon a bench, at a street corner, and watching the excitements of traffic. This would be the same street corner where the youngsters always stood, dreaming of one day escaping from the tyranny of rain and empty mountains. Before the trap shut tight. And the three unlikely companions would sit every dry day upon this bench, like those wrinkled old men in faraway lands, and gossip only of death.

Why, Dafydd wondered, as he reached the edge of town, was the chief planner sending cornflowers to the mayoress? And what could be meant by *Hoping that we can stay friends*? Other, of course, than code for the sentiments of post-coital trauma. Yet something was awry, and Dafydd could not decide what. He struggled, as always, to master the mystery of mutual attraction, but could make no sense of Mr Pritchard and Mrs Edwards. For Dafydd, sex was in many respects like Lego, and required all interlocking objects to be of roughly similar size. If this indeed were mayoral misbehaviour, he felt the need to know more about the sexual habits of town planners.

Nor did he find the next floral tribute any

less perverse. Miss Powell's fancy man continued to send her a dozen red roses every other week, and as Dafydd drove them down the drive he half-expected to meet her eloping. The messages had got ever more urgent, ever more pleading, and the impassioned cry of 'Not much longer' now had three exclamation marks. No more did Dafydd have any doubts that this was a married man awaiting his divorce — a liaison confirming what all the books said about ice maidens being goers. He just wondered where she did it.

Dafydd liked to say to those who asked — and they were few — that little now surprised him, that he had seen first-hand the human heart in all its wayward forms. To a man of limited imagination, this no doubt seemed true. He had been witness, as it were, to many kinds of unconjugal coupling, and the go-between for the most ill-suited of suitors. Although he personally favoured the sexual technique of a moth, whose scent alone brought dogged mates from many miles distant, he had learnt something of the labyrinthine lengths to which lovers often go. He now knew that conquests and orgasms came from stratagems and sieges, and that objects of desire succumbed to lust laced with trickery.

He carried the six yellow roses up the short path to his terraced cottage. Their arrival had given him much pleasure. Amanda and June had shown considerable interest and, he reckoned, some early signs of jealousy. He would give it another ten days before he ordered himself some more.

29

'Item 12,' announced Mr Capstick, the butcher. ''Any Other Business.''

The church hall was silent. By silence, those present hoped soon to be home.

'Nobody? Then *I* have another urgent matter to raise,' he continued.

Their numbers were now down to eight — seven in practical terms as old Mr Chigley, the deaf corn seed-merchant, was asleep — and the closest scrutiny of the Chamber of Commerce proceedings was coming from the hall's caretaker, who was breathing heavily and trying to make two Yale keys jangle.

'A matter which arose too late for inclusion in the main agenda,' clarified Mr Lloyd. Secretary, treasurer, carwash owner, and pedant.

The butcher opted for a brief pause, as Mr Lloyd was known for addenda, and then — not for the first time that evening — prepared to address the meeting on a matter of moral import for Abernant, possibly with reference to the works of Edward Gibbon.

Hubert — also not for the first time that evening — prepared to heckle. His mood was such that he would have heckled silence.

The change of venue, the move from alcoholic fug to spartan draughts, had for several been a culture shock too far. The publican of the Brown Bear had boycotted the meeting because beer profits would be down, and the off-licence owner had a phobia about evenings spent without a pint of lager in his hand; Celtic Militaria were believed to be ideologically opposed to a meeting with no prospect of violence; and old Mr Fortescue, the homeopathic chemist, was thought unable to find the suburbs in the dark.

The other problem was the chairs.

No-one had known about the children's playgroup . . . and their nursery-size chairs, placed in a little circle for little people with icky-bicky legs and a size 1 bottom. So nice for listening to stories about Little Red Hiding Hood and the Bears. Less nice for listening to Mr Capstick.

And unfortunately Hubert, with a passport that claimed him as six foot, was the tallest of the committee members. Who, one by one, had been citing pelvic disorders and cramp and disappearing into the night. Only venom and a belief in eternal vigilance had kept Hubert still in place, still squatting, knees above his bum, like a turkey waiting to be trussed.

'We're being invaded,' declared short Mr

Capstick, for once finding status in standing. He waved a finger for Churchillian effect. 'Invaded.'

The evening's dwindling band of contortionists was understandably surprised.

'And,' he went on, 'the council does nothing!'

'Invaded by who?' queried Mr Benyon the haberdasher, whose sensitive mind had quickly led to a vision of aliens.

'The great unwashed, that's who,' retorted Mr Capstick. 'There's a field full of them out there. Somewhere. We know their type. Illegal vehicles, illegal drugs, illegal sex, illegal . . . other things. And what happens? KwikSave! A public scandal at KwikSave! What type of degenerate uses a range of meat products as a toilet? In the middle of the day? Trade is going to be hit hard if we don't get the police to round them up, and drive them right out the area. Whatever the by-laws say! These Bolsheviks are out there right now, saving up their urine. You mark my words, KwikSave is only a dummy run. Any one of us could be their next target.'

'But mine's just a clothes shop,' said camp Mr Devonald. 'Why would anyone urinate in a clothes shop?'

'Tight corsets?' suggested Hubert.

Hubert knew what had really got the butcher's goat. Urine was a secondary issue.

The man was piqued about the poet. His wild claims that honouring a bawdy writer would bring Bacchanalian debauch to Abernant had failed to persuade; his plan for a petition had gained more yawns than signatures. Item 1, a call to ban the statue, had bit the church-hall dust. And now his moral zeal was short of a mission.

Hubert had a hunch that hubris might be afoot. Still bruised from his overthrow, the deli-owner had of late found few chances to fly the flag for freethinkers. Now, the ageing rebel sensed this might be his moment — not just to mock but to wound, not just to provoke but to offer up a more expansive, Hubertian world-view. He tried to summon up as much dignity as a man could when his bottom was only four inches from the floor.

'In my opinion,' stated Hubert, 'speaking as a small businessman, I personally think there are few better places for excess urine than KwikSave.'

As opening remarks go, it was up with the start of *Pride and Prejudice*. He had the attention of the floor. And he got a small titter from the caretaker — now leaning threateningly against the exit door.

'On their next visit, I would like to see these chaps extend their pissing range to cheese.'

Hubert was pleased to see that Mr Capstick was not amused; had he been less fit, the butcher would have gone blue-veined.

'We're all small businessmen. We share a common enemy. The supermarket.'

These words of Hubert struck a chord. There had been much wailing and gnashing of teeth when the supermarket was nigh. There had been many forecasts of the end of the world for the shopkeeper, and a small anaemic boycott still lingered on.

'And so I welcome radical action. Anything that encourages customers to use the local shops has to be good for business. Maybe we should form an alliance with these New Age travellers.'

'And do what?' spluttered Mr Capstick, now wary of being wrong-footed.

'Oh, I don't know . . . how about a mass piss-in?'

Old Mr Chigley stirred, as if woken by the unfamiliar words that were washing over his slumber.

'Perhaps the start of a National Urine Campaign? 'Support Your Corner Shop — Piss on a Grocery Chain.'' Hubert raised a teasing, interrogative eyebrow as he spoke. 'Obviously, not everyone can be an activist. But most could donate to the cause. Those who are housebound could send in some bottled urine . . . and have it thrown over any cheap sliced meat for sale.'

'I don't think this should be minuted,' said Mr Capstick furiously.

'Why not?' asked Mr Beavan the bookseller, always sensitive to issues of censorship.

'It's hardly the image we want the Chamber of Commerce to project,' he snapped back.

'And freedom of the borough to anyone who pisses in KwikSave,' added Hubert, now on a roll. 'That's b-o-r-o-u-g-h,' he said to the teenage minute-taker, who was struggling with her giggles, and enjoying work experience for the first time.

'It's unconstitutional, not minuting,' advised Mr Lloyd, the secretary.

'Well then I want it on record that these hooligans are a threat to the business community,' insisted Mr Capstick. 'They don't wash. They don't work. They're vegetarian. They carry diseases. They don't pay tax. They walk ten abreast. They park in disabled bays. They frighten old ladies — '

'And they play the flute all day,' added Mr Bufton bitterly, the ironmonger more than ever resentful of the mayoress.

'Stocks!' announced old Mr Chigley. 'Put these youngsters in the stocks, and piss over *them*. That would stop it.' And with this sole contribution to the evening, the deaf seed-merchant struggled up out of his miniature seat and left for home. Mr Lloyd made a small note on his pad.

Hubert knew he had the butcher rattled. He could see it in his little piggy eyes. Gauleiter eyes. Somehow Hubert knew that the man had been hated at school, his elongated head shaped by years of being thrust down toilet bowls. But whereas Capstick loved order, and needed order, Hubert always hankered after a bit of anarchy — provided it were no threat to profits. Age and Abernant gave him too few traces to kick over, and he savoured the rare chance to be provocative, regressively childish even, for he knew it disconcerted his enemies.

And when Capstick was his enemy, he always had the feeling that righteousness was on his side, as it was still Hubert's hunch that he had lost his role as leader through the corrupt distribution of sausages.

'Perhaps we should ask Dev's Dainties for some sheets?' suggested Hubert. 'And if our chairman could bring along some burning crosses, we could all have ourselves a lynching. I'm sure that would solve the problem of youth.' He smiled at the minute-taker. 'That's lynching with a y.'

Mr Capstick bridled. He suspected the

237

underhand use of wit. But he did not respond. He always found the most effective way to deal with wit was to ignore it. There lurked the danger it could become laughter. So he pressed onward, eager to table a resolution, keen to play a leading part in public policy. And to make a lasting mark as chairman.

'I propose,' he said, slowing his speech for effect, 'that we request the police to use all reasonable force to immediately remove these undesirable young persons from the vicinity of the town of Abernant. Now, if I could have a show of hands, please. In favour?'

But before a hand could be raised, Mr Lloyd intervened. On a point of order.

'Yes, Mr Lloyd?' the chairman said wearily. 'What is it?'

'We have no quorum, Mr Chairman.'

'What do you mean, we have no quorum?'

'We lost our quorum when Mr Chigley went home.'

'We did what?'

'We're down to seven — we need eight.'

There was a moment of silence in the hall as half a dozen grown men, wedged with great difficulty into kiddy chairs, tried not to look rather stupid.

'So we can't vote?' said the chairman.

'I'm afraid not,' said the secretary.

'How sad,' said Hubert.

Mr Capstick sucked tightly on his already thin lips. Twice in one evening he had been thwarted, first over the poet, and now over this. He had never realised how difficult it would be to rid the world of sin.

'Right. Right. Time for home, then.' His voice had gone cold and hard and very quiet. 'I vote we declare this meeting closed.'

'On a point of order!' called Hubert.

Which was a surprise as Hubert did not believe in points of order.

'What?' snapped Mr Capstick in a most unchairmanlike manner.

'Well, correct me if I'm wrong . . . but if there's no quorum,' Hubert said in the polite and tentative tones of a man seeking enlightenment, ' . . . how can we vote to declare the meeting closed?'

'A good point,' said Mr Lloyd.

'I mean, as I understand the rules,' said Hubert, his helpfulness a triumph of deceit, 'the meeting has to continue.'

'Er, well, constitutionally, yes,' agreed Mr Lloyd. 'I suppose it does.'

'It what . . . ?' said the confused butcher.

Hubert heaved a great sigh of regret.

'Rather poor chairmanship, Mr Capstick,' he said ruefully. 'It seems we may never be able to leave the room.'

'Oh for fuck's sake!' cried the caretaker.

30

Mr Blake was not sure where best to put his penis.

'Sugar?' called Elenid.

'Just the one.'

Roderigo blew his pencil shavings on to the floor and laid aside his hunting knife. Then he took yet another long swig of beer. He did not believe that art flourished under conditions of sobriety.

'Stare out the window,' he ordered, and picked up his pad.

Rain was the default weather of the month, and the heat of the log fire left little to see but condensation, yet the reclining bank manager turned his head without demur, complying like a pet. Indoors, the afternoon light needed artificial aid, and a 60 watt bulb gave extra definition to cheeks that had newly lost their colour, in a face that masked concern.

'The lean-to leaks!' said Roderigo bitterly. As if in explanation of why a nude man was on his dining-room table.

He swept the tin-tack tip of his 4B pencil across the first blank sheet. 'And,' he went on, 'it's got no heating.'

Mr Blake did not speak, perhaps from a sense that silence offered a protective shield. Why he had agreed to come he did not quite know. He had let the days drift by as though in hope that the last conversation had an expiry date, whereupon their words would be tactfully wiped. Yet in the end, true to his form as a charmer and a chancer, it was a sort of vanity that had lured him back.

'But then, of course, I'm not an *English* artist,' said Roderigo. Pressing hard, and often, he laid down several dense black lines in the torso area.

Mr Blake's pose gave him no eye contact, no benefit to a quizzically raised eyebrow. Instead, he just gazed ahead at six small panes of misted glass. He was glad of their opacity for he had suddenly remembered the right-of-way through the yard. The prospect of blinking at ramblers, of seeing them check their maps for indoor zoos, would have been one indignity too many.

'Me, I live in the wrong sort of valley,' sneered Roderigo, rubbing hard at the lines with his thumb.

'Oh, not that again,' sighed Elenid, standing in the corner waiting on the kettle.

For the first time, Mr Blake had begun to question his ribcage. Or more precisely, the flesh overlaying it. Normally the flesh was kept at a similar angle, hanging like a tight suit in a well-ordered wardrobe. But in becoming semi-recumbent, he had found his flesh a little too keen to explore, too ready to take up attitudes independent of his body. He wondered if this would be captured in the art. He wondered if Roderigo was fully focused on the art.

'Wrong valley, wrong accent, wrong country,' Roderigo rasped, his drawing hand now given up to wild whorls in the neck area. 'Wrong money.'

A faint but steady whistle began in the corner.

'I'm just Welsh. Just fucking Welsh!'

Mr Blake knew little of the etiquette of modelling, but even that little had led him to expect a bit of sensitive chat, some attempt at cultural bonding. In exchange for the hours of muscular stress, he had imagined there would be interest in his life history, questions about his favourite colour. He knew that the Queen got asked about her horses, for hour after hour, and so it had seemed not unreasonable to assume he too be put at his ease, if only by some light banter over banking.

'You want to be an artist, you've got to be English. Second-class citizen, the Welsh artist. Always has been. You're English, you get the awards, the shows, the acclaim. And your cock sucked. You're Welsh, and it's the cold shoulder. You could be Rodin, and they wouldn't want to know. But do a few scrawls, admit to an English mother, and it's welcome to the club.'

The whistling grew more determined, more unpleasant on the ear.

'It's the jackboot of colonialism. Art's one big private club, run from London. Doling out the dosh to their mates. Quality doesn't come into it. Just your blood-line. Yet one more conspiracy against the Welsh. To try and trample their culture underfoot. A thousand years of art, and nothing but love spoons to show for it.'

As he ranted, Roderigo's exotic accent had all but gone, and the Heathcliff of Myfanwy's wet dreams had given way to a more local churl. Here now was the voice of a man from Merthyr, a man who had gone from Rhys to Roderigo at the age of twenty-three, and had taken on piratical airs to make himself a person of intrigue, with better sales.

'It's criminal! I could be world-famous, if it wasn't for the English. Instead I'm in a hovel. Third-class citizen, the Welsh artist. Always has been.'

The kettle boiled and the screeching steam forced a pause. Elenid let the boiling have its head, and waited until her lover's own steam was spent. Then she poured Lionel his coffee.

Elenid moved over to the table, where Lionel sat with his legs splayed open, his body arched back, and his head turned in profile.

'You'd look good on a coin,' she said softly.

'What value?' asked Lionel.

'Oh, big,' she replied. 'Very big.'

Elenid leaned across to where he faced east and helpfully raised the mug to his lips, so that the pose could be kept intact.

'Of course, I've been on coins,' she confided, trickling the hot coffee down into his throat. 'As Cleopatra.'

Despite Lionel's best efforts, some of the beverage misrouted.

Elenid leaned over him, and dabbed tenderly at his chin with a doily. She had on a loose midnight-blue shift, as often seen in pyramids, with a central gold-embossed panel enlivened by linear black snakes; its sharply angled V-neck gave an 85 per cent view of her breasts, and little hennaed arrows guided the eye down to her nipples.

'I like being on a coin,' she murmured. 'I love the thought that my body is rubbing around in people's pockets.'

Lionel's own silken charm had usually had the promise of lower interest rates as its most seductive feature, and he lacked a ready rejoinder.

Elenid stepped back, and appraised him in the round.

'Photos,' she said. 'Photos for the maquette.' And she hurried to the cupboard for the camera.

Mr Blake had never been a sex object before and had severe doubts it was a fit role for a man. He wanted to raise objections but felt his status was undercut by being stark naked. A lifetime of penetrating housewives added to his confusion. Credit and debit, men and women, they had their own columns. Each sex came supplied with set rules for sexual order. But here was a world where even zips and bra-hooks served no function. How was he to organise his manly lust? How was his will to be exerted? Yet though he felt the pangs of a puzzled libido, he had not entirely lost his ability for preening, his capacity for self-regard. He might be cornered, he might be conquered, but he was also secretly rather flattered — for he, middle-aged Lionel Blake, was desired by a woman used to having the pick of all the men in Egypt. Over very many years, it would seem.

'Head and shoulders first?'

And she aimed the Polaroid.

'Very nice,' she purred to Lionel. 'You'd have a great career as a bust — you could sex up one of his Indian restaurants.'

'Fuck off!' said Roderigo, who was now in a foul mood.

Elenid ignored him and, flaunting the camera, she moved steadily around the table, capturing Lionel's essence from all angles.

Not allowed to move, not encouraged to talk, Lionel fell back upon thinking. He was not a natural thinker, his thoughts were usually about himself, but his brain was being taxed by the ties between the other two. And by the search for clues as to what kept them together. He couldn't get much further than Beauty and the Beast, although an ignorance of Cocteau and big gaps in his social anthropology soon left him struggling with their storyline.

As a man of cashmere, it baffled him to find that churlish and scruffy was a turn-on. The romance of the garret was fine when a youngster, but a draughty lean-to lost its sex appeal when over forty. And whilst artistic fame might be for her an aphrodisiac, this was surely best when it arrived *ante mortem*. Neither did Lionel see the allure for him of living with Elenid. The free-loving temptress can not have been the bringer of much peace of mind. Her willingness to party elsewhere must surely have taken the bounce out of their bed.

'Last one,' she said, three feet away. And fired the final flash.

She had taken some dozen Polaroids, and Lionel's loosely rippling body could now be said to exist in 3D.

But, being under artist's orders, Lionel had to hold his pose, stare straight ahead, and listen to the sound of her looking at the photos. Some twenty years her senior, he was nervous of her judgments. Her personality seemed to depend on the whims of the moment, the shock of the new and the naughty, and his mind struggled for purchase. Lionel's secret wish was to get her on to home ground, to play to the strengths of his bungalow.

'You look lovely,' Elenid announced. 'I think you should put your phone number on the plinth.'

Relieved, he laughed, though Roderigo winced like a man for whom laughter was the enemy of genius. Elenid then moved quietly to Lionel's side, carrying the final Polaroid photo, which she flicked like wet washing. She held it up before him, and together they stared into its sludgy grey depths. Gradually, as the Polaroid dried, and the sludge receded, Lionel could see emerging into view the unmistakable outline of his genitalia.

Roderigo sketched on, grunting and grumbling as his latest 4B made heavy weather of the thighs. Like an Inca chewing coca to perceive the divine, he slurped hard at the beer to help him create his visceral vision of the godlike. And all the while, a yard away, Lionel and Elenid shared a long and intimate moment as they wordlessly watched the bank manager's private parts take glorious technicolour form. Which was perhaps not one for the album.

Elenid smiled, and laid a little kiss upon Lionel's cheek.

'Definitely your best feature,' she said firmly, with the authority of centuries.

Lionel sat and basked in a warm glow of minor sexual triumph . . . until he became all too chillingly aware that his best feature was irresistibly, monstrously, growing in size.

31

Clydog gazed with mild curiosity at the appearance of a plinth below his office window.

He had been charged with catchy stories. Or failing that, catchy headlines. And no doubt the type-setting lads had been charged with catchy lay-out. No one had yet suggested calling the paper *The Catchy Mid-Walian*.

But, as he always said to the editor, and hoped the editor said to Miss Nightingale, Abernant and its valley were simply not places where drama and scandal and catchiness occur. Clydog had a theory the cause was climatic, and that for passion you needed heat. Indeed, he had once proposed an article correlating sex and violence with low rainfall. Miss Nightingale, however, had not been enthused, and had insisted the article be just on the subject of rainfall.

Now, though, their proprietor — their proprietor for just a few weeks more? — was coming round to catchy. She had even visited the newsroom, traditionally a Christmas event, and given what she believed to be a pep talk. Liberally laden with sporting metaphors, it was really only of use for a difficult bunker shot. But beneath her impeccable manners, hidden by her immaculate clothes, the two old hacks claimed to detect the signs of fear and sweat. Clearly, multiple kitten births were no longer news enough. So, from editor down, each was on the look-out for stories that might have some connection with the modern world.

Clydog wondered again about the plinth. He had been watching it all morning: watching the lorry arrive with it, watching the men unload it, watching the men move it about, watching the men sit down, watching the men move it some more. It had been hypnotic, but was it news?

Sales had surged a couple of times in recent weeks, but not enough. The outrage in KwikSave had been a most popular read, albeit cause for some confusion. Since urine was a substance not mentioned in polite reportage, much of the shocked readership were uncertain what they were shocked about. But none was keen on empty freezers. Counter-culture was new to Abernant, as indeed was culture, and hairy men in shops were a body blow to civic pride. This disconcerting story had also led to vigorous activity on the Letters Page, revealing a previously unknown section of the readership

250

with strong views on death squads.

By mid-morning, Clydog had despatched young Auberon, the nephew and neophyte photographer, downstairs to the square. The advantage of a plinth is that it makes no sudden movements, and was ideally suited to Auberon's few skills. Clydog had watched for over an hour as Auberon stalked the plinth, repeatedly capturing it from unexpected angles.

A spate of wheelchair accidents had also been good news for the sales figures. In all his pedestrianising proposals, the chief planner had overlooked the correct angle of inclination for ramps. As a result, there had been an increase in runaway old people, whose frail spouses had lost control on the down slope. *The Mid-Walian* even had a go at something called a campaign. This gained extra publicity when — faced with a looming pensioner — a bus had taken evasive action and collided with the replacement heritage bus-shelter. The subsequent provision of remedial ramp concrete was marked by a rare self-promoting headline: 'Cripples Roll Safer Thanks to Paper'. But this too was not increase enough.

By late morning, the plinth had caused a small crowd to gather in the square. Events like plinths were rare in town, and Wednesdays were traditionally a slow day. As were

251

most other days of the week.

Clydog gazed down from the first floor and reflected that he knew almost every person in the crowd. And their immediate relatives, and their distant relatives, and their dead relatives. And even relatives they didn't know they had. He found it a timeless scene of reassuring familiarity. Of depressing reassuring familiarity. His life was on a loop, its characters destined to wind and rewind into view, like rotating targets in a fairground. Targets that he daily embraced. He briefly wondered what it would be like to live among strangers, where abuse and rudeness could be a life choice, with no fear it would sour the harmony of a small and interwoven world.

Provincial life, he had recently concluded, all came down to big frogs and small ponds. This was not exactly an original thought, but Clydog had done some extra philosophical tinkering with it. Lately, in the middle of the night, the thought had come to him that he might well be a frog that had outgrown its pond. And that the solution was for him to change ponds . . . Or was it to fill his pond with more water? . . . And what exactly did that mean? It was also around this time of night that he would realise the limitations of abstract thought.

Clydog decided to potter down to the

square, and ponder on the plinth. And perhaps feel the pulse of his people. A hundred words at most, he reckoned. The statue had been good for column inches, but the debate was over. The 'don't knows' and 'don't cares' had won. As was traditional. The little knot of watchers had been equally riveted by the laying of cobbles, and the siting of the poet roused no angry ardour.

In the interests of catchiness, Clydog would have liked perhaps an angry placard. Ideally, he would have liked a sneak preview of the statue. Yet apparently even the mayoress had been barred from the artistic process, such was the sacredness of art. As the man whose waste bin had set the sculpting in motion, Clydog would have liked to follow up the work-in-progress. But, in truth, his nose for news told him that Ieuan Owen Owens was no longer a story.

He stepped out into a rare patch of sunlight, and watched whilst Auberon took a picture of plinth with shadow. Then Clydog gazed across the square, as he had done almost every weekday for forty years. He gazed across at the newsagent, where his words were delivered to the world, at the delicatessen, where he sourced his scoops, at Dev's Dainties, where he outfitted his mother, at the homeopathic chemists, where his allergies were spoken of in awe. Nothing new sprang to mind.

It was the day before the paper went to print, and he still had nothing solid or exciting. There was a rumour that a television series was to be shot in the valley, but facts were hard to come by, and made little sense. Apparently it involved jeeps. Driving up stairs. During the end of the world. Sceptical, Clydog had asked around. Only to hear that the rumour had come from the Commodore, a man whose contact with reality had ended with the war.

Clydog turned and slowly went back into the newspaper building, to see if inadvertently he had thrown anything of interest into his bin.

The Second Spring

32

Gareth snorted himself awake, and found straw up his nose.

He had no idea of time, but guessed that dawn had yet to come. It was his third night in the barn and his head was telling him little. His nose was telling him that he smelt. He yawned, and the yawn ran into another yawn, and he knew he had days of yawns backed up. The world did not look steady and his skin felt glazed with grime. He reached for the smelling salts.

Outside it was the first day of spring.

The barn air was solid with noise, the pain and joy of lambing a tumult of overlapping bleating. Pools of light from arc lamps lit up the bonding pens replete with twins and triplets and worn-out mothers, their overweight wombs a triumph of remorseless science and selective breeding. Waiting outside the wooden hurdles, membranous string dangling as they stood stamping their feet in the ante-natal scrum, were the bulging ewes that the thirty-a-day ram had turned to at a later date. And over everything hung the myriad smells of sheep, from fetid fleeces to slithery after-birth, the animals infused with fear and disinfectant.

He used to catnap in the house, rising every four hours to check on amniotic sacs and mucus, but — as with so many little disciplines in his life — he had grown lax of late and stayed out in the hay, and said to hell with the body odour. And why should he care about comfort?

The lambing season, that magical moment when his subsidies first saw the light of day, now only brought Gareth a heavy heart. Lambing alone was a draining task, and a badly timed blink of the eye could turn life into death. An airway with no air left a lamb with no hope. To him the long days and long nights were like forced labour, which had as goal the survival of the fittest *and* the weakest, and his were the shoulders on which all weight rested.

Not a man noted for his interior life, he had always had one farming fantasy. He had dreamed of a bride who loved the life, and who would want to lamb *à deux*.

Together they could have shared the tasks. For him, the lambing gel, for her the antibiotic pessaries. His job, the disposable syringes, her job, the iodine spray. He would get to use the plastic funnel, she would get to handle the colostrum. Hand in hand they would watch for the burst water bags, that tell-tale sign of labour. And acting in union, they would truss any prolapse.

It was perhaps an over-romantic vision, a throwback to the days when all the family ran the farm, yet it softened his soul to dream. And now it would never happen. Moira would never return.

So he tried to focus on the good news as he lay blear-eyed upon the prickling straw. As of midnight, his months on probation were over, his unjust debt to society paid. No more need he fear that a binge in a pub could put him inside. No more would Bob ask him questions about the state of his emotions, innermost or elsewhere. No more would he stumble over five-step and seven-step plans, or try to locate his anger. His life could return to what he sadly called normal.

And, give or take an embryotomy, the lambing would shortly be done. Leaving him free, for the first time in over seventy-two hours, to have a few drinks.

33

The sacking had stayed there all day, tied on tightly, teasingly, waiting till the mayoral words of welcome were heard.

The new civic landmark had arrived early morning, unseen and unsung. Four men and a fork-lift truck had manoeuvred it into place. Some said. A small crane on the back of a lorry had lowered it into position. Others said. The mountain rescue helicopter had winched it down as part of a training exercise. According to a third version. Given time, the help of aliens seemed likely to gain credence.

A light dew covered the municipal grass, which had been mowed to a military shortness by the parks department, who had little sympathy with nature. Attempts to make the gravel look smart had been less successful, as the dog shit clung like chocolate round a walnut and neither blowing nor sucking was fully persuasive. At the War Memorial, a respectful brush had been applied to the marble and chewing gum removed from the names of the dead. And, being a special occasion, the green rail which ran shin-high around this little haven — a square almost French in its formal baldness — had seen generous quantities of paint applied to its rust.

A seagull was the first to visit the statue, pleased to reach a perch far from stormy weather, but not quite certain about the sacking. On and off, she wheeled and screeched above the square, like an avian town-crier announcing the coming of trouble.

Before long, below her, the day's first humans gathered to gawp at the mystery object, unsure whether prodding was permitted. With its shape hard to determine — did it stretch outward or tip upward . . . or lean backward . . . or bend forward? — they usually settled for a nervous joke, fearful of looking foolish or philistine.

At around nine-thirty, two men with fluorescent yellow jackets arrived on the square. They approached with the regulation walk of Abernant officialdom, unhurried and vague and ponderous, as if recceing a route for a hearse. Then they did some standing. The taller of the two had a file, which he twice checked to make sure he had the right statue. Much of their remit was pacing, and they made several slow circuits, clockwise and anti-clockwise. Then they halted in front of the plinth and stood for a while with furrowed brows, trying to invest their purpose, if not with majesty, at least with . . . well, purpose. And then they left.

Abernant was no stranger to grand occasions. The highlight of the year before last had been the ceremonial opening of the town's first cash-point, an event involving a velvet cushion and special scissors. And watched by nearly all the town council and several surprised tourists.

It was the Agricultural Show, though, which was the annual triumph, a cornucopia of rosette-packed events. Held every year on a wet August Saturday in mud, it was an afternoon-long carnival of everything agricultural, from wind-chimes to double-glazing. It had a beer tent and hamburgers with onions. Parts of the town brass band would play things. Tractor salesmen would give slide shows. Glove puppets of sheep were on sale. And up and down the rugby pitch there paraded a cavalcade of award-winning animals, many of them with enormous testicles. For additional entertainment, men with chainsaws cut tree trunks into interesting shapes. As was traditional, the proceedings were accompanied by a witty commentary over the Tannoy system supplied by Edwards Electrics. Nor did the range of attractions end there, as a wide selection of leaflets on topical aspects of animal husbandry, from slurry to organophosphates, was freely available. And, on stands throughout the show, there was the opportunity to join over a dozen local societies, prominent among them the Samaritans.

At midday, a council lorry arrived at the square, with a podium. And out got two more men with fluorescent yellow jackets. The pace of events was quickening.

And the level of interest was hotting up, though it would be hyperbole to describe a scattered dozen as a crowd. But the sacking did have the effect of a curtain about to go up on a stage. Passers-by would pause from passing by, and stand in vague anticipation. It was as though they expected the object to have a life of its own, and perhaps be about to glow or hum, and announce it had come in peace.

Next to arrive were crush barriers. This was a form of street furniture new to the town, ordered by the modernising wing of the council. Overkill would have sprung to mind, but budgetary constraints had restricted the number of these barriers to three. Thus requiring any crush to be of a limited and genteel nature. Uncertain how to organise the barriers to best effect, their yellow-jacketed escorts left them resting against the back of the plinth.

By mid-afternoon, the first councillors were drifting into view. This was about as sexy as the job got, and they did not wish to miss the flashing of the cameras. There was a wall in the town hall, between the toilets and the cloakroom, where a winding line of grainy photographs immortalised the seminal moments in Abernantian history. These were the events that had made the town what it was today, and these were the people who had helped with the making, and here they had been memorialised for ever, though the lighting in the corridor was of poor quality. (This municipal memory lane had as its aim to honour, *inter alia*, the replacing of the outmoded Guildhall, the removal of the unwanted railway station, the filling-in of the superfluous canal, the bulldozing of a redundant Roman wall, and the demolition of an impractical stone bridge over the Nant: in sum, a long roll-call of exciting urban leaps into the twentieth century.) This afternoon, these eager and anonymous councillors, freshly scrubbed for the public unveiling, were nurturing the hope that one day they too would be remembered for their role; that in years to come, posterity, as it walked to get its coat after a piss, would look upon ill-lit photos of their faces and recognise them as the visionaries who had brought culture to their people.

By late afternoon, the sides of the square had the sort of turnout one would expect for a good car accident. The onlookers now were less fickle, scenting the pleasures of a civic soap opera and unwilling to wander off. The dramatis personae were beginning to mingle meaningfully, to form a line that faced the hessian-hidden features of Ieuan Owen Owens.

The mayoress had been hoping for a three-tiered seating block, an idea she had picked up from a visit to Horse Guards Parade. After rancorous negotiation, she had settled for three plastic seats, folding. These were to be for herself, the leader of the council, and the dignitary from the faraway Cardiff world of art. The Chamber of Commerce had drawn a blank. The butcher had been fatally indecisive, torn between the moral high ground of a boycott and a more lowly longing for the limelight. The sculptor, as is the fate of artists, had been overlooked altogether, and was expected to linger by the plinth.

By the hour of the unveiling, Miss Nightingale herself had descended from her eyrie, joining the good and the great with distaste. Clydog and Auberon had been here mopping up the human interest since lunchtime, and had left no boring opinion unheard, no banal profile unsnapped. Clydog had even interviewed Dafydd, and obtained his views on modern Welsh literature, despite neither of them having read a book for several decades. But he had drawn the line at an interview with a bizarrely dressed woman claiming to be Cleopatra, reluctantly recognising that there were some things which had simply got no news value. Still to come, however, was his big exclusive: the moment when he interviewed Roderigo standing beside his new statue.

The crowd was moving from eager to restless, attention now shifting towards the statue. There was, of course, the urge to see this much-publicised poet soon to occupy the centre of their town. But there was also interest in the knots, and how best to untie them. And a number of farmers had their eye on the sacking, which can be so useful in a farmyard during the winter.

But first a hurdle, that *sine qua non* of every local shindig, the speeches. Mr Arts Council was to expatiate on the fever for sculpture that was now sweeping mid-Wales; the council leader was to reminisce on his love of the arts since childhood; and the mayoress, resplendent in a pond-green tent, had prepared a few thousand words on '*converting the world of dreams into solid form*'.

266

34

At about the same time Philip and Greg were struggling along in bottom gear, edging on to the Westway out of London. Somewhere behind them were the crew, clogging up the rush hour with rented vans, overloaded by all the kit that comes with film. And scattered elsewhere on road and rail were the C-list stars whose gift for the genre of apocalypse had so impressed at audition.

'So this ice-cream van kept ringing its chimes. *Every* time we started to shoot. Round and round the rec ground goes Luigi's Cornettos, and then there'd be a sudden burst of '*O Sole Mio*'. Again! The bastard! So in the end I go over, and I say '*Ciao! Come sta?*' And I hand him a couple of tenners and I say '*Tutti frutti* for all the crew, *signor*'. And I look him straight in the eye, and I say 'And then it's *arrivederci!* Know what I mean, mate?' So Luigi buggers off, everybody's happy, and we get it in the can!'

Greg laughed, pleased with his triumph. He had a lot of triumphs. Sometimes it was bent police in foreign lands, palms greased for permits to film the forbidden, sometimes it was moaning old ladies, pacified by putting their dog in shot.

Philip was thinking it was probably a mistake to drive down on a Friday evening. His shooting schedule was due to begin at first light, an arduous day not made easier by the cannibalism scene. And he had not been sleeping well lately. Life at home had become rather stressful. His wife had been showing little sympathy for his heavy workload. She had even been voicing criticisms of his script. The frivolous world of fashion gave her little understanding of the rigorous disciplines of film. Sometimes he was tempted to keep *her* in a locked room.

'We were being plagued by yobs, this one time. In a park. Usual nonsense, whistling and waving. So I say, ''ere, mate, wot's wiv all this bovver?' And they give me some lip, so I say, 'Waddya reckon to bein' a star then, eh?' And they go 'Oh yeah?' and I say, 'Straight up!' And I wave a couple of fivers. And I get this pair of delinquents on to a tennis court — as a background shot — bashing a ball back and forwards over the net! For an hour! Problem solved. Except they were so damned useless it looked like a scene from a cripflick!'

Philip wondered if there would be time to make some last tweaks to the script, not that it was in anything but good shape. But he had it in mind to enlarge the role of Mrs Igor, make her a symbol of something. He wondered how good the old lady would be at taking direction. All down to the bottle, he supposed. Perhaps — and he was not cineaste enough to know — this would be a filmic first, to have a drunken ghost. And Philip briefly felt excited, for he sensed *Aftershocks* was breaking new ground for Channel 4. He was making a multigenre series.

'We were once under this flight path for learners, and every five minutes they'd do a circuit, one mile this way, one mile that. So every five minutes they'd balls up our sound. We were trying to film a sex scene, and it sounded like the Battle of Britain! So I figure out where the airfield was, and I ring up the control tower. And I say, 'Morning, Air Traffic Control. Major Featherby here. I'm making a training film for the MoD. Five miles west of you. And I'd like to have some hush. Would you shift your planes somewhere else, please?''

Greg paused for the punch-line. 'Five minutes later it all went schtum! And we got our lovers bonking away as per the script.'

He laughed at the memory, a little too pleased, a touch too triumphant.

Gradually, as dusk fell, and the city was left behind, the motorway traffic began to gather pace, and soon was forming an unbroken tidal wave of vivid red tail lights, moving mesmerically through the night.

The dark blue Jaguar, all leather and luxury and padded silence, seemed to subtly confer status upon their mission, and insulate them from any problems to come. And with Greg as lieutenant, Philip felt he was in the hands of a master fixer. He had glimpsed Greg's wallet at the petrol pumps, and it bulged with bribes for a dozen nations. Even the boot was set up for PR, with a crate of champagne ready for the popping, and deckchairs handy for the lounging, in case there were temperamental stars to pacify or truculent locals to placate. Philip's one slight unease — an employer's unease — lay in the feeling that 4.8 litres was an unusual engine-size on the salary of location manager.

'So, you reckon there shouldn't be too many problems, then?' he said, fishing for Greg's reassurance.

'No. Be a doddle.'

'I hope so.'

'Always nice and quiet, the back of beyond. No inappropriate noises for the end of the world.'

'And there's rooms I haven't even been in. So there's plenty of scope.'

'That's right. And if you need some scary

extras, there's a valley full of village idiots.'

They lapsed into silence, not being natural companions. Philip could never fully warm to a man who wore two-tone driving gloves.

'How much longer d'you reckon?' he asked, after some time had passed.

'Abernant? A couple more hours yet. I thought we'd eat once we're into Wales.'

'Know of anywhere?'

Unsurprisingly, Greg did. His location hunts always began with the *Good Food Guide*.

'Yes, nice little place. Very Welsh. Indian restaurant with a harp.'

'OK, fine by me. Fine by you, Françoise?'

Françoise stirred from where she lay dozing across the back seat.

Philip helpfully moved his hand to his mouth and made eating noises.

Françoise murmured approval with a sleepy sultriness, and then closed her big brown eyes again, not seeming very excited by the prospect of Wales.

35

The goat was playing up. It was never a great one for speeches, although, as a ceremonial goat, much of its life required a patient reverence for oratory. Seamus always preferred the marching, if possible along the high street in front of an oompah band. For that he got a coat, in bright dragon-red, and some leeway for a bit of prancing. But speeches just meant standing about, attached to the tight leash of the Traffic Warden, a man who lacked empathy for his town's mascot.

The bribe-taking Traffic Warden might appear an inappropriate choice for Master of Ceremonies, but some years ago the council had discovered him to be their only employee with a uniform. A middle-aged martinet, whose uniform seemed to have more braid than was strictly necessary for parking offences, he relished the pomp of parading round town at the head of anything (with or without a goat). Endowed with the perfect chest for civic occasions, he could also do pomp standing still.

Like most of the town, Seamus was not keen on the Traffic Warden. From a goat's perspective, the man was over-zealous on discipline, too anal on the leash. From the locals' viewpoint, they disliked his ambition to be Napoleon.

Grand meter man and frisky goat, the pair were stationed beside the podium, esoteric symbols of civic tradition, and an unlikely audience for the higher flights of rhetoric.

★　★　★

The mayoress constantly shifted from one overhanging buttock to the other, visibly impatient for her moment of glory. Mr Arts Council, a fey, donnish sort, with the *pince-nez* that adds ten points to your IQ, had made the mistake of assuming his audience were interested in the subject of sculpture. He might have better grasped the intellectual concerns of the crowd had he heard the cry of 'poof!' as he approached the podium. Instead, he offered those few who were listening a starter module for the Open University, placing the commission at Abernant within an Indo-European context. By the end of his third peroration, the scattered hand-claps were drowned out by the bleating of the goat.

The leader of Abernant Council, for whom overarching visions were not part of the job spec, then spoke of his record collection, which was mostly Country and Western, in an attempt to establish his artistic credentials. He also spoke of a visit to a museum somewhere. And then he read a poem that he had learnt as a child, which he said had guided him through dark days (and which close colleagues took to mean the adultery incident in a lay-by). Finally, sensitive to the forthcoming elections, he launched into a long and inclusive vote of thanks, climaxing with a name-check for the men in fluorescent yellow jackets.

By now the mayoress was worried about her bladder, always her Achilles' heel when waiting to address her public. It was little comfort that, in the time her fellow dignitaries had spent on their *tours d'horizon*, she could have visited all the toilets in town. But she pushed such thoughts away. Her campaign was complete, her tireless, selfless years of talking were about to bear artistic fruit at last, and she could almost smell the OBE. The big heavy woman rose slowly to her feet, with as much dignity as is possible from a bendy plastic chair. And then, notes in hand, she made her noisy way across the off-white gravel.

Gazing down upon the crowd, Myfanwy felt she was born to stand on podiums. As she spoke of the honour she was bringing to the town, the mayoress beamed at the sight of the subservient faces, so many with little faith and lesser vision. Lined up at the front were all the familiar actors in the town's daily dramas. Mr Pritchard the planner had the false smile of a man claiming credit; Miss Nightingale had the tight lips of a woman not returning phone calls; Mr Capstick had the fixed frown of a man opposed to life; and Hubert had the encouraging leer of a man hoping for a pratfall. She was determined not to oblige him. The mayoress would for ever associate Hubert with the psychic trauma of the parking meter ceremony, and she saw today's success as her revenge.

As the champion of Ieuan Owen Owens, his encomium fell to her, and she put her heart into a wordy, windy appreciation of his genius, struggling heroically to disguise the fact that she had yet to read a single line of the celebrated poet's work. Partly this was because she had been so busy trying to celebrate him. And partly because, if the awful truth be known, the mayoress was not that keen on poetry. Indeed, the dog-eared translation supplied second-hand by Mr Beavan did not even correspond to her idea of a proper book. When it came to art, her real field of expertise was TV soaps (despite claims to have sticky-taped over her ITV button in protest at the lack of quality programmes) and the secret lives of their stars. It was not an expertise she made widely known.

Instead, eager that the speech maintain her standing as a cognoscente, the mayoress offered her insights into the Arts Council mission statement 'of converting the world of dreams into solid form'. But, failing to appreciate that this referred to the mysterious process of creation, Myfanwy took as starting-point her life as mayor, and rendered a glowing account of how ego had triumphed over adversity. How strength of will had vanquished petty officialdom. How belief in artistry had shamed the bureaucratic and mundane. How breadth of vision had, etc, etc. To the more cynical, it could have seemed the occasion was a celebration of *her* life and works, and the speech a grandiloquent proposal that she be put on a plinth. ('Woman and tent', as Hubert had less than quietly whispered.) It was a long ten minutes before, reluctantly, she had to recognise that the unveiling hour was now upon her. That the grand ceremony for the late Ieuan Owen Owens was finally due, and history was breathlessly waiting in the wings.

The mayoress drew herself upright, melodramatically turned toward Roderigo's hidden opus, paused for effect, twice, and then gave an imperious wave of the mayoral arm. Two men in yellow fluorescent jackets, now much motivated by the name-checks, started to loosen the rigging on the poet.

The mayoress turned to the impatient crowd and began to read out the rubric, '*With preference given to concepts ...* ' Below her, a bored goat bleated loudly and turned its thoughts to butting; above her, she was challenged by the screeching of seagulls, who now numbered a flock and were wheeling around in a rising wind. Mayoress Myfanwy Edwards raised her loud voice louder and proclaimed to the crowd ' ... *or individuals that best expressed the nature of their locality.*'

The hessian fell away. The two men stood back. The mayoral mouth stayed open. The crowd gave a communal gasp. Roderigo gave a big grin.

For some, the shock was the roughly chiselled granite where they had expected smooth Italian marble. For some, the shock was the informal, sprawling pose where they had expected a more dignified posture. For some, the shock was that a local poet should be covered in sea-shells, for reasons which were not clear. For the remaining 99 per cent, the shock was the size of the penis.

* * *

The gasp of the crowd gave way to silence, except for a titter or two from those not employed by the council.

Roderigo leaned against the plinth in the fading light, leering at the mayoress as he raised a frothy can of beer to her, his gesture a two-fingered toast. He had his notoriety and he was happy. He had successfully re-evaluated the mythic figure within a modern context, fusing the godlike and the pagan in a style certain to piss off the bourgeoisie. He saw himself in the tradition of Duchamp's urinal, as a man ahead of his time and changing the course of Abernant art for ever. Next goal was to corner the money man from the Arts Council and lay out his proposal to emblazon the Welsh landscape with more of his mythic figures, in what he planned to call the Roderigo Williams Sculpture Trail.

Clydog hesitated beside the War Memorial, no longer certain what questions he should pose, and unsure what answers would be printed. He supposed it would be safe to ask about the seashells, but it was always possible they were an obscene fertility symbol . . . or some rather rare gonorrhoeal disease, inflicted upon the body as a penalty for gross sexual

278

practices. Yet had he known he was looking at a sea-god he would still have struggled for a pertinent question.

It was the penis that was preoccupying the butcher. At a deep and subconscious level, he was not in favour of penises of any size, public or private, but the presence of such a large penis in close proximity to the War Memorial was an outrage which called for public protest.

'It's an outrage!' protested the butcher.

'What is?' enquired Hubert, with the airy innocence of an *agent provocateur*.

Duly provoked, the butcher burst out, 'This is Abernant, not Ancient Rome!'

'Now that would be a city worth twinning with,' said Hubert. 'We could have toga weekends.'

'I tried to warn people. But nobody would listen. They buried their heads in the sand. The council don't seem to realise that most artists are perverts.'

'I fancy one of those Coliseums myself,' mused Hubert. 'So hard to know what to do with surplus Christians.'

The butcher tried his best to ignore him. 'If the people had listened to me, the town could have had a nice fountain.'

Still upon the podium, and unsure whether to come down, the mayoress watched the scene below with growing dismay. A crowd forming into small knots and pointing — sometimes laughing, shoulders shaking — was not a sign of art appreciation. A double line of tight-lipped councillors, no-one moving, was not a sign of mayoral appreciation. And several tons of granite lying in the middle of the town was not an ephemeral event, easily forgotten. For the first time, Mrs Myfanway Edwards harboured doubts, and wondered whether she should have gone for the street theatre, with hay-wains full of farmers doing a fertility dance in Greek smocks.

A few yards away, the butcher's moral outrage was gaining ground.

'I don't care if it's by Michelangelo himself, the people of Abernant are not ready for a naked man. People walk their dogs here.' He kept his eyes averted as he spoke, as if not to be complicit in the sin. 'That's what they have art galleries for, to keep filth out of the way of the public. Not put it next to a war memorial. Built for heroes. Men who have died for their country. And who don't expect to end up next to . . .'

Mr Capstick struggled to go on, though the difficulty was not emotion but linguistics, for righteousness had left him with no usable language for genitalia. He was also in earshot

280

of Mrs Capstick, a plain and obedient woman, who was rarely seen with him in public. She had fancied an outing, expressing an interest to see the goat. Her husband now much regretted that he had agreed to this request and wished she would go home.

'That statue dishonours the memory of these brave — '

'Oh, bollocks!' said Hubert, wishing he had worn his medal, if only to trump Mr Capstick's brief time with the scouts. 'The soldiers I served with, if they'd had the choice of being a name on some memorial or a high-profile flasher on a plinth . . . Well, it'd be no contest!'

The butcher reddened, never before having heard sex and patriotism in juxtaposition. He felt it an argument too tricky to pursue, though he remained sure the dead would be on his side. Especially if, as the poetry hinted, the writer was that ultimate horror, a *pacifist* nude. But Mr Capstick was not defeated.

'And where will people eat their sandwiches at lunchtime? Have you thought of that? Or the shock a blind person could get? And what about the effect on visitors? Who want a family experience. Don't you care if this town gets a reputation?'

'Be about bloody time!' said Hubert.

'Could be our trademark. Like with Wordsworth. We could sell little replica poets, and T-shirts, and little gingerbread poet men. We could have a Naked Poet Day. Think how many lamb chops that would shift!'

The mayoress decided to descend, judging that her finest hour was probably over. Already she was rather regretting that her speech had put so little stress on the *joint* nature of the project and the vital, constantly supportive, role played by the council and the planners. Perhaps, she reflected, this could be a matter usefully addressed by a press release. In the meantime, she would have to mingle, taking soundings of the mood. Her spirits sank as, from the midst of the crowd, she could hear the familiar voice of the butcher, crying, '*And* it's a traffic hazard!'

To which Hubert had shouted, 'Only if you masturbate while driving.'

By now some of the crowd had started to move forward, to be shocked at closer quarters.

'Your health food may give you a healthy body, but it doesn't stop you having a sick mind,' retorted the butcher. Which he felt was rather clever. And he added, 'You've no respect for anything, alive or dead.'

'And which category do you fall into?' enquired Hubert.

'Is there *anything* you don't make cheap jokes about?'

'Is there anything you're not a self-righteous twat about?'

'At least *I* don't have a dirty shop — with out-of-date food and rude service.'

'So I'm an acquired taste. It's called niche marketing.'

The butcher's barbed darts had bounced off, as so often. Always very wary, he was now very vexed.

'I've won awards for my hygiene, and certificates for my customer care, and rosettes for my butchery, and my shop has been in business for over 135 years.'

'And I've got friends.'

'Well, I've got principles.' And with that stout riposte, Mr Capstick turned and set off determinedly toward the statue of the poet.

Close behind him followed the mouse-like Mrs Capstick. He tried to wave her away, tried to order her back to the house. But still she persisted in following him. As did Hubert, reluctant to abandon the lifetime collection of witty invective that he had been storing up for just such an occasion as this.

At the statue, the Traffic Warden and the goat had lost interest in their ceremonial duties. Indeed, the warden had, without authority, moved to the side of the plinth, sensitive that standing in direct line with loins could demean his office, and make life very embarrassing in pubs. The goat was now hungry and had lost all decorum, tugging and twisting to be free of his captor. Nearby stood the men in yellow jackets, vaguely watching the sacking and uncertain of their role.

The butcher pushed his way to the front of the crowd, distaste etched upon his face at the sight of Ieuan Owen Owens in close-up, his sea-shells everywhere except where decency demanded. Mr Capstick had the look of a man upon a mission, but before he could move, Mrs Capstick appeared. This took him by surprise, for his wife was rarely independent.

'I said to go home.'

'No way am I going home,' she said.

Embarrassed by her presence, puzzled by her disobedience, he repeated his request.

'I'm fifty-two years old, you bigoted little bully!' she shouted back. '*And if I want to look at a decent-sized penis for once, then I will!*' Public interest shifted from the statue. 'So I am going nowhere.'

And there she stood, arms folded, six feet from the plinth, staring straight ahead.

This was uncannily like the social disintegration that the butcher had so feared, and had warned so presciently against. And now all eyes were upon him, for the first time in his life. He was finally the centre of attention for more than the quality of his meat, and this could, he realised, at last be his chance to take on the role of a leader. Then, at just that moment, the evening sun began to slip the shadow of the War Memorial over the poet's privates, and Mr Capstick knew that God was calling. With his wife gazing fixedly at the giant granite genitalia, the butcher's rightness of purpose was confirmed, his resolve to act fully strengthened.

'Well, Mrs Capstick,' he yelled, 'take a good look, because it's going right back under wraps.'

And he began grabbing up the hessian from where it lay on the ground.

Hubert was transfixed, as were those around him, all enjoying this folly far too much to intervene.

'The man's mad. His meat's gone to his head.'

'Oh, he's not mad, he's bad,' said the mayoress, who had now squeezed in beside him at the front of the crowd. She and Hubert had not spoken — at least not civilly — since he ruined her last civic ceremony with a riot, but on the statue campaign there had at least been common cause. And a common dislike of the butcher.

The hessian sacking had not been folded tidily, and lay in crumpled heaps. It was not conducive to decisive action, and the butcher was forced to rummage about in an unleaderly manner, looking for a loose end. This unseemly scrabble not only attracted the full attention — and derision — of his audience. It also attracted the goat.

The goat had been standing around for nearly an hour, with nothing ceremonial to do and nothing goatly to distract it. It had also not eaten since lunchtime. The Traffic Warden was a curmudgeonly creature who never kept so much as a boiled sweet in his uniform pocket. And even the tonsured grass was out of reach. So the rustling of nutrient-rich hessian came as a menu of interest.

Seamus jerked the leash from his keeper's hand, bolted toward the butcher, and planted his front feet on the sacking. Then he lowered his head, with its fine pair of horns, and clamped his mouth over a choice portion. The butcher tugged, but Seamus resisted. Finding the taste of sacking to his liking, he went for more. Again the butcher tried to wrench it off him, to save the sacking for its higher purpose. But he failed again, the protuberant jaw not yielding an inch. For a man whose whole life had been at the service of animals, albeit dead and in sections, it was a hurtful irony that now, in his finest hour, he should be obstructed by a goat. Eyeing each other warily, they paused in a stand-off.

''Bad?' Why'd you say bad?' Hubert asked the mayoress.

'Remember when he ran for mayor against me . . . ?'

Hubert nodded.

'He had a secret weapon. Specialist sausages. On the side, no questions asked.'

'Did he now!' exclaimed Hubert, with the joy of vindication. 'Did he now!'

He still remembered the scorn that had greeted his bribery claim in the deli. But here was the proof that his patrician nose had been right all along.

'Thank you for that, Myfanwy.' And then, with the full power of his sixty-three-year-old lungs, Hubert cried out, '*Come on, Seamus! Up the arse with those horns!*'

Distracted by the cry, Mr Capstick looked around, taking his eye off the goat. Which charged him. Winded, the butcher stumbled backwards, but caught his foot in the sacking, and half-fell to the ground. Instinctively, he grasped hold of the horns, and tried to wrestle the goat to its knees. But the goat twisted and bucked in defence of its dinner, and the pair fell sideways in a tangled heap of hessian.

Watching the butcher struggle to get upright, and try to gain some dignity, Hubert was assailed by *déjà vu*, and dark memories of his parking meter trauma. But where he had had the gutter, Mr Capstick had the goat. And the goat was giving no quarter. The pair tumbled to and fro like washing in a laundromat, with grunts and bleats as a backing track. The drama made the mayoress feel jinxed, destined never to cut a ribbon or loosen a rope without unleashing the forces of social disorder. In all the Queen's long years of unveiling, the mayoress had never seen a report of a riot, or even a minor fracas with a dog. Now she feared her track record for trouble could have destroyed her driving dream to be *grande dame* of the mid-Wales art world.

And once again pimply Auberon was on hand, camera clicking, trying to capture the defining action shots of local government. He had been on a course, a course that taught how to focus on more than disconnected limbs, and was hoping for a picture with some inner truth and a recognisable face. But the cut and thrust of man-goat conflict did not make for easy framing. Every time Mr Capstick tried to manoeuvre Seamus into a submission hold, the action became too fast. And every time Seamus tried to mount Mr

Capstick, the action became too shocking. But very keen to make amends for his one-eared mayoress, Auberon just kept on snapping, kept on trying for a close-up of Mr Capstick's unChristian expressions.

And finally Auberon's photographic course paid off — he perfectly positioned the camera at the climactic moment when Mr Capstick made a tactical error and the goat got him in the groin.

Unfortunately Auberon had come to the end of his film.

Which left *The Mid-Walian* with no record of a fallen Mr Capstick groaning on the hessian, his face being licked by the long tongue of a conciliatory Seamus.

Overall, the contest quite took the audience's mind off the king-size penis.

Not a person had gone home early, though few would claim artistic uplift from the day's events. Most members of the council could claim some sense of pleasure, as the day had so delightfully discredited their mayoress. The Chief Planning Officer felt he could probably now locate an airport in the high street without fear of her interference. And the leader of the council felt he could now safely look forward to an art-free town. As for Roderigo, he felt the unveiling could hardly have gone better, as he always liked a good ruck. Even Mrs Capstick was observed to have a small smile on her face. But Elenid had missed most of the fun, as she had popped off for a quickie with a councillor.

Mr Arts Council, however, had a report to write, and it would conclude that some of the remoter provinces were not yet ready for the civilising influences of sculpture.

No one knows what Ieuan Owen Owens would have made of the day, but readers of his poems might well conclude he would have penned a stanza full of joyous ridicule — even if it might not have rhymed.

★　★　★

As the crowd slowly slipped away to start their weekend, Miss Nightingale beckoned her hapless nephew, belatedly reloading his camera.

She was standing by the statue, which now dominated the square. Naturally, he had at no time aimed the camera in that direction. Even Auberon knew *The Mid-Walian* well enough not to waste film upon a lost cause, on a subject that would never pass the test of taste.

He looked questioningly at his aunt.

She pointed at the penis. Then, with the twinkle she kept for her favourites, Miss Nightingale said, 'I think that could be catchy.'

36

'Another eight pints of scrumpy!' bawled Adrian. A touch of posh slipped into his plebeian tones as he struggled to be heard above the drunken rumpus in the Brown Bear.

A week of lying about in a tepee full of smoke in a field full of mud is an exhausting form of social protest, and by a Friday evening the non-travelling travellers were always ready for a convivial drink. Pubs were almost the only places where their suspect money was still welcome. Barred by the faint-hearted and the fascist from the leading retail outlets in town, the New Agers found that the opportunities to practise their anticonsumerism were more widespread than they wished. But the Brown Bear was a rough old alehouse, once a coaching inn, and not much short of a highwayman ever fazed the landlord.

'Coming up!' cried Mr Clement, wiping a streak of blood from the counter.

Outsiders were here seen as little threat, as the town had its indigenous *demi-monde*, many of whom were brawling between Adrian and the bar. In a ritual sort of way. Trouble on a Friday night in Abernant was booked into the diary of the town's drunks with the same dependability as a dental appointment. Not so much the rural poor as the rural bored, these tanked-up young men with their tank-topped young women had only the dullest ideas of mayhem. Five pints was an excuse to puke. Ten pints was an excuse to puke over a friend. These were the lowgrade yobs who had cast such a blight upon the career of Bob, whose Sisyphean role was to persuade them of the hidden pleasures of a life without public indecency and criminal damage.

Not that there was a lot of entertainment choice. Evening social life for the youth of Abernant offered a view of the mountains and a visit to the chip shop, excitement that was easily exhausted; even the joys of watching traffic go by had been reduced by Mr Pritchard's one-way system. (There was also an old cinema which had become a duplex but, as that meant watching one film while listening to another, it was not a box office success.) Yet ambitions for less boredom were low. When a 'survey of youth' had asked what social amenities they would like to have provided, the answer was a weekly beer festival.

In the meantime, it was down to Mr Clement — and the landlords of Abernant's sixteen other pubs — to selflessly fill any shortfall of alcohol. And tonight he was a happy man. News of the goat's victory had been brought by runners. No more would Capstick's reign of teetotal tantrums have any moral force. The poky, smoky upstairs room (above the poky, smoky downstairs rooms) might once again house the Chamber of Commerce and normal service and sales could perhaps be resumed. With decisions informed by alcohol.

Adrian and his look-alike rebels crammed into a corner with their scrumpy, gulping fast before the next pit-stop on their pub crawl. There was a demanding routine to the work of inebriation. The Brown Bear, the Black Bear, the Blue Boar, the Red Lion, the Yellow Cockatoo, the progress to being blind-drunk was colour-coded. Completing the circuit was rare, and cause for insensate celebration. Tonight the target was twelve pubs, with a possible pizza.

But the next port of call was the square, always the focus for early evening japes and doing witty things with gravel. In the warmer weather, there was usually a queue for sex against the War Memorial. And tonight there was a new attraction. The regulars had heard

293

from the landlord about Ieuan Owen Owens, and the packed public bar had echoed to cock jokes. The local lads were already starting to leave for a look, stumbling their way to the door as they set off for their first-ever art appreciation. Three hours gone, and the statue was proving to be not quite the amenity that the mayoress had had in mind.

Quickly belching down the murky remains of their scrumpy, Adrian's lot got up to follow. They tumbled out into the dark alleyway, and started to noisily walk the few hundred yards to the square, gobbing on windows as they went.

★ ★ ★

'Any requests?' asked the harpist.

For once, Philip had no ready answer. No favourite harp airs sprang to mind.

The restaurant was empty, apart from the two media men and the one mistress. For ninety minutes, the balding middle-aged man with a gut had provided a non-stop stream of unknown tunes on his Celtic Harp. He spoke now in response to the pint of Kingfisher which Philip had felt obliged to send over.

'It's difficult to know what's suitable for an Indian restaurant,' explained the overweight harpist, lilting strongly.

'Can you do 'Land Of My Fathers' on a harp?' asked Greg.

'Not really,' he replied, giving him a weary look. 'You need a choir for that.'

'Of course,' said Greg, and relapsed into silence.

Philip focused on his after-dinner mint.

Françoise focused on Philip.

The waiter focused on the middle distance, not looking keen on an encore.

'My girlfriend used to sing,' added the harpist.

'Right,' said Greg.

'Until she left me, that is.'

'Oh,' said Greg.

'She felt the harp was holding her back.'

'I see,' said Greg.

'Yes. Said its range was too limited.'

Philip meticulously rolled his mint wrapper into a small ball.

'Which is nonsense, of course.'

'Of course,' said Greg.

'But then, she secretly wanted to do folk clubs.'

Philip gave his mint-wrapper ball a push and watched it run around his saucer.

'She had no feeling for her national culture.'

'Quite,' said Greg.

The man began to harp again, and Philip

decided to call for the bill.

Outside it was dark and cold, and there were fifty miles of Welsh countryside still to go.

'What's the suicide rate in this country, any idea?'

'100 per cent. Shall I drive?'

'No, I'm fine.'

Françoise made the yawning noises of a beautiful woman ready for bed, and Philip helped wrap her white fur coat tightly around her. Like her predecessors, she came well scented, with the dress sense of finishing school, but her views on the world were a mystery, and she never spoke out of turn, if at all.

'So,' said Greg, flexing his gloved fingers, 'Where's this hotel? The Dragon's Whatsit?'

'In Abernant. I've put the crew in a motel on the bypass. They won't like it much, but it'll save a few quid!'

'Quite right too.'

'We're pretty central, on the square.'

★ ★ ★

Like lagered-up wildebeest, the local youths charged down the dark high street, raucously chanting. The exact words were unclear, but the body language was not respectful. Which perhaps explained why the bulk of the citizenry had opted for a quiet night in with the telly. As on every Friday. And Saturday. And most other nights of the week.

A couple of lads paused at Mr Beavan's. They had it in for the bookseller, on the grounds that he sold nothing useful. Quite often there was a queue of three or four waiting to urinate through his letter-box. But the focus was elsewhere tonight and he got off with a light sprinkling. Mr Devonald was also spared on this occasion as no-one had so far eaten. The owner of Dev's Dainties was judged too camp for Abernant and thus was never safe from the more bigoted vomiter. The sight of ladies' chemises in his well-lit window was often sufficient to summon up a curry that was several hours old. There was no known deterrent for the little lords of misrule. And had the perpetrators known their deeds were noted in uncensored minutes, a rare form of fame, the high street would soon have been awash with waste products.

The mini-mob ran on past the baker's, kicking over all available bin-bags and cascading gungy rubbish along the street. The lead kicker sent a dustbin lid high into the air. It landed with a clang and became a football, clattering erratically over Mr Pritchard's new cobbles. In a brief and frantic free-for-all, the heritage bus-shelter became a goal, and was left with putrid fruit and used nappies spattering its mock-Georgian glass, while gobs of rotting meat ran down its timetable.

Arguably this was a breach of the peace, but around this time of night the two-man police presence would make their excuses and leave town for the hills, patrolling the country lanes in search of criminal sheep up to no good. Many hours later, the occupying army gone, an early morning contingent of the men in yellow jackets would arrive from environmental health to reclaim the streets for the citizens. And thus make sure the Georgian streetscape had back its picture postcard looks in time for any tourists.

By the time that Adrian and his mates staggered into the square, two people were already astride the statue, egged on by a crowd in party mood. Others were posing by the poet's legs, and several girls had knelt in front of him to amuse their boyfriends. A beer-can had been wedged in his loins. (Though the attempt to stuff a cigarette up his nose was ongoing.) The alleged iconoclasm of Ieuan Owen Owens' life was being revisited upon him in death. But this time round there were just jeers, no poetry. And gradually, after barely ten minutes, the crowd was running out of inventive mockery. Or even unoriginal mockery. So a few just pelted him with gravel. Then the kicks of the new phallic toy began to pale when compared to the old call of ale. And the local drunks started to drift back to the seventeen pubs.

But the New Age mindset was of a wittier, more sophisticated constitution. It was alternative. Freethinking. Subversive. It aimed to remake the world, if possible overnight.

'The granite's a mistake,' said Adrian, examining Roderigo's work more closely.

'A mistake? What sort of mistake?' asked Daisy, who was expecting his love-child.

'It's dull. Old hat, too trad,' replied Adrian, who had plans to study fine arts.

'Bit late now,' said Jonathan.

'Just needs a little livening up,' said Adrian.

He put his mind to this for a moment. And then, searching as if for something specific, he looked around him, at what now appeared to be the scene of a dustcart accident. Suddenly, his eyes settled upon his pavement pitch, where he passed the mornings tooting his flute in front of ironmongery.

'Of course!' he cried. 'Mr Bufton!' And there was a malevolent tone to his voice. He had not forgotten the attempt to move him on with a broom. Of such trifles are revolutions made.

He looked around again. This time, his eyes settled upon the three crush barriers, still leaning against the plinth to no purpose.

'They'll do!' he cried.

Adrian hurried across the gravel. He put his hands on their cold metal and tested their weight. Then he urged his fellow travellers to stand at either end.

'Right, now, all together! One ... two ... three!'

And they lifted aloft the nearest of the crush barriers, which had been waiting all day for a chance to enhance health and safety. It wobbled a little in such unsober hands, and several had a question for Adrian.

'Now what do we do with it?'

'We chuck it through his window.'

'Oh. Right on! Another blow for anarchic nihilism!'

'Not really,' said Adrian. 'It's to get some paint.'

37

Gareth patted his dog goodbye, turned on the outside light, and crossed the farmyard to where his Land Rover had stood for a year.

Bob had said he should celebrate. He was not, by nature, a celebrating sort of a person. He felt he was better suited to suffering. But he had finished his time on probation, and not got into further trouble; his driving ban was over, and he had his licence back; and his divorce was soon to come through. It was, he was told, time to move on. Bob had said he was doing well — though Bob was grateful for anything short of utter failure — and had told him that he should be kind to himself, whatever that meant. He had also just pulled the last of the lambs out of the last of the wombs. So if there was ever a time to celebrate, Gareth guessed it would probably be about now.

He would have gone down to his local, and drunk with the mole-catchers, but the village pub was on sale as a second home. He would have stayed in and drunk alone, but he was short of six-packs. He would have gone out to a friend's and drunk, but he was short of friends. So he put on his better Barbour and went to town.

★   ★   ★

Gareth was not keen on towns, and visited as few as possible. Towns filled him with unease, the world suddenly a series of multiple choice questions. With noise. Everywhere, the constant threat of the unexpected took the pleasure out of life. Worse, he found himself faced at every turn by people and talking. And his sessions on personal growth had clearly identified his weak points to be other people, and talking to them.

In his home town of Abernant, though, his abiding fear was that other people were talking *about* him. A reticent person even at birth, he had come to bitterly regret announcing to a busy bank on a market day that his wife was, at that very moment, indulging in extra-marital activities with the manager. Adultery, especially when it involves adventurous practices, is best kept on a need-to-know basis. Sharing the news with one's neighbours, in a catchment area covering many miles, does not improve one's sexual standing — or any other aspect of one's standing.

He slipped into the Market Tavern, where

302

he knew they did cheese nibbles. This was the farmers' pub, the pub where he drank to celebrate the sale of his sheep for slaughter. This was the pub where the auctioneers and the breeders lunched, and animatedly discussed the latest price per carcass. This was the pub that was the hub of all that was hot in agrigossip. And this, it now turned out, was the pub that was all but empty at night. As was the stockyard it stood by.

He ordered a pint and, for some reason, a chaser. He tried to remember the last time he had behaved with abandon. In the end, he reckoned it must have been his jiving moment, when Farmer Gabriel, who still DJ'ed at age seventy-five, had done his Elvis impression in a barn near Llanfihangel. Farmer Gabriel had one of the best collections of fifties records in the valley, as well as a number of fairy lights, and his disco evenings were always oversubscribed. His Brylcreemed black hair and spangly black shirt were guarantee of a good night out. However, since Gabriel's slipped disc, his Elvis had had no movements.

Gareth ordered a second pint, and a third. And thought some more about a hobby, though not very fruitfully. Competitive hedging was not giving him the pleasure he had hoped. He sometimes wished he had pursued his childhood daydream — to be a rugby referee. It was not for the companion-ship, the travel to other valleys, the singing in the coach, but because he was drawn to the power of a whistle. He had a few ball skills, he was used to mud, and his Saturday afternoons were always free, so he could have played for a team — except that what appealed to him most was having the authority to send someone off. Off, and away to an early bath! For refereeing brought a guarantee that he be obeyed. Be respected. Or at least be taken notice of. Gareth would perhaps not have perceived this as a secret desire to be dominant, but he did often think that the business of living would be easier with a whistle.

He ordered a fourth pint, though reluc-tantly, for fun was not a feature of the barn-sized bar. The evening's trade was a handful of solitary farmers, bonded by monosyllables and silence. Life on the hills did not breed conversationalists.

After a fifth pint, Gareth decided to move on, and try the Hog's Head, where he had heard they sometimes had singers.

Back out in the evening air, he began to feel the effect of days and nights with little sleep and less food. And five pints. His was not the folly of a drunk, for six-packs were second nature, but lambing and liquor were leaving him slightly light-headed. Walking as though on rough pasture, he threaded his way through the narrow side streets that led to the centre of town.

He was torn between a desire for company and a dread of it. In his madder, more despairing moments, Gareth had come to see himself as part-hermit, part-pariah, a man grown weary of the world and its ways. Seeking isolation, he had abandoned all interest in the daily doings of his valley and he no longer even read *The Mid-Walian*. His life now having little time for humans, the actions of the town went unnoticed.

The Hog's Head was heaving, with bodies half out the door. A heavy-duty sound system was shaking the air with the wayward notes of a wannabe rock star, his lungs vibrating to a forgotten hit of yesteryear. And the room regularly erupted with tumultuous and undeserved applause. The bar was a long and sweaty fight away, through an audience packed tight. Gareth was not to know it, though the four-foot poster gave a clue, but something called karaoke had finally arrived in Abernant. It was, ironically, ideal for lonely menopausal farmers, offering them a platform to discordantly pour out their hearts. But it was unlikely to offer Gareth much solace as he, a lonely runty figure amid this chanting and cheering, saw only the intimidating happiness of youth. Theirs were not the celebrations he had in mind, and he gave up on the struggle to push his way through for a pint.

Out on the pavement once more, Gareth found he had gone from light-headed to rather woozy, and the world seemed prone to spin.

He felt the need for cool air and a cold flannel, and the chance for his mind to stop churning. Alone, and suddenly unstable, he had the urge to sit, or at the very least to lean. By now, he was less than a hundred yards from the town's only open space. And so, hoping to bring some peace to his turbulent innards, Gareth weaved off toward the square.

★ ★ ★

It was the green glow he saw first. A bright luminous green glow, to the left of the War Memorial. Like a sort of hovering vomit. Gareth tried closing his eyes and re-opening them. He was finding it difficult to focus, and several strange colours had already swum in and out of his vision. But each time he looked, the green glow was still there. Still biliously shimmering in midair, to the left of the War Memorial. Where there was meant to be just grass and gravel.

Gareth stood unsteadily on the edge of the empty square, pondering the possibilities. Or trying to. The night was strangely silent, the drunken populus away on drinking duty, maximising the last minutes of the opening hours. There was not a person in sight, no-one of whom he might make enquiries.

He had the thought it could be fireflies, though the green was a puzzling colour. He tried to judge whether the light was moving, up or down, or side to side — but much else was also moving, including the War Memorial, so it was hard to be conclusive. For a hazy moment, he wondered whether he was in danger, though how, or from what, was also too taxing to work on for long.

After several drawn-out minutes of drunken indecision, Gareth decided to approach the green glow.

The critical hurdle was the shin-high rail, which required the lifting of each leg. In sequence. With planning. It took two false starts and a stumble before he made it on to the grass. Only then did he remember that the path into the square was but a couple of yards away. He crossed to its gravel, and crunched cautiously forward, like a man who thought he might be on an obstacle course. Repeatedly fearful of falling, he kept his eyes cast down on the ground just ahead. Which is how he arrived at the plinth.

Much surprised at the presence of a plinth, he glanced up ... and for the first time learned that the square had a statue. And thought it looked rather godlike. And was indeed reclining in a godlike way. In a nude and godlike way. And, at that moment, he realised that the green glow was coming from its genitalia.

Gareth immediately turned and glanced nervously around the square, queasily uneasy that standing so close, even to granite private parts, might be cause for re-arrest. But the square was still empty, he and the statue were still alone. And now his mind was racing, wondering just how drunk he was. Slowly, woozily, he turned back to re-check his senses and look again.

And it was as he looked again that he realised the genitalia were familiar.

And that the last time he had seen them they had been entertaining his wife.

This was a lot of information even for a sober man to absorb, and it is small wonder that Gareth slumped to his knees. The memories that he had spent the last year attempting to bury came rushing fresh to the surface. Try as he might to forget his wife, he had never forgotten the proportions of the penis that had come between them.

Counselling sessions, personality development, emotional sensitivity training, everything now bit the dust. Issues of isolation and mental health were back with a bang. It was a year that had been wholly in vain. He had been advised, assisted, and befriended, but never allowed to talk about the bank manager. And the bank manager was all he ever thought about.

For a long, long minute he was numb. Until the gravel began embedding in his knees and the desire to be sick won through.

And then, slowly, through his fog of inebriation, the full, humiliating horror of his plight, and the dreadful significance of the nude and godlike Mr Blake, dawned gradually clearer and clearer to him. Not merely had his cuckolding been the tawdry cause of whispers and sniggers, the cheap excuse for sneers and jokes, but the occasion had now become famous — now it was the grounds for public celebration! And in order to mock him the town had made a hero of his tormentor, had erected a statue as monument to his fame. Hailing his godlike powers as seducer.

The prospect that he be forced to see this

Lothario triumphant — his phallus thick and mocking — every single time he came to town made Gareth's alcoholic blood run cold. Nor did his dread stop there. Before long, he feared, paranoia growing, that the man would become not just a town hero, but a national hero, a Nelson of the bedroom. And then, in honour of his actions, statues to the man who cuckolded him would be erected in squares throughout the country. Until, like a jubilee celebration, giant models of his glowing penis would pulsate like beacons right across the land. Erected on prime time television. In years to come, lessons would be given in the local schools about Mr Blake the Big, Lionel the Luminous. And Gareth the Cuckold. His name would be a cautionary tale of the times.

He needed to take action, direct action, but could not think what action that might be. Bob's advice, though, was fatally flawed. A public monument celebrating the penetration of his wife would make it difficult for him to move on. He had to be a man, and that meant violence. The seven-step plan to manage his anger had had insufficient steps. But these days he was a farmer who had no shotgun, and no obvious way to terminate a quarrel. Slumped against the plinth, his head going round in circles, he struggled to find a solution.

Suddenly, he knew what he must do — although he did not yet know how he was going to do it.

Like Adrian, he too looked around the square for inspiration. Then, he saw the carpet of broken glass glinting at him from the pavement. And, like Adrian, his eye too was drawn to the ironmonger's shop. To the looted premises of poor Mr Bufton, now nearer than ever to bankruptcy, and watching in bourgeois terror from his flat above.

'Aaaaaaah!' slurred Gareth excitedly.

He scrabbled clumsily up from the gravel, and started to weave across the square.

38

'Paris,' said Philip. 'She comes from Paris.'

'Oh,' said Greg.

'And she loves film.'

'Right,' said Greg.

'Anything artistic, she loves it.'

'Really,' said Greg.

'She wants to be a writer.'

'Great,' said Greg.

Greg could not work out the source of Philip's sex appeal, for the man was too languid for testosterone. And he showed little obvious sign of captivating humour. Did his charm come from class, or clothes, or the aphrodisiac of producer power?

'That was another village with no fucking vowels,' he muttered, as his car swished effortlessly through the darkness.

'Of course, in France, finance wouldn't have been any problem,' Philip went on. 'They love film, the French. I could have got funding just to film a couple of middle-aged intellectuals sitting around talking. About anything probably. Though most likely it would have to include a bit of angst. Angst and adultery. But that's the great thing about

French films. Nothing has to happen, as long as it looks super-cool. And very Gallic. No call for any plot, and it all gets shot in bars. Or while they eat five-course meals.'

'What happened to Ulrika?'

'Too German.'

'Oh.'

The Jaguar was steadily climbing, scarcely easing its pace as they moved through the mountains, ever closer to their home for the next three weeks. They would be far from any urban treats, and have little time for distractions. At the back of both their minds were the tricky logistics of the rural shoot, and whether or not they would work well together.

'Why did you choose Wales?' asked Greg.

'It ticked the ethnic box at the channel.'

'Right.'

'And the Welsh are usually cheap.'

'True!'

'Except for bloody Dilys.' He laughed.

They both laughed.

'Ees far?' asked Françoise, stirring from sexy slumber in the back.

'No. Just a few miles more,' said Philip, turning to squeeze her hand.

'Eet ees my first time in Gaul.'

'I know, darling.'

'So, Françoise, what has he told you about

the land of Gaul?' asked Greg.

'Ees full of dragons. Red dragons.'

'Very good,' said Philip.

'And *des châteaux* . . . castles.'

'Excellent, my dear.'

'And everybody *chantent*. And *jouent au rugby!*'

'Bravo!' said Philip.

'Knows enough to take a coach party on tour, then,' said Greg. 'Does she know about having to wear a leek?'

'I thought it best to leave out the coal-mines and the constant rain or she'd never have come.'

'One look at the Powells' place and she'll go back.'

A 40 sign appeared, and soon was followed by the first street-lights. Françoise sat up and began to brush her hair.

'Have you ever been tempted to move out of London, Greg? Go rural?'

'Not this rural, no.'

'Not in the blood?'

'Well, I am a city lad. Though I don't mind the odd spade of lightly spread manure. But out here? No, not for me.'

On their left, they passed the boarded-up Elim Tabernacle and then drove by Mr Lloyd's carwash, Soapy Heaven. On their right was a semi-derelict stuffed-animal shop, next to the Pensioners' Memorial Garden with a browning monkey-puzzle tree.

Greg slowed to 30, as Abernant was grateful for careful drivers.

'I like a bit of a buzz. That's why I do this job. Period drama one day, end of the world the next. Soft porn the week after. Keeps you alert, alive.'

'Exactly,' said Philip. 'That's why I always chose to do a very varied range of training videos — so as to stay fresh, and stimulated.'

The road narrowed as they moved on to the only remaining stone bridge across the River Nant, and Greg slowed further. Françoise leaned forward, and started to take an interest in her surroundings. In the distance, the illuminated town-hall clock said 11.20.

'But live right out here?' added Greg. 'Back of beyond, nothing to do except bet on raindrops sliding down a sheep?'

The Jaguar moved off the bridge and started up the short, steep hill to the square with their hotel, the Dragon's Head.

'I reckon,' Greg continued, 'every second death certificate in this sort of place must have 'Boredom' as the cause of snuffing it. Me, I could never take the tedium of nothing ever — '

And then he slammed his brakes full on.

' . . . *What the fuck is that?*'

All three of them stared in disbelief at the scene that was lit by his headlights.

'Jesus Christ!' said Philip.

'Fucking Ada!' said Greg.

'*Sacré bleu!*' said Françoise.

39

It was perhaps Françoise, who had been expecting dragons and castles and daffodils, that was the most surprised.

Although, being Parisian, she was born of a centuries-old tradition of revolution, and although she was steeped in the French custom of twice-daily demonstrations, and although such matters as riots and tear gas and baton charges were second nature to her, Françoise found that Abernant had a form of political protest she had not previously witnessed. And whose meaning she had trouble in grasping.

Why, late at night, in a public square, in a small provincial town, was a short and angry middle-aged man sitting in the lap of a statue of a male nude, with hammer raised in one hand, chisel in the other, vigorously trying to sever a huge glowing green penis (made greener and more glowing by Greg switching to main beam)? And why was he surrounded by cavorting younger men singing 'Delilah' and exposing themselves?

'It's how the Welsh celebrate the coming of spring,' suggested Philip.

'*Mais c'est bizarre* . . . why ees he . . . ?' Françoise mimed the hammer and the chisel.

'Probably an English penis,' said Greg. 'Symbolising centuries of colonial repression.'

'Oh . . . So what ees he . . . er . . . ?' she pointed to her mouth.

'Shouting?' offered Philip.

Françoise nodded.

Philip and Greg were uncertain on this point.

'I hate green . . . ?' suggested Philip.

There was time for various theories on these events as granite is an unyielding medium and Gareth's strength was dissipated by drink and growing exhaustion. The backing group of flashers, however, had higher energy levels and they danced around the square with phallic abandon, several now naked from the waist down, their private parts public in a tribute to the influence of art.

'Wish I'd scripted this,' said Philip. Several times.

They sat in the car, headlights on, like an audience in the front row of the stalls. Françoise leaned forward over Philip's shoulder, nuzzling his neck, and for several minutes the three of them enjoyed some of the most original entertainment they had seen in years.

'*C'est formidable! C'est Dadaiste!*' said Françoise.

The crowd did not seem unfriendly, if one regards waving one's bollocks about to be a gesture of mateyness. When not performing freelance obscenities, they formed and re-formed a daisy-chain, which wound around the War Memorial and the plinth. To give encouragement to Gareth, some joined hands in a circle around the well-endowed poet, chanting in time to the blows of the hammer. It had the look of an ancient fertility rite in reverse, though not one ever likely to make the mayoral shortlist.

'Worth a few photos, this!' declared Greg, whose camera was always to hand.

'Odd sort of collection you must have,' said Philip, as Greg reached into the dashboard.

Greg laughed. 'Oh, I'm thinking more of the public record.' With that, he slipped out the car and was off.

Philip and Françoise watched as he circled the statue (as Elenid had once circled its model) and snapped away at the work-in-progress. Gareth seemed unaware of his presence, as he seemed unaware of anything except the focus of his attack. It was an attack made tricky by paint still sticky, and most of the blows slithered their way to the scrotum. But he kept on hammering, and he kept on shouting, determined to have his revenge.

And Greg kept on clicking, determined to capture the moment. A quality amateur, he caught not only the hammer in the air, and the chisel on the pubis, but the venom on the face. Then, when he had several sequences to his satisfaction, he turned his lens to the supporting cast, to the raggle-taggle chorus of amateur orgiasts. The provincial drunks were the puritans, with their manly traditions of piss and puke, while the New Age performers were the liberati, with no constraints upon their debauch. The whirling of their bodies, and the twirling of their privates, and their joy in the shock of the lewd, all combined to create a rare counterpoint to the serenity of the Georgian backdrop.

However, just in case of a censor's dead hand, Greg finished with an arty shot of a crush barrier upended in an ironmonger's.

But he was glad to be soon back in the warm of the Jaguar, for the wind was still rising, and he had had no alcohol to help him deny the coming cold.

'So what's the guy shouting?' asked Philip.

'That was the oddest thing,' said Greg. 'It sounded like . . . well, 'Take that, you bloody banker!' '

' 'You bloody banker?' ' repeated Philip. 'What's that supposed to mean?'

'I've no idea.'

'Perhaps he was refused a loan.'

'By a statue?'

Philip took his point, and shrugged. Welsh rural life was proving more multi-layered than he had realised.

'So then — Dragon's Whatsit next?' said Greg. 'And bed?'

'Sounds good.'

Françoise yawned agreement. It had been a long and culturally challenging night.

The Dragon's Head stood facing *The Mid-Walian* with all the unilluminated anonymity of Britain during the Blitz. Greg joined Mr Pritchard's one-way system and, give or take a flying beer-can, drove unimpeded round the square. An old hotel, its two stars had been annulled by black adhesive tape, a fact not mentioned on the phone. He squeezed the Jaguar into its small car park, avoiding several bodies, and the three were quickly across the plastic-fibred Welcome mat.

But bed was elusive. No one was at reception. No one was in the lobby. 11.35 p.m. was an hour when the only arrivals were the undead.

For twenty minutes they took it in turns to beat the hell out of one small hand-bell. Eventually an unhappy man with a limp appeared, who claimed the hotel was full. This was easily proved to be a lie, but he was not a good loser. He gave out their room keys without a smile, and made no offer of help with their bags.

'Front-facing,' he said glumly. 'The extra fiver's for the view.'

It was midnight when finally they reached their rooms with a view, the moment noisily marked by much striking of the townhall clock.

And followed by a lot of cheering from the scene outside.

Philip opened his tinny shutters to see what had happened. His room had a token balcony, supported by what appeared to be token concrete, and he gingerly stepped out upon it. From where he looked down upon the little town of Abernant.

Below him, the numbers in the centre had grown, and Gareth was no longer seated in Ieuan Owen Owens' lap. Now he was being carried aloft by a triumphant semi-naked mob, in a lap of honour around the square. His runty hands no longer held Mr Bufton's looted hammer and chisel. Instead, with palms green and glowing, his arms were outstretched to the skies as, like a winner with a victory cup, he raised high the great luminous penis of Lionel Blake.

'*Aah, mais c'est Zola! C'est Germinal!*'

An excited Françoise had joined Philip on the balcony.

Fortunately, her lover was familiar with the role of the penis in nineteenth-century French literature, and immediately recognised the reference. (A small but telling point, which revealed those social skills that had escaped his location manager.) *'Ah oui, ma petite. Comme les mineurs.'*

When Zola's striking miners had taken their revenge upon a hated exploiter, they had excised his penis and marched through the cheering streets with the thing trussed, bayonet-like, to a stick. Gareth Richards, however, had lacked the social realism to chisel away at a live bank manager, so the analogy was not perfect. But it nonetheless had intellectual piquancy. Philip kissed her approvingly.

A cheer went up from below. Philip waved. Another cheer came back. And this time Françoise waved. And the penile procession took on the air of a march past, with the well-dressed man and his mistress standing upon their little balcony waving at the barbarians as they celebrated their rout. Philip had a brief temptation to salute, but wisely resisted his impulse.

Then, bit by bit, the rout began to edge toward a riot. Bored by triumphalism, the crowd turned their attention to the cobbles, that essential for all successful riots, so thoughtfully provided by Mr Pritchard; and to the paint, that essential for any artistic riot, so thoughtfully liberated from Mr Bufton. The crowd were not short of targets, with an organ-free poet, a buffed-up war memorial, and a heritage bus-shelter all within range. Plus a wide spectrum of petit bourgeois shop windows.

As Philip watched the mayhem commence — and wondered how much yobs cost as extras — he grew increasingly depressed at the creative shortcomings of his debut film script. His own sex and violence were far too predictable, far too restricted in their vision. He suffered the social deprivation of being trapped within a narrow metropolitan elite. He had not realised that, in small market towns the length and breadth of the country, the end of civilisation was being enacted on a weekly basis. But with flair and imagination.

Then, in a final decorative flourish, the storm forecast by the émigré seagulls arrived. The first fork-lightning of the night lit up the windswept debris and the dissipated mortals in a violent flash of vivid white, as if to reveal a secret snapshot of a forbidden world. And a rumbling thunder offered the imprimatur of the weather gods upon the Bacchanalian townscape.

40

In the early morning sunlight, Sharon Bellacuzzi stood signing autographs while she waited for the off. Occasionally she would sign them leaning forward, as this was a position favoured by her fans. It is possible that some of those seeking autographs were not her fans, had indeed not heard of her, but merely liked to start the day by looking down a cleavage. Not that Sharon minded, for this was the way to fame. And, keen to be famous, she was always ready to sign when thrust a scrap of paper, though she did wish her publicity agent had given her an easier name.

She would love, as she said whenever near a microphone, to do more films, because she was a film sort of person. And *Aftershocks*, she was quoted as saying, was the type of film that she loved to do, as it gave her a chance to develop. So far she knew little of the plot, since she was more an instinctive actress than a scriptreader. But she hoped there would be some lesbian vampire work in it, as this was a forte of hers.

The other cast members were lesser known and so they were waiting inside their cars, queued along the square. And behind them were lined up the vans of the crew, already wondering whether, ten minutes out from the motel, it was time to take their first break.

To drive to the Commodore, along the road that had so flummoxed the mayoress, Greg had arranged to lead a convoy from the Dragon's Head Hotel, the no-star, no-staff standard-bearer of local tourism.

Except Greg was a no-show, and the deadline for departure was now past.

Philip looked up and down the cavalcade that awaited his command, and yawned from lack of sleep. What should have been a night of *amour*, had been a night of rewrites. And ideas had come thin and slow. He sensed a lack of structure, the need for a unifying story line. At 3 a.m. he had even toyed with marauding mutant sheep, and only dawn had made plain this was folly. (His most recent training videos had been hygiene in hospitals, and the creative leap was a struggle.) Writer, producer, director, was at least two hats too many and the pressure was telling.

Some forty people were waiting, many of them artistic, and the delay did not help his attempt to look professional. Nor did Françoise's repeated request for a kiss. He was just wondering what would make him seem dynamic when he spotted Greg on the other side of the square. Walking toward them with no great hurry.

'Didn't have you down as a tourist,' said Philip, trying to be both jocular and just a touch critical. 'What have you been doing this time of day?'

'Oh, a bit of ducking and diving,' said Greg, offering an enigmatic smile. And slipping smoothly behind the wheel of his Jaguar without further word. A moment later he was into gear, and laconically waving a wagon-train hand out of the car window.

The other vehicles moved off behind him, and all slowly circled the sorry-looking square, where green graffiti now adorned the war dead and cobbles lay like grape-shot. Further on, the high street and its heritage had suffered body blows beyond the remit of the men in yellow, and pot-holes jarred their way out of town. The commerce of the day had yet to begin, but early window-shoppers were already gathering to shake their heads and tut in groups.

'Could have been worse, I guess,' said Greg. 'One of us could have become the Wicker Man!'

Burned alive, reflected Philip ruefully. Another good plot idea he had not thought of.

As the convoy made its way through the

narrow streets of Abernant, Philip was still struggling to improve his plot-lines. The trouble with the end of the world was, he had recently realised, that it was not a very original idea. Most of the angles had been covered in the preceding centuries, and by some seriously big names. Not least Milton. And nowadays cinema was always crashing planes on desert islands leaving a motley bunch of thugs to fight over the last can of sardines. So the scenario of survival skills needed fresh insights. Philip had briefly been tempted by the concept of the human race having to start again from scratch, post-holocaust, with a brand new Adam and Eve — except this time, with each of them middle-aged and very ugly and needing to psyche themselves up for mating. Interesting, but not box office, he had been told.

'I've counted six charity shops,' said Philip, apropos of nothing except a wish to talk and hide his nerves. He was on the verge of a jokey remark about 'stopping to see if they had any second-hand scripts', but drew himself up short, suddenly fearful of what hidden — and unfunny — truth this might convey.

Abernant had been a random choice, one of a dozen towns where he had placed his advert. Most responses had, however, been in the Homes and Gardens category, from people eager for their décor to be seen by a wider world. He had quite fancied going to Aberystwyth, so that his doomed characters could have done something with boats — like built them or drowned in them. But the only reply had been from a man with a small terraced cottage who wanted to interest him in a movie about his cycling holidays.

So now here he was, months later, driving through a time-warp town in the mountains en route to gentry retards. With a film crew in tow. And a fear the script was scrappy.

'Thought I might beef up the ghost sequences . . .'

He paused, but Greg had no comment.

'Yes, reckon I'll try and get Mrs Igor to walk through a few more walls. And aim for extra-spooky!'

Greg had no thoughts on extra-spooky.

'I doubt it'll affect the budget much. Old girl will probably be too pissed to charge us for staggering about!'

He gave a forced laugh, but Greg did not join in. They were passing the library, and his attention had turned to its avant-garde concrete-and-rust architecture, which in sunlight resembled a mausoleum.

'Assuming they'll unlock her, of course,' continued Philip. 'And slip off her shackles!'

After a short distance the road forked, and the town began to dribble into a brief suburbia of bungalows, where old farmers downshifted from tractors to lawnmowers and tried to look happy for their remaining urban years.

'And maybe,' Philip added, 'we could sneak a few shots of the Commodore looking cadaverous. He's got a touch of the Draculas about him.'

'Should have brought my glider,' said Greg.

'Sorry?'

'Sign to a gliding club back there. I've got shares in a glider.'

'Oh.'

'Syndicate of four.'

'Right.'

'Always fun flying near mountains.'

Philip said nothing. Somehow it irked him that Greg had time to have other things on his mind. And his ownership — even in part — of a glider was socially unsettling.

But equally unsettling was the day ahead, and Philip's worries were becoming legion. He had creative gifts that were on the wane, he was running late, and now he had to deal with the wrong weather. He had relied on the certainty of rain, the grim grey relentless slash-your-wrists rain, to help establish the onscreen mood of despair and other downbeat emotions. He was therefore not happy at the sight of sun — a low morning sun so bright and bothersome that at times they both had to squint to see the road in front. He hoped all this was not a taste of troubles to come.

'Oh bugger!' said Greg.

'What is it?'

'A hearse.'

And the convoy slowed to accommodate the pace of death.

Ahead was a hearse and a single funeral car, as yet to collect its mourners. It was a modest death, with just two wreaths, but maximum respect and minimum speed was being accorded the dear departed.

The Jaguar idled along in first. 'Not what I expected from you, Greg. Thought you'd flag 'em down, give 'em a quick blessing and a shot of holy water, then slip them two tenners to give it some welly.'

Greg did not know how to respond, uncertain whether this was praise or mockery. 'Oh, it's just a couple of hundred yards, and we turn off up the Nant Valley.'

After just a couple of hundred yards, the hearse turned off up the Nant Valley.

Its cortège was now unusually large. As the slow, steady climb through the Welsh landscape began, its mourners included a double-decker catering bus, two vanloads of props, a rental van of sound engineers, a rental van of electricians, several carloads of soap opera extras, and a soft-porn star who insisted on waving. (Which was much to the surprise of Clydog, who now took early morning walks for his blood pressure; he reached work and filed an exclusive report that a James Bond movie was indeed being secretly filmed in the area. And was given the byline of The 007 Correspondent.)

The Nant Valley had awoken to a rare absence of louring cloud, and its woods and hills were invigoratingly crisp in the still morning air. It was the first time that Philip had had sight of these views, indeed even knew there were views. The landscape was uncompromisingly stark, as spring arrived here late, and green had yet to soften the land. The white fuzz of hawthorn was weeks away and the beech hedges were still playing dead. In this austere beauty, the only mark of spring was the gambolling lambs, their date of birth mechanistically dictated by man's control of the ram.

The rites of death were also being rigorously observed, and the lead undertaker repeatedly turned down chances to let his coffin pause in a lay-by. There are few obvious joys to funeral work, and the power to delay traffic ranks high. His black-gloved hand could be seen in his wing mirror, and he had hold of the wheel with a God-given gravity, displaying no desire whatever to wave anybody by. The man had blanked out all expression and he drove with the stillness of one of his corpses, but just occasionally his eyes would dart sideways to enjoy the view of the vehicles behind him.

And the vehicles behind him wound round and round the B-road's bends, dawdling through the countryside at the speed of knackered ramblers. Half-hidden by hedgerows, and stared at by cows, the crack troops of television were forced to form a straggling crocodile and learn the rural virtue of patience.

This unconventional cortège slowly snaked up the valley for several miles. They passed the verge where the mayoress had stopped her Daimler and had tried to make sense of her map; they passed the bungalow where the bank manager was living in seclusion, but now with the fear that his penis had become an icon; and they passed the sign that said the next bend — Dead Horse Bend to locals — was dangerous.

And then they reached the Land Rover, buried in a hedge.

Unlike the road, the 4 × 4 had gone straight on. It had demolished the chevron board, crunched into a telegraph pole, and toppled down a ditch. Its off-road capabilities had been of little benefit, for it had careered along on its side. The bodywork looked as though battered by a bull, and a forgotten number plate was lying on the tarmac garnished with broken glass.

'Never a dull moment here,' said Greg. 'What are these locals on?'

Philip shrugged, and looked in vain for the driver.

'We'll be attacked by a male voice choir next.'

A tractor was starting to winch the vehicle up and even the undertakers turned their heads, acknowledging quality drama. The police, who had been hiding overnight in the hills, were now boldly back on patrol, and keen to look useful. One stood staring at skid marks, one stood staring at a tape measure, and the other stood waving at traffic to slow down, a superfluous gesture in the case of a hearse. The funeral procession ground on past, burial of the dead taking precedence.

'And the day is still young,' said Greg.

'Not that young,' replied Philip.

Philip had grown familiar with this long and winding road, and knew there was no overtaking to be had. He was paying wages for this scenic tour in slow motion, and even the sound of birdsong was poor compensation for that. So he was much relieved when the distant eyesore of the tarpaulined roof at last came into view, and then watched with nervous tension as it gradually grew closer. Before long, the bulk of Chateau Powell could be glimpsed through the trees. Next to become visible was the terraced garden . . . and after that the rhododendron bushes . . . and finally the old gates of the long gravelled drive.

Into which turned the hearse.

'Oh Christ!' said Philip.

'This isn't in the script,' said Greg.

'Oh Christ!' said Philip again.

And fell into the silence of trauma.

For some seconds, the only sound heard in the Jaguar was the loud and persistent crunching of gravel as the motorised retinue of forty assorted strangers followed the dead body up the drive.

This was not an occurrence that lay within the realm of Greg's rich and varied work history, normally so full of inspirational anecdotes, and it was a while before he spoke.

'Are we insured?' he asked.

'Against what? 'Unreasonable dying'? I doubt it.' snapped Philip.

Had he not been in the Jaguar he would have kicked something. Repeatedly. A full year in the planning, months in the writing, weeks in the casting, and seconds in the abandoning, his project would now be hard to salvage even with the most polished of press releases. Not so much The Now Company as The Never Company. And the *Zeitgeist* felt like shit. No mistress of any nationality could bring balm to bear, or hope to re-puff his ego. He was undone.

'We need a fall-back plan,' said Greg, reverting to the mantra of the fixer.

'Obviously,' said Philip.

'And quite fast,' said Greg astutely.

'So, what d'you suggest then? Give the stiff the kiss of life? Or tip the morgue man a couple of hundred smackers to drive the body round the block for the next three weeks?'

'I'm thinking.'

Greg continued to think as they processed between the rhododendrons, as they passed along the crumbling brick wall of the kitchen garden, and as they observed the Queen Anne portico come into view. And as the hearse glided to a respectful stop.

His thinking continued, but to no noticeable effect, as the pair sat opposite the site of their shoot and gazed glumly at the funeral cars and the wreaths lying on top of the coffin.

'Must be the old man. He looked a

hundred and ten,' said Philip.

'Just hope he didn't die of black mould. That woman'd sue us.'

'Ulrika reckoned he was already dead. Held together by formaldehyde.'

The sombreness of the setting made Philip very conscious of the decrepit vans and old bus that were accompanying him, indeed were now in full view behind him. They looked like a travelling freak circus that had just come to town, and on the wrong day. He worried how best to frame his sympathy, for etiquette offered little guidance in a situation such as this. He fervently hoped that Miss Sharon Bellacuzzi knew not to wave or offer to sign autographs when the bereaved came out of their home.

'Pity we didn't bring any flowers,' said Greg.

'Bugger flowers! What about the film?'

'Film's fucked,' said Greg, who had given up his attempt at thinking.

Then the ancient front door slowly opened.

And Dilys came out and waved.

'We are deeply sorry to learn of your loss, Miss Powell,' said Philip.

'Thank you.'

He shook her small gloved hand.

'A tragedy,' said Greg. 'I'm sure it's a great blow to the community.'

'Thank you.'

He too shook her small gloved hand, but added a squeeze for good measure.

The head undertaker stood waiting with stock funeral face, the limousine door held discreetly ajar.

'And I speak for everyone at The Now Company,' said Philip, 'when I say you will be in their thoughts.'

'Thank you,' said Dilys, who looked surprisingly elegant in black dress and coat.

Philip and Greg turned to go.

'Where are you going?' asked Dilys rather sharply.

'Back to town,' said Philip.

'Back to town?'

'We need to try and reschedule.'

'Reschedule what?'

'Er, well, the filming.'

'Why?'

'Why? Er . . . Well, because — ' Philip gestured imprecisely at the hearse.

'You can't leave now.'

'Sorry?'

'We need the money. You signed a contract.'

'But I thought . . . ' Philip struggled with the knowledge that the body was but five yards away and not long cold.

'And we're waiting for our new roof.'

'Oh . . . ' said Philip. ' . . . Right.'

'And a new candelabra.'

'Er . . . right,' he said, and he realised the gentry would for ever remain a mystery to him.

'And the redecoration of our reception room.'

But then, as Philip absorbed this triumph of greed over breeding, the consequence for *Aftershocks* made it through to his brain, and triggered a great surge of relief (though to film amid a wake could be a challenging first).

And he said again, though now with vigour, 'Right!' And added, 'Well, we're ready to roll!' He only just resisted the urge to punch the air and shout, 'Sweet Mother of Jesus!'

Dilys's expression discouraged a big wet kiss and Philip was wondering exactly what words would go down well when, at that moment, the old black labrador emerged from the house.

He had aged in the weeks since they last met, and looked a sadder dog. Beset by rheumy eyes and rheumaticky legs, Rupert plodded out into the sunlight with a lurching determination. Gazing dimly about him, and ignoring Philip's friendly fingers, he made his rickety way to the hearse and its coffin.

The two men watched the dog's progress across the gravel.

'Always very touching, the power of that bond,' said Greg, as they witnessed his final farewell.

Man's best friend stood unsteadily, and sniffed the redolent air just one more time.

'Yes,' agreed Philip. 'The dog's got a sixth sense, even now.'

The dog raised his leg and widdled over the wheel arch.

'No! Not there, Rupert!' cried the Commodore, emerging from the house looking equally rocky and gaunt.

Surprise had become the default expression on Philip's face since arriving in Abernant some ten hours earlier. It did not desert him now.

'Heel, Rupert, heel!' called the Commodore.

But Rupert was too deaf, too blind, and too bloody-minded to heed any commands. Which was not a bad description of his master, who, as he half-dragged his old dog back into the house, glared at the men from TV with his usual mixture of disapproval and confusion. And then disappeared.

'He's not used to being bereaved,' explained Dilys.

'Yes, death can be very difficult,' murmured Greg silkily.

Philip said nothing. He too was finding

death very difficult as he slowly rethought who had been bereaved. For this brought a personal trauma. *Aftershocks* was now short of its ground-breaking gin-swigging ghost. And had a spooky hole in its script.

Dilys also said nothing. It was a habit at which she had practice.

'Of course, losing a loved one is never easy,' said Greg, attempting empathy again.

'No,' replied Dilys.

'Though it is a journey we all have to go on,' said Greg.

'Yes,' replied Dilys.

'And hope we end up stronger,' said Greg.

This time Dilys had nothing to add to his insights.

And Philip had no insights at all.

The three were left in an awkward little group on the gravel, midway between hearse and porch, their only option to wait. Lacking the temperament of the funeral director, who had mastered invisible breathing, they all were impatient for the Commodore to come out from the house. Philip and Greg were eager to get set up, but invasion by a dozen hairy crew with half a ton of cabling would not be helpful to the process of grief. And going in to chivvy the old guy along could be as tricky as rounding up geese. Dilys meanwhile was anxious to be off to the funeral as she had other things planned for her day.

The sun inched higher. Expressions of sympathy flagged.

'Had they been married long?' enquired Greg.

'Too long,' said Dilys. 'Far too long.'

'Ah.'

Greg decided the point was best not pursued. Dilys pursued it.

'Child bride,' she said. 'Child everything, in fact.'

'I see,' said Greg.

'They married in the war,' she went on. 'His mad period.'

'Oh.'

'Well, his first mad period.'

'Right.'

'He should never have married. He should have stuck to fish and dogs.'

'That's what life's about, I guess,' said Greg. 'Difficult choices.'

'She drank away the furniture.'

'Oh dear.'

'And the fox-hunting portraits.'

'How sad,' said Greg, looking to Philip for help.

'It's been years since she had solids.'

'Terrible.'

'He should have shot her. Claimed it was an accident.'

' . . . Oh.'

Dilys looked at her watch.

'Where is he? I suppose her last wish was to be buried with a gin bottle.'

Seconds later, her hapless brother re-appeared in the porch, brushing dog hairs off his suit. On his face was all the gloom of the house, and he was muttering quietly to himself.

'Ready now?' said Dilys.

'It won't be the same,' he said. 'Not now all the bones have gone.'

He ignored Greg and Philip, seemed scarcely to know who they were.

'Ten generations of bones, all gone in a night.'

'I know, dear.'

'Every Powell in the Nant. Who would have thought it?'

Dilys touched him briefly on the arm, the only contact Philip had ever seen.

'In the old days, we each had our own shelf when we died,' he said.

'I know, dear.'

'With some Latin on it.'

The old Commodore looked out across the terraced garden, down to where the family church once stood, to where the family's grand tomb had been.

'It won't be the same,' he repeated. 'Being buried next to people who are not Powells. In somebody else's church.'

'It can't be helped, dear,' said Dilys. 'Floods are sent to try us.'

Her brother seemed not to hear.

'I used to go down there at night sometimes. The ancestors liked a bit of company. But that's all over now.'

And he hobbled toward the hearse.

Dilys took Philip aside, and said, 'After the woman's buried, I think we'll be away at our cousins' for a couple of weeks. A little change of scene.'

'Probably for the best,' said Philip, sombre-faced to keep hidden his pleasure.

Then somehow, licensed by this discreet exchange, he heard himself quietly say, 'A word of advice, if I may.'

Dilys reacted as if to lese-majesty.

'These mad periods . . . '

'Yes?'

'When you go through town . . . best not let the Commodore look at the War Memorial.'

She was about to ask why, but the undertakers had moved into full-blown obsequiousness, and doors were being held open by ushering arms, and formulaic words of encouragement were being whispered.

The funeral director waited on the Commodore as he took a lingering look at the church ruins below.

'I've had their bones in the net,' he said sadly. 'Could have been anyone. Pater, mater, great-uncle Albert. No way of knowing.' He sighed. 'Last laugh to the trout.'

And then Julian Powell climbed slowly and awkwardly into the funeral car.

★　★　★

'Gor blimey!'

There were a lot of Gor Blimeys as the horny-handed craftsmen of film crash-banged their way down the entrance hall, recceing its eighteenth-century features for where best to nail their twentieth-century kit. The giant oil painting of the last cavalry charge by the British Army, the huge urn with the cracked Chinamen, the defunct chandelier, the baroque barometer, the forgotten croquet mallets, all came in for raucous shouts and laughter. The old decaying mansion echoed to more noise than it had heard for many years.

Philip, though, was quieter. He stood with Greg at the bottom of the grand staircase up which he had once strode with confident gestures and Potemkin references, and thought hard about the problems with his script. Today was cannibalism day and already they were running late. Tomorrow was ghost day and they had no ghost. The next two days were sex days and he held grave doubts that Sharon Bellacuzzi could remember any lines. He had also been left a dog to feed daily.

'Greg,' he said, remembering that his location manager was a man of many talents, few of them unsung.

'Yes?' said Greg.

'What do you reckon are the chances of getting hold of some jeeps?'

A Few Weeks Later

41

'An all-time record?'

Hubert and Dafydd were seemingly united in disbelief.

'Yes!' said Clydog defiantly.

'More copies than the end of World War Two?'

'Yes!'

'More copies than the start of World War Two?'

'Yes!'

'More than the death of Lloyd George?'

'I don't — '

'More than the Relief of Mafeking?'

'Oh now you're both being silly,' complained Clydog.

'Thought you'd never notice!' said Hubert.

And reluctantly Clydog joined in their laughter.

He felt pressure to be convivial as their exchanges were more public than usual, with the three men standing in full view of the street. For over a week now, they had been forced from their normal smoky nook and latterly they lingered near the door. This was ten yards closer to the butcher, and put

Hubert within easier gloating distance, though he denied this was his motive. The real cause was practical: his deli window was boarded up, and so natural light was in short supply. Hubert's anarchist sympathies had, unfortunately, not impressed the cobble-throwers, and — no doubt enragé by the price of his asparagus — they had reduced his plate glass to shards the size of a shaving mirror.

'It was the supplement that did it,' said an almost animated Clydog. 'The special eight-page pull-out souvenir supplement. With the twenty-four photographs and eye-witness commentary.'

'Shame it was past your bed-time,' said Hubert. 'Or you could have reported it yourself.'

Clydog did not rise, perhaps did not even notice the bait, such was his focus on his news.

'The pictures have been syndicated, you know. And Miss Nightingale has been on a chat show.'

'What, Parkinson?'

'Late night Radio Wales.'

'Wow!'

'She said the edition was a tribute to a hardworking, experienced staff with solid, traditional news values.'

'Oh, that's very nice. Well done, Clydog,' said Hubert, but privately feeling that the news he was nurturing was of much greater interest.

'Yes, well done,' said Dafydd, but privately feeling that the news he was nurturing was of much greater interest.

'Thank you,' said Clydog, wary of their warmth.

'But there's never been a supplement before,' said Dafydd, a little puzzled. 'Not even when we nearly came runner-up for Mid-Wales in Bloom.'

'Ah, well . . . ' said Clydog, and here defensiveness noticeably altered his voice. 'Apparently some bloke wandered in early the Saturday morning, just as she was having her herbal tea, and sold her three rolls of film. Of all the action highlights, so to speak. And then they divided up the sales rights. It . . . er . . . ' Clydog hesitated to mention his early-morning power-walks for fear of weeks of ridicule. 'It happened before I got to work.'

'So that's why the pictures were so good!' said Hubert. 'A passing amateur.'

Clydog ignored him. 'We've never had so many letters. There'll be three pages of letters again this week. And follow-up articles. And exclusive interviews, like with the man who laid the cobbles. And what he feels about having to lay them again.'

'You missed a trick, though,' said Hubert.

'What's that?'

'Well, I kept turning the pages hoping to find a piece of in-depth analysis from you — something to help readers understand the underlying cause of all these strange goings-on. From Our Penis Correspondent.'

'Ha-ha,' said Clydog. And this time did not join in the laughter.

'These sales figures, Clydog, have they reached what Miss Nightingale needs?' asked Dafydd.

'Still don't know. It's not been officially audited yet, but according to Ted — Ted's that old guy who takes the paper from the printers and runs it over to the newsagent's each week — we're six wheelbarrows up on normal.'

'And the man from Birmingham thinks you're not an efficient modern newspaper. Amazing.'

'I doubt Mr Trench ever gets as much news in one week,' said Clydog. 'Ceremonies, riots, a scandal, a film, a death among the gentry, and now the Best Kept Village Award.'

'You're not the only one with news,' said Hubert, trying not to sound peevish.

Bastard, thought Dafydd, beaten to the draw.

'Is it worth a supplement?' asked Clydog.

'It's Crapstick.'

'What's he done now?'

'Been forced to resign. With immediate effect.'

'Well I never! Because . . . ?'

' 'Unbecoming behaviour with a goat, of a manner likely to bring the business community into disrepute.' Auberon's photos were dynamite.'

'Is that why his shop's closed today?' asked Dafydd.

'Probably. That and the fact someone sprayed a picture of a goat on his window. In a compromising position.'

'Goodness gracious!' said Clydog. 'How appalling!'

'Yes, indeed. Who, I wonder,' said Dafydd, 'would do something appalling like that?'

'I just can't imagine,' said Hubert. 'But it's the sort of thing I would put a stop to if I were re-elected President . . . which I gather I might be.'

'What a surprise,' said Dafydd.

'And what will you be bribing them with?' asked Clydog. 'Patisserie or prosciutto?'

'I thought I'd try principles. First time for everything.'

'Any particular principles in mind?' asked Dafydd.

Untypically for Hubert, he looked slightly abashed. It had not been an easy few days, unpicking the glass from his high-class comestibles. Glass was a subversive substance, difficult to detect and quick to wound. More than once, he had sliced his fingers and bloodied his produce. All of the meat and much of the cheese had gone into the bin, for fear a sliced glottis would lead to a lawsuit. Even long hours with a broom had not seen the last of the slivers. And then there had been a lot of time lost with the money-men of Lloyds. A boarded-up window is bad for business, the semi-darkness a loss-maker. Customers do not like to shop if reminded of the Blitz, and Hubert was eager to return to normal. But he had waited in vain for his cheque of reimbursement. And neither complaint nor abuse was successful. Redirected to the small print, and to the large matter of liability, he had learned to his cost that he and his premises lacked any insurance cover . . . in the event of civil insurrection. And so now he was greatly out of pocket with no obvious means of redress.

'I think something needs to be done about yobs,' was Hubert's answer. 'We're being invaded by yobs. We need new by-laws to curb their behaviour. To help the police ban them from the pubs. And perhaps put them on an island somewhere.'

This was an aspect of anarchism he had never expressed before, and it caused some surprise to his audience. He did not mention his new membership of Celtic Militaria.

'Was that an election speech?' enquired Dafydd.

'Might be.'

'I think I'd prefer Capstick to slip me his sausages.'

'I think the paper's too full to cover such dull local issues as a new President of the Chamber of Commerce,' said Clydog. 'Perhaps if you had a brawl in the meeting room of the Brown Bear I could spare you a couple of lines?'

It was rare for Clydog to be witty, so this confused Hubert and he briefly fell silent.

'I've got the sort of story you'll want to print,' said Dafydd, seizing his moment with graceless speed. 'Perfect for the new *Mid-Walian*.'

'If it's more disgusting details about my doctor, I don't want to hear it,' said Clydog.

'No, no. It's hot news, just hours old.'

'What is?'

'Gareth's been given bail.'

'Bail! What's your source?'

'I gave him a lift home. He was on the road this morning.'

'Does he know he's a folk hero?' asked Hubert.

'No obvious signs of that, no. The magistrates told him he was a danger to all civilised society.'

'Well, fortunately there's not a lot of that around here,' said Hubert.

'What did they charge him with?' asked Clydog.

'Enough to make his probation officer despair. Drunk driving, disorderly conduct, criminal damage, and possession of stolen property.'

'Stolen property?'

'He still had the penis.'

'Oh.'

'Apparently he glowed. Staggered from his crashed Land Rover, glowing.'

'He doesn't have much luck, this Gareth, does he?' said Clydog.

'Well, at least he's put the town on the map,' said Hubert. 'He's the one that deserves a statue.'

'Is that a manifesto commitment?' mocked Dafydd.

'Certainly not. Even if he keeps his Barbour on.'

They all laughed, the easy laugh of companionship, if not of any great friendship.

The ex-postman had one more story to tell,

but now did not seem the moment. Life for the other two was starting to go well again, and he felt ashamed to be seen despondent. Soon it would be the anniversary of the day he departed the Post Office, sacked for being too slow, too keen to stand and talk. And now history had repeated itself. The girls in Forget-Me-Nots had struck. Dafydd had given one lift too many, and been spotted with a passenger, a sin which was sackable. In fourteen days' time, he would once more be unemployed. And on that final downward slope . . . to pizza delivery man.

Dafydd leaned back against the meat counter, and quietly watched as the ribbing continued. It was hard to avoid self-pity. He had always liked to think of himself as the Wells Fargo of gossip. But in life, he bitterly reflected, you sometimes have to pay a high price for making sure the gossip gets through.

42

Clydog was short of an adjective, and the obituary had come to a pause. For a while he stared at the pattern on his Parker fountain pen and after that he toyed with his blotter. Then he slipped a shoe off, and scratched a foot. Through the frosted glass partition he could see the back of the editor's head as he talked upon the telephone. Clydog looked at his watch again. Soon it would be time for an apple.

He gazed out of the office window as the latest coach party of Japanese tourists stopped in the square below. He had noticed before that all the photos they took were of each other, but in front of things. In front of shops, in front of mountains, in front of locals. But, of course, most of all in front of the mutilated statue. He himself had several times been asked to take a family snapshot as he crossed the square for a little light reporting. They were always smiling, always polite, and grateful to have a record of Welsh cultural customs to take back home. Often they asked if there were other mutilated statues in the area that they could visit and he had to disappoint. He had suggested the idea to Hubert, who had suggested the idea to the council, who had said the Dragon's Head couldn't cope with the extra tourist numbers.

He still sometimes regretted that the offer of America had never come to pass. On some days, when he wanted to smother his mother, he thought of applying on spec, of winging his CV across the Atlantic. Perhaps, on reflection, inner-city Chicago was too great a leap, but he reckoned Manhattan sounded good, and he'd heard the women were sassy. He liked the idea of Central Park, where there would be both crime and greenery. He might need to buy new clothes as no doubt his lifestyle would be different, but that was an adventure he was up for. With forty years in journalism to recommend him, and the fresh perspective of a Brit, he felt that his transatlantic chances would be good. And his recent knowledge of riots was sure to be a plus point.

Trenchant. That was the word he wanted. Trenchant. He liked the clever word-play, apposite for the death of a Mr Trench. The man had never recovered from his stroke, brought on by the shock of defeat. Aidan and Theo said he had become apoplectic and unpleasantly sweaty before collapsing over their desk, and that his last words had been very rude about their sister. No doubt the ribald nature of her success had added irony to insult. Then, as the man from Brum lingered on for a month or so longer, it had grown ever more galling, and harmful to his bank balance, to see the dowdy little paper become a cult — some issues were even snapped up on news-stands in Knightsbridge. So Miss Nightingale had judged it only fitting that a small farewell tribute be paid to Eddie Trench and his unforeseen role in transforming the *Mid-Walian* fortunes.

Miss Nightingale herself remained quite untransformed, though she would visit the newsroom a little more often, and occasionally bring cakes. She said that longevity ran in the family, and her traditions would see out the century. As the spinster grew older, however, and with brothers that no longer spoke, it was obvious to all that *The Mid-Walian* itself had become her family. And that she worked in an office which was almost her home. Yet even family would always come second to the game of golf, for — although she now struggled with the long par fives — her heart still beat fastest when standing on a tee. And nowhere was she happier in her declining years than when up on a podium, proudly presenting her Nightingale Cup.

Clydog finished the last lines of the brief obituary, seeking in vain any final oratorical flourish. It was not easy to be nice to a man who would have squeezed the life-blood from the staff and crushed all character from the paper. With his dedication to the bottom line, the new owner would never have published circulars from the Arts Council, or found room for tiny adverts from far-off TV companies. And he would have refused to do so on the grounds that such things were dull.

Clydog laid down his Parker pen, and gazed out of the window and across the stone bridge to the sunlit Nant Valley, to where the hawthorn was finally lighting up the landscape with its brilliant bursts of white. He leaned backwards in his office chair and stretched his arms, and noticed that for the first time in years he did not need to undo a waistcoat button.

We do hope that you have enjoyed reading this large print book.

Did you know that all of our titles are available for purchase?

We publish a wide range of high quality large print books including:
Romances, Mysteries, Classics
General Fiction
Non Fiction and Westerns

Special interest titles available in large print are:
The Little Oxford Dictionary
Music Book
Song Book
Hymn Book
Service Book

Also available from us courtesy of Oxford University Press:
Young Readers' Dictionary
(large print edition)
Young Readers' Thesaurus
(large print edition)

For further information or a free brochure, please contact us at:
Ulverscroft Large Print Books Ltd.,
The Green, Bradgate Road, Anstey,
Leicester, LE7 7FU, England.
Tel: (00 44) 0116 236 4325
Fax: (00 44) 0116 234 0205

Other titles published by
The House of Ulverscroft:

THE VALLEY

Barry Pilton

It is the 1980s and in mid-Wales the inhabitants of the Nant Valley are holding out against the modern world. Then outsiders discover the valley, and wrongly believe it to be an idyll. Mysterious Stéfan buys a derelict manor house and sets about becoming a squire. Jane and Rob, poor arty urbanites with an enthusiasm for alfresco nudity, buy a tumbledown farmhouse. Meanwhile, Dafydd the postman doubts the valley is ready for outsiders — and as they struggle with sexual scandal, hostile artisans and a corpse, the omens are not good.

THE CROWDED BED

Mary Cavanagh

Joe Fortune, a Jewish GP, has been married to Anna for twenty years; they enjoy a passionate and happy relationship. But there are dark secrets in their lives. Joe has long nurtured a desire to murder Gordon, Anna's father: a motive born of past events and involving revenge, mutual hatred, and Gordon's deep prejudice against Joe's faith. Anna too is hiding deep, painful secrets. The reader is led back and forth over the last half century to discover love, lies, passion, religion, cruelty and violence. And while Joe is angry and resentful, Anna's quiet dignity discloses her own shocking revelation.

MINDING

Chris Paling

Now that Billy lives with his foster family, he and his mother, Jane, only get to see each other four times a year. These visits are all Billy dreams of and they're the reason why Jane struggles to get up every day, and to try to behave 'normally'. But when Jane receives a sudden and violent reminder of her troubled past, she ends up missing a precious appointment. There remains one possibility that they can be with each other again — but this will mean evading the authorities and finally confronting the legacy of Jane's own damaged childhood.

WOUNDED

Percival Everett

John Hunt and his Uncle Gus live in the high desert of Wyoming. Although a black horse trainer is a curiosity, he's a familiar curiosity in these parts. It is the brutal murder of a gay man, however, that pushes the small community to the edge of fear and tolerance. Then, as the first blizzard of the season rages, John copes with the daily burden of unruly horses. But he faces many difficulties, including a father-son war over homosexuality, his own uncertain chances of love, and the increasing unease hanging over a community, now a victim to random hate crimes.

JOURNEY

Jae Watson

Following the break-up of her relationship, unsure of her life's direction, Marianne leaves a London still reverberating from the terrorist bombings to travel for a year with the mysterious and beautiful Sara. However, deep into the chaotic and mystical heart of India, events take a dramatic turn. In the Holy City of Varanasi, Sara's body is discovered floating in the Ganges. As the investigation ensues, unexpected and shocking revelations cast a new light on Sara and take Marianne on a painful but vital journey to uncover the truth about her friend and also her own life.

MY FRENCH WHORE

Gene Wilder

It is 1918, the final phase of the war. Paul Peachy, a shy young amateur actor from Milwaukee, realises that his wife no longer loves him. He joins the U.S. army and boards ship for the trenches of France. There, captured by the enemy, he survives by impersonating Harry Stroller, a famous enemy spy. Peachy is feted as a hero by the German top brass, but the mounting suspicions of his German hosts force him into ever more outrageous deceptions. However, as Peachy falls in love with Annie, a beautiful French courtesan, she seems to see through his artful disguise . . .